Once
A
Tyme

Stefan Jakubowski

To
Jaqui

Published in 2009
Reprinted in 2012
by Zygmunt Stanley

ISBN 978-0-9554244-3-4

© 2009 Stefan Jakubowski

Cover illustration by Pat Moffett
www.patriciamoffett.com

Cover and pages designed and typeset by
Rachel Jones
Absolute Design Solutions
www.absolutedesignsolutions.co.uk

Printed by Gomer Press, Wales

For Fun

The Author

Originally from Reading Stefan Jakubowski moved to Wales in the latter part of the last Century. (He wishes to point out that he is not as old as that makes him sound). He now lives in Pembrokeshire with wife Nia and their owner, Peaches the cat.

Now a confession and an apology.

It would appear dear readers that I have been living a lie.
In earlier books I professed to have never owned a bicycle.
It appears this is not true.
It has been pointed out (by my wife) that I won one in a raffle once.
But I did sell it on the same day I picked it up.

I have never ridden a bike that I have owned.

Special thanks to
Rachel Jones
and
Pat Moffett.

The last thing you need, when your time machine is one of those plastic portable toilet jobbies, is for it to turn upside down when you are in it.

'Ugh!' groaned one of the two occupants aboard, as it did just that. The second occupant managed to dodge the falling "mayhem" by clinging grimly to one of the plastic walls.

'What's going on?' wailed the wall clinger, as she dodged a fetterless toilet roll of the rough medicated kind.

'It has to be them!' the other shouted back, wiping at the blue liquid, matting his grey hair.

The other, an elderly chap who could call an octogenarian, kid, struggled upright and stood, unsteadily, with arms braced against supporting walls, on what was, just a moment ago, the ceiling. His name: Rufus. His occupation: time traveller.

'How?' enquired the wall clinger, having to tighten her grip as the toilet jobby suddenly lurched and righted itself.

The wall clinger, a cat who could call the elderly chap a somewhat recent event, leapt onto one of two handy shelves. Her name: Cat. Her occupation: loosely described, a familiar; a being not of the black arts but bestowed with white magical qualities. She wasn't keen on cat food.

The old man landed with a thump on the floor. As he lay there, groaning, the door to the toilet jobby swung open. 'I believe', he observed, between groans, 'we have arrived somewhere.' He squinted towards the light flowing through the opening.

'Somewhere we no doubt shouldn't be,' warned the wall clinger, as the old man again got to his feet.

'That is to be seen,' said the old man, gravitating towards the open door.

'Rufus!' To the wall clinger's horror, the old man had shot forward as if propelled by an invisible force. The old man now clung perilously by the fingertips of one hand, the only part of his body now visible. 'Rufus!' the wall clinger now screamed, frantically inching her way to those straining digits but afraid in case she too followed the old man into whatever unknown was waiting for them.

'No, Cat,' yelled the old man, his voice sounding strangely distant, 'save yourself!'

'Rufus!'

'Home,' the old man ordered, 'home!'

The wall clinger made a desperate lunge for the old man's fingers, but it was too late. They slipped from view and to her dismay the door slammed shut. The portable toilet jobby had been ordered home and that is where it would now go.

'No!' wailed the wall clinger, clawing at the door. 'No!'

Chapter 1

'Mum! Granddad swore,' tattle-tailed Marc, miffed, eleven year old, video game is my world, grandson.

'Dad!' groaned Lucy, harassed, single parent holding down job, daughter.

'But there's some disgusting goo stuck to my backside,' bewailed Tom, disgruntled, stuck in his ways and won't be told, granddad.

'It's not goo,' protested Marc, 'it's my stringy cheese.'

Ignoring was chosen as an acceptable way forward by Lucy as she tried to concentrate on the road ahead.

'Why's Granddad here?' asked the silent, until now, car's other passenger, Kate, enigmatic – her words – moody – her mum's words – fourteen year old granddaughter.

Lucy, realising sadly that ignoring was not after all going to be a viable course of action, sighed and related the reason Granddad was with them that morning. 'He wants to collect his first pension in person.'

'I thought they'd stopped that,' said Kate, frowning. 'Don't they pay it into a bank account or something now?'

'Try telling your Granddad that,' said Lucy, hoping for all their sakes that her daughter wouldn't.

Kate turned in her seat and gave her Granddad, sitting in the back, a long, hard stare. He returned her stare by crossing his eyes. Kate resumed her forward position.

But Tom was going to have his say anyway. 'It's my right,' he said.

'But you haven't even got a pension book,' said Kate, taking the bait. Lucy's shoulders sagged a little.

'It's the principle of the thing,' said Tom, getting into gear, 'I'm making a stand.'

'The cheese won't come off him,' wailed a voice from the back.

'What principles?' asked Kate, swallowing the hook.

Lucy's shoulders were now so low she was having trouble steering.

'Post offices,' said Tom.

Lucy took a moment to cast a despairing glance at her dad in the rear view mirror. 'I thought it was about your pension,' she said. Dammit! she thought, sucked right in. But before she had time to fully rue her mistake and acquire an ear-bashing lecture on the rights and wrongs of anything and everything Tom thought was wrong with the world, they arrived at their destination; or Tom's at least. Lucy pulled the car up to the kerb and stopped alongside the village post office cum mini-mart. Tom alighted with cheese stuck to his backside.

'See you this evening then?' said Tom, leaning down to the driver's side window.

'Like I said,' said Lucy, 'if I've got time. I've that video conference scheduled for six. Don't know how long that will go on for.'

Tom peered beyond Lucy at the kids. 'What about you kids?' said Tom, putting on a look of frailty, 'you'll visit yer ol' granddad this evening. On his birthday. Won't you?' Katie?' Lucy half expected humble hand wringing to materialise. Thankfully it didn't.

'It's Kate,' corrected Kate, 'and I'm going to Zoë's until Mum gets home.' She folded her arms and adopted a "stare ahead at any cost" position.

'Marc? You'll visit your old granddad.'

'Suppose so,' Marc started, something approaching a look

of disgust on his face, but before he could say anything else he was interrupted by Lucy.

'Not so fast young man, you're going to Andy's until I get home.' Lucy looked from Marc to her dad. 'Sorry Dad, would have asked you to look after them, but I thought you might have plans.'

The look on Marc's face brightened as he remembered Andy had the latest "shoot 'em up and make as much gore as you could" console game. 'Take that alien scum!' he suddenly spouted, followed by an eruption of sound effects.

Lucy took to frowning at her son.

'More of that fantasy rubbish,' Tom harrumphed, scowling. He backed from the window. 'Don't know what goes through kids' heads these days? Well, sorry for existing. It's only my birthday. The special one. The one where I have to learn to survive on meagre handouts from the government. Perhaps I'll call in on the council on the way home and see if they have any of those old folk visitors with nothing better on their hands. Perhaps they'll find time to visit a lonely old man in his dotage.'

'Don't be so melodramatic Dad.' Lucy put the car into first. 'You've probably more money than the Queen.' She looked up at Tom and weakened a little. 'Look, I can't promise anything, but I hope to be finished with this meeting by eight. If I do I'll pop round. Bring the kids. I've a bottle of plonk in the fridge, I'll bring that and we can drink your health.' Beside her Kate's eyes had taken on a mischievous look. 'At least we will,' said Lucy, noticing.

'Could be dead then.'

'I'll drink it myself then. See you about eight.' Without waiting for further comment, Lucy took advantage of a gap in the traffic and pulled away. She tooted as she went.

'Do you think he suspects?' asked Kate, as she waved at her granddad who wasn't looking.

5

'Not a thing,' smiled Lucy.

'Did you get the cake?' said Marc, hoping it would be sponge and not fruit.

'Picking it up later.'

The car disappeared into the distance.

Chapter 2

Tom chuckled to himself as he tried to pull on the door even though the sign beside the handle said push. They think I'm stupid, he thought, but you can't put one over on old Tom, no sirree. He had accidentally discovered the receipt for his birthday cake a couple of days ago and further research, of the undercover kind, threw up certain plans that were secretively afoot. You just couldn't fool an old fool; or something like that. Tom stopped pulling and after a cursory glance to see if anyone had been watching, pushed.

Inside the post office cum mini-mart the owner, Mister Smokowski, was donning his trademark grocer's apron. He didn't really need one, but felt that one should follow tradition when able. He looked across at Tom as he stumbled through the doorway.

'Morning, Mister Tyme,' breezed Smokowski, on seeing his first customer of the day. 'Door sticking again?' he enquired, smiling. The question was met with a grunt. Undaunted, Smokowski retained the services of his smile. 'And what can I do you for this bright and sunny morn?'

'You can cut the crap for one thing, Smokowski,' growled Tom, playfully, as he peered outside at the rain threatening clouds that were gathering, 'and get me my pension as the law and my lifetime contributions to the state dictate I should on this, my sixty-fifth birthday on God's good Earth.'

Smokowski became grave faced. 'The Principle?' he said.

'Damn right, the Principle.'

The smile returned. 'Happy birthday, Tom.'

7

'Thank you.'

'Having a party?'

'Would seem so,' said Tom, exchanging grins with the shopkeeper. 'You coming?'

'Can't, stocktaking.'

'Shame. See you about eight then.'

'Wouldn't miss it. Now, what can I really get you?'

'Give me a second class stamp and the saddest birthday card you got. One with an old fool fishing or something.'

'Birthday card?'

'For me.'

Smokowski raised an eyebrow.

'Should have at least one card on yer birthday,' said Tom, looking as sad as he could.

'From you?'

'Of course.'

'Stamp?' queried a frowning Smokowski.

'Gotta make it look as if it's been delivered.'

'You could write, "delivered by hand" on the front. Save a small fortune. Also make you look even sadder.'

'Good man, Smokowski,' laughed Tom.

Smokowski went to a display of assorted cards and had a rummage through. 'No fishermen,' he said after a moment, 'but I have got this one.' He showed it to Tom. It had a picture of an old squire or the like leaning on a fence and a rustic looking walking stick. The dog at his feet looked quite dead.

'Good choice,' said Tom, clearly delighted.

'No other post yet then?' asked Smokowski.

'Postie hadn't arrived when I'd left, but I suppose he'll be empty handed when he does. Unless of course I receive that letter from the Prime Minister I'm expecting.'

The shopkeeper made a phew-wee sound. 'The Prime Minister eh?'

'Yeah. Rumour has it everyone's going to get one.'

8

'Really?'

'On my oath,' said Tom, trying to keep a straight face. 'Called a fiscal recovery request, so I heard.'

'Ah!' said Smokowski, 'a begging letter.' He started laughing.

'So,' said Tom, moving swiftly on, 'told you to keep them back, has she?'

'Lucy popped in the other day.' Smokowski started to put the card in a bag. 'She said she'd pick them up later this afternoon.'

'As mean and as sly as her old mother, that one, God rest her soul.' Tom put his hands together and raised his eyes skyward.

'She's living in Crewe isn't she?'

'One can only hope,' said Tom.

'That'll be one British squid then please.'

'A whole squid?' said Tom, feigning horror, or not. 'But it's crap.'

'The best crap I've got in the shop,' said Smokowski, holding out a hand.

'Fair do's,' said Tom, rifling a pocket. He pulled out a coin that wouldn't have looked out of place in a museum.

Smokowski took it and took a moment to look at it.

'It's real,' said Tom, narrowing his eyes, 'bite it.'

The thought of putting it in his mouth was the last thing on Smokowski's mind. 'I'll trust you,' said the shopkeeper, sliding the coin into the shadows of the till for later and closer inspection. 'Anything else I can do you for?'

A thoughtful look stole across Tom's face. 'You don't sell flat caps, perchance?'

'You are going downhill fast.'

'The Principle,' said Tom.

'Sorry, no,' said Smokowski, 'but you could try the farm shop. Or failing that, you could ask old Missus Dewhurst.'

'She sells hats?'

'No, but her hubby, Arthur, used to wear them. Mayhap she'll still have the odd one lying around.'

'Old Arthur died years ago,' said Tom, wrinkling his nose at the thought of ancient headwear.

'You could always wash it,' said Smokowski, helpfully. 'Besides, the worn effect will add to the look.'

Tom couldn't argue with that. 'I'll be off then,' he said, making for the door.

'Don't forget your card.'

'Ah, yes,' said Tom taking the proffered card. He took a quick peek at it. 'Smashing,' he said, 'the old fart's wearing bi-focals.'

'Talking of,' said Smokowski, 'where're your bins?'

'Only need them for driving,' said Tom, pushing the door. 'Pull.'

Tom pulled open the door, wished Smokowski a woeful day and left. Next stop the farm shop.

Chapter 3

Tom T. Tyme; sixty-five today. Prone to dressing mostly in distressingly old-fashioned grey corduroy trousers and jacket; not usually matching. Divorced. Hasn't worked for five years; if pressed, known to quip he was in training for looming retirement. The truth: down to the demise of one Great-Uncle Rufus who expired at the ripe old age of one hundred and twenty. Abode: a cottage called Hope End; again down to Great-Uncle Rufus who bequeathed it along with the shedload of money keeping Tom from honest work. The shed being an offshore account, that houses a sum of money with more noughts in its number than that of the account number. Tom likes the cottage's name. He thinks its name befitting of an old codger.

One child; a daughter, Lucy; personal assistant to someone who thinks they are important. Deserted and divorced; her ex-husband somewhere in the Arctic Circle; so it's rumoured. *Good riddance*. Two grandchildren; Kate, a normal four-teen year old; whatever that was, and Marc; eleven and not normal. Well, how can he be? All that interest in fantasy and stuff. Should be outside doing what comes natural; conkers and that.

All in all Tom was an otherwise quite unspectacular man, a straight man, a no-nonsense sort of a man, a man of reality, a sensible man, who had thus far lived an equally unspectac-ular, sensible, normal life – if you didn't count the shedload of money – and who could often be found finding solace in his garden shed,* where there could be found a numerous amount

---

* Not to be confused with the one full of money!

of things not to do and an equal amount of things to ignore. He has also been known to saunter. Mostly in a straight line to the local hostelry; the line back not always as straight!

Tom sat at the kitchen table in a spare pair of cords, staring through the kitchen window into the garden beyond as he absently picked at the cheese stuck to the ones he had been wearing. His search for a flat cap had been a fruitless one. The farm shop a waste of time and Missus Dewhurst, sweet but strange old dear that she was, had been more interested in making tea and asking him what he was going to do with it when he found one. But that didn't mean the end of the world. No, he didn't need a flat cap to prove he was an old codger; he could do that all by himself without the need for props. He stopped picking and idly tapped his fingers on the table top to the rhythm of the music emanating from his old radio.

He liked his radio; you didn't have to look at the presenters. Tom didn't like presenters. *Overpaid tossers*. He knew it was the same for radio but at least he didn't have to look at their smug faces as they spouted their spiel. And woe betide any poor soul that mentioned the licence fee. Television tax, more like. This is what Tom thought.

Tom had other pet hates. He didn't like the government. *Overpaid tossers*. Not that he was political. He disliked all governments, whatever the colour of the rosette. He wasn't a career moaner though, not by a long chalk. And he didn't totally think of himself as an old fart; he just liked playing the part. That was his excuse. Other hates were so many he could fill a book, but perhaps no more than your fellow Joe or Josette – to be politically correct – which was another hate – when it came down to it. He was just a little more vocal than perhaps other people might be. Tom stopped his tapping and looked at the shed.

His most favourite place in the whole wide world was the shed. It was large, airy and chock full of contraptions he

12

didn't, and didn't want to, understand. That was Uncle Rufus for you. Eccentric to the end; Tom guessed. And not being able to understand, meant he could wile the hours away and not be disturbed by the world and its distractions. He didn't like distractions. *Waste of time.* He didn't like newspapers. He didn't like the phone ringing. He liked the uncomplicated quiet of the shed.

He now turned his attention to the other "building" in the garden. This was way past being hated. A portable loo. Tom scowled at it. It was a monstrosity, but it had to stay. For some reason only known to him, Rufus had stipulated in his will that it could not be removed whilst Hope End stood. Tom narrowed his eyes. There was a perfectly good toilet indoors. Salmon pink in colour yes, but perfectly serviceable. Why the thing was there in the garden he would never know. The thing was ugly. Took up too much of the garden and was... was... useless. Its once white roof was yellowing under the weight of the lichen growing there. As for the blue of the body, well, that was fading fast. Tom hoped it would fade into oblivion. He had tried to clean it, but it seemed impervious to all his efforts and just shrugged them off. He had tried to open it, but the blasted door was stuck fast however much he tugged or levered; perhaps for the better. Goodness knows what might be growing in there. He had even tried to camouflage the damn thing by planting shrubs etc. in front of it, but all had died off quite quickly. Tom suspected something nasty was seeping from it and was poisoning the ground. But that didn't explain the fence he had erected mysteriously blowing down. It was as if the flaming thing wanted to see what was going on. It was downright creepy, but Tom wasn't one to dwell too much on the strange or weird. There had to be a perfectly plausible reason for it all. There was no room for fantasy in his life. He suspected there might be some scientific reason for it all, but he hadn't the faintest idea what that could be.

13

So he just put up with it; begrudgingly. Tom, when all said and done, was your ordinary down to earth kind of guy; a practical man. Hungry: food. Cold: more clothes; usually a cardigan these days, or chop wood. Strange goings on: ignore them. The phone started ringing. Ignore that too. Time to visit the shed.

Chapter 4

Outside, the weather was still undecided. Tom shut the back door behind him and started down the garden path. Dotted along its edge and spilling onto it stood dwarf lavender bushes almost five feet in height. Obviously no one had bothered to tell them. Tom could remember hiding behind them as a kid, from his brother during a game of hide and seek. Tim was sadly long gone. Tom did wonder sometimes if they were still the same plants. Did lavender live that long? The threatened rain started to fall, large lazy thunder spots landing on the concrete path. Tom gave himself the hurry up. The path was about a hundred feet long and he was only just halfway along it. It would be a sod if the heavens opened up before he got there. They could do what they liked when he did.

Doubling his pace, Tom made it to the shed door just as the clouds decided enough was quite enough and let terra firma have it big time. As he shut the door, Tom glanced up at the sky. All was black, grey and heavy. The rain was here for a while.

Because of the darkened sky the shed was veiled in gloom. Tom felt for the light switch. The sixty watt bulb bloomed into life and attempted to illuminate the assemblage of weird and wonderful objects Great-Uncle Rufus had seen fit to store within the shed's four wooden walls. Most covered with tarpaulin, the rest with dust.

Tom took in the sight and headed for his seat; a deckchair, held together only by the grace of whatever saw fit to keep such ancient things in one piece. It had been "borrowed" some time ago from Brighton seafront. He carefully positioned his posterior over it and gently lowered away until contact was made. This was always a tense moment. A sigh of relief as the material held. Tom relaxed, now for a little Tom time. Tom closed his eyes.

He spent the next ten minutes or so like that. Gently drifting. Not asleep, but not awake. Meditating some would call it. Then there came the scratching.

At first Tom managed to keep his eyes shut to it, but it wasn't going away and after a couple of minutes of gently growing insistency, he could ignore it no longer. Tom opened an investigative eye. He couldn't see anything untoward in the immediate vicinity. He continued with his meditating with his eye open. He could sleep that way too; a trait that ran in the males of the family. The women of the family, so it was rumoured as no man had ever seen it happen, could sleep with both eyes open and even cook a full breakfast while doing it if they put their minds to it.

The scratching continued but now accompanied by a mewling sound. Tom flicked open his other eye. What did a man have to do around here to get a bit of peace and quiet?

Tom shifted in his deckchair and tried to place where the sound was coming from. He homed in and if he was right, someone or something was scratching at the shed door.

Chapter 5

The door inched open. Rain spattered on the threshold. There followed a gasp. Followed by an exclamation of what could have been relief.

'Oh, it's you!'

'Well that's a nice welcome,' said Lucy, shaking her brolly. She stepped in and placed it by the door, 'perhaps I should take my trade elsewhere.'

'Sorry,' said Mister Smokowski.

'It's okay, I'm only joking. Are you all right?' Lucy gave Smokowski a concerned look. The man looked positively ashen.

'Yes,' said Smokowski, distractedly, then appeared to pull himself together, 'yes, sorry. What can I do for you Lucy?' There was just a hint of emphasise on her name. 'The post?'

Lucy had taken the day off work, dropped the kids at school, run a couple of errands, finished a couple of chores to clear the decks and was now ready to start the preparations for Toms birthday bash. 'Has it arrived yet?'

Smokowski wasn't properly listening. He was standing behind his counter like a rabbit caught in headlights.

'Mister Smokowski?'

'Eh? No...sorry. Er...I have to do something. Is there anything else I can help you with before you leave?'

Well there's a brush off if ever I heard one, thought Lucy. Old Smokowski came across as an odd one to Lucy at the best of times, from a different world or time on occasion, but she couldn't ever recall the man being on this form, or looking as agitated. 'I…' she started, then, thinking better of getting involved, 'no. No thank you.' She had wanted a few more candles for Tom's cake. Wanted to overload it, a Michael take she was sure he would enjoy. But she could always pop into town. It wasn't an emergency. Time to leave. She picked up her brolly and went to give Smokowski a last concerned look before she left when he appeared to almost take a jump back from something behind the counter; a peculiar look on his face.

'You sure you're okay Mister Smokowski?' said Lucy, trying to peer behind the counter, which she realised was impossible from where she was. She took a step closer.

Smokowski noticed the movement from the corner of his eye and quickly moved through the open gap left by the raised counter flap to cut her off.

'Yes, yes,' he said, running his hands nervously across his apron as if smoothing it, 'just busy, that's all. See you this evening.'

'The post?' said Lucy, wondering how she was going to get it if Smokowski was fudging her off until this evening.

'I'll bring it with me.' Smokowski shook his head. 'Tut-tut, the postal service these days but what can you do?'

He's rambling, thought Lucy, backing away. 'You won't forget them?' she asked, letting Smokowski show her to the door and outside.

'What?' said Smokowski, taking a quick glance behind him. 'No. See you later then.' He then as good as shoved Lucy out into the rain.

Lucy turned to say something but the door was already closed and the open sign turned to shut. Inside Smokowski pulled the blind on the door. She heard the click of the door locking.

Stranger and stranger, thought Lucy, managing to put her umbrella up without getting too wet. She ran for the car, which she had had to park a little distance away. Once inside she sat for a moment taking in what had just happened. Odd, is what she concluded, plain odd. She gave a shrug and started the car. Should just be enough time to pick up those extra candles.

Chapter 6

The scratching continued without any sign of stopping or introduction of the culprit. This meant that if Tom wanted to know whatever or whoever was making the noise, he would have to get up and go see for himself. He toyed with the idea of just ignoring it. It would have to stop sometime. But what if it didn't? What if it ate into his "me time"? He couldn't have that. Perhaps it was a rat. Tom looked for a sturdy stick. No rat was making his sanctuary its home. He found one in the shape of a dusty old cane and reluctantly struggled from his resting place.

Cane held in defensive mode, raised slightly behind his head and ready to be dropped in conciliatory fashion the instant the size of the foe loomed larger than reckoned on, Tom slowly advanced on the door. The scratching appeared to intensify, as did the mewling, as if whatever was outside sensed him coming. Tom tightened his grip on the cane. He concentrated on the mewling; he had never heard a rat make that noise before. Then again he hadn't been faced with the prospect of a mad, starving, man-eating rat before; one that obviously regarded Tom as a rat buffet. Tom arrived at the door and gripped the handle. The mewling and scratching stopped. In the seconds that followed, as Tom turned the knob, his senses heightened, he regained control of them. He started to feel a little foolish. Where the heck had he got the rat idea from? Note to self: don't get up so quickly when still in the mists of relaxing; mind tricks imminent. Need to loosen up. He let his arms fall by his sides, shoulders relaxed

– he had seen it done on one of his rare incursions into the world of television, some geezer had said it was good for you, relieved tension – and shook them. The cane hit against the door and the scratching started all over again. 'Bloody rat,' growled Tom, tensing, cane rising. He gripped the handle, turned it and pulled the door open in one swift – but hardly fluid – movement.

But what he'd expected to find on the other side wasn't there, whatever that had really been. After a moment or two of surprised looking this way and that his sight alighted on what was really there. Sitting, almost demurely and surely smiling up at him, was a cat. Cats couldn't smile, could they? thought Tom, bending a little so he could get a closer look at the feline.

The cat returned Tom's stare and mewed at him, though in truth it sounded more like a refined titter.

Tom straightened his back and scratched at his head. 'What have we here then?' he said, as all good detectives did spout when faced with the blatantly obvious. 'You had better come in out of the rain.' It occurred to Tom as the cat accepted his invite and ambled over the threshold and through Tom's legs, brushing against them as it did, that the cat didn't look remotely damp, considering the ongoing downpour situation outside. Tom shut the door, noting that it and the doorstep were both soaking wet. Strange, he thought, but it was nothing more than a passing one. Tom supposed it had managed to keep dry somehow; cats were good like that; always landed on their feet.

The cat meanwhile had found the top of an old sideboard and was sat amongst the dust atop it cleaning its paws.

Casting no more than a cursory glance at the cat, Tom reclaimed his seat. It was time for Tom time again and with a bit of luck, now the cat was out of the rain and looking as if it had just wanted somewhere dry to hang out, he would now be able to drift into it without being disturbed. But Tom found to his chagrin this wasn't going to happen.

Tom shifted uncomfortably, grumbling as he did; something wasn't right. It wasn't the deckchair per se, it was still its old comfortable self, but he just felt there was something wrong in its general demeanour. He sat up and shifted his bottom from side to side to see if he could find out what was disturbing him. Nothing. He sat back again. Nope, it was still the same. Then it dawned on him; it wasn't the chair that was uncomfortable, it was him. He was making the chair uncomfortable. That didn't make sense. Tom gave it a moments thought to try and clarify just what it was he was thinking. Something was making him uncomfortable, which he decided, was perhaps foisting itself on him on a subconscious level, which in turn was causing him to put blame on the chair. There, everything made perfect sense if you gave yourself chance to think about it. Except it didn't really, did it? Tom's mind turned to the cat. So did his head. It was watching him.

No, it wasn't just watching him; it seemed to be studying him. Tom felt an involuntary shudder travel through him. He considered the cat for a moment and decided he had found the real cause of his discomfort. Shame on him, how could he have poured blame on his old friend like that?

Tom continued his considering. Why was the creature giving him the heebie-jeebies? The cat was still staring at him. It had to be the staring, it… it was a little unnerving. Perhaps he'd accidentally stepped on its tail at sometime or other. He raked his brain but couldn't recall seeing this particular feline before. Not that that meant anything around here, he supposed, what with all the farms about and the comings and goings of city folk, as they came and went like a dose of salts through the countryside, moving in and out of villages as the whim took them or fads changed, or they just got bored. He couldn't really expect to remember or even know of every

22

cat that was or had been in the neighbourhood. Anyway, they all looked the same to him. Except this one didn't. There was something about it. He felt that if he had seen it before, this one he would have remembered. He hadn't seen this particular breed before. It didn't strike him as your common or garden moggy. This one looked to have breeding. Mayhap it was one of those pedigree ones. Now they could be odd; barking ones and ones with no fur, not natural, or maybe it was. But this one had fur. And spots, not blotches but proper ones like you would find on something in the wild. But it didn't look wild. Its colour was different as well, a mix of blue and pewter, the spots a darker version of the rest of its fur. Tom, without realising it, was in danger of falling forwards from his seat, as curiosity took hold and he started leaning closer and closer to the furry one. Why, it even had what appeared to be a worried look on its face, almost a frown. Could cats do that? He was no expert, but he didn't think so. And what was that mark between its ears? If he didn't know better he'd swear it was in the shape of a beetle. Tom leaned a little further and only just managed, with a lot of jerking about of arms and legs, to stop from tipping out of the chair and onto the floor. On the sideboard the cat looked on, unperturbed.

Tom gathered himself and decided he needed a drink of something, rain or no rain. He stood up and gave the cat a stern look. It too would have to face the elements.

The cat, as if sensing something was afoot, stood up and wandered over to the edge of the sideboard. There it proceeded to give, what Tom took to be, a try it if you dare look.

The shudder returned, this time making Tom shiver. It wouldn't hurt to leave it in here, thought Tom; wouldn't do any harm. Tom started to slowly, nonchalantly he hoped, move towards the door. Perhaps the cat was wild after all. Tom had been scratched as a child; by a kitten. He wouldn't admit it, but there was a scar, psychologically. Oh, he could

23

laugh about it now, but this was different; a wild cat.

Tom got two steps and then it happened. His world of reality, of no-nonsense sensibility, of normalness, collapsed about him.

The cat, who had watched Tom's every exaggerated, tele-graphed, awkward, nothing like stealthy, move towards the door with something akin to amusement, had decided enough was enough and that there was never going to be any good time to do what it was about to do. So it did what it had to do. It spoke. Not a mew or meow you understand, but words, a sentence in the Queen's English.

'I think you should sit back down,' it said.

Chapter 7

'Do you have to sit there?' asked a pouting, disgruntled, Kate.

'I can sit anywhere I want,' said Marc, parking his bottom, 'it's my playground too.'

'Child,' Kate sniped. She glanced up at the sound of barely refrained giggling. Mouths behind hands; her friends were laughing at her. She was seething, angry. He always did this. It was at times like this she wished she was an only child. Why didn't he sit with his mates and annoy them? She decided she would ask.

'Why don't you go sit with your mates?' she said. But Marc wasn't listening. Sandwich halfway to mouth, he was staring blankly into space.

'Marc?' said Kate, now annoyed that he was ignoring her.

But Marc still wasn't listening; he had his mind on other things. Something had caught his attention. As if in a trance he placed his untouched sandwich back in his lunch box.

'Marc!'

For a fleeting moment Marc re-entered the here and now. 'Eh?' he offered, looking at his sister as if she had suddenly appeared from nowhere. He started to pack his lunch box away. 'Got to go,' he said, his face a picture of distraction.

'What?' said Kate, confused for a moment, but then what he had said finally seeped into her brain. 'Should think so too,' she said, sternly. Hoping to regain some credibility within her little clique, she added, 'And don't come back.'

'Bye.' Marc threw his bag over his shoulder and started walking away.

Frowning a little, Kate watched her brother go. He was heading towards the corner of the main hall, towards out of bounds. He would be in trouble if one of the teachers saw him. Why was he acting so weird? Was he acting weird? She watched for another moment or so and then decided perhaps he wasn't; he was a *brother* after all; weird was in the contract. She then realised someone was talking to her. She turned; it was one of her friends asking her who she thought would win the latest reality show. She answered, but then threw a quick glance her brother's way. He was gone. She frowned then shrugged. Brothers! Who'd have them? She returned to the conversation and within a short while thoughts of annoying brothers were lost in the swirling mists of girl talk.

Chapter 8

Tom almost fell backwards. If it wasn't for the door he would have. His eyes bulged from their sockets as he tried to get a grip on what had just happened. *Couldn't have happened!* Tom drew a shaky hand over his thinning grey pate. He went to draw on his reserves of no-nonsense commonsense. Get a grip lad, cats can't talk. *But this one just had!* Have to sit down. Tom, with one wary eye on the cat, carefully reached over to his deckchair and pulled it towards him. He placed it as far as he could against the wall, as far from the cat as possible. It had to be the drink. Was tea that strong? He hadn't come out of Tom time so quickly before. Perhaps he was hallucinating? First the irrational rat thingy and now talking cats. It could have been brought on by pressure. That was it! Pressure put on the brain by oppressive weather. Tom couldn't remember if it was caused by low or high pressure. High he suspected, because that's how he felt; high and light-headed. But Tom's mind kept racing. Perhaps he'd been drugged? Perhaps it was a senior moment? He'd had a few of those the last few years. Come to think about it, he'd had them for as long as he could remember. But this moment in time hadn't been lost, it had been right here, right here in vivid colour, backed by surround sound. What he realised he was trying to tell himself, was that it *had* really happened. The cat had really spoken. He sat down. It was all becoming just a little too much for a man who prided himself on his lack of imagination.

On the sideboard the cat looked on, seemingly unconcerned by Tom's attempts at rationality. It had sat down to wait. It had known what would happen. What always happened the first time it introduced itself; or rather its ability to utter more than the odd mew and meow. The trouble was, the cat reflected, the job needed typically unimaginative, realist types. A steady enough lot and generally trustworthy, which was fairly top of the list, but it was always hard for them to take. It was literally pulling the proverbial carpet of how they thought they knew the world, from under them. It was hard to take but hey, tough titty. It was a hard universe. The cat lay down; this looked like it might take a while.

In the chair Tom was struggling with his conclusions. On one hand the evidence was irrefutable. This wasn't some second-hand story passed from one barfly to another, he had seen it, or rather heard it, with his own ears. But on the other hand he had played the old "didn't hear you" trick so many times perhaps he really was going a little "Mutt 'n Jeff"? And there lay the problem; could he trust them? Of course he could. Who was he trying to kid. Tom appeared to have finally come to a decision about what he had witnessed. He opened his mouth to say something and… nothing. His bottom jaw just hung there. Tom's eyes began to glaze over.

Damn, thought the cat, who had been splitting its time between watching the rain trickling down the window and Tom, he's shutting down. She had heard of it happening, but never to her yet. And it wasn't about to either, not on her watch. The cat suddenly leapt from the sideboard to Tom's lap and back again in one fluid movement. Unorthodox, but she had heard tell that it worked.

Noises of the groaning type now emanated from the direction of the deckchair. In it Tom was noisily nursing his unmentionables and quietly mentioning the need for a nurse; Tom didn't trust doctors; not since the kitten episode. But however painful it had been Tom was now back in the world of the unbelievable. He wheezed, coughed and, as if surfacing from a stint below water, gasped and grasped at the words trying to form in his mouth. 'You spoke,' he eventually spluttered.

'Give the man a cigar,' said the cat, sounding for all the world the most sarcastic cat that ever spoke.

Tom returned to shifting uneasily in his chair, but to be fair he had a good reason this time. When he had found something approaching a comfortable position he fixed the moggy with a stare that would have had lesser cats turning on their little furry heels. This moggy though dug its heels in and stared back.

Tom was the first to break eye contact, which was understandable as they were watering somewhat. But even so, it was doubtful he would have won the stare down contest. 'What do you want?' he said, after a moment of hesitation. Hesitation because asking the question would prove one of two things; he was either going mad and talking to a cat or he actually believed he had heard what he had heard. Neither choice filled him with comfort.

The cat stood and stretched, its front legs pushed out in front of it. It yawned as it did it. It was thinking it was time to get things moving. Get the old ball rolling. Take the bull by the horns. Grab the old boy by the goolies. No – that had been done; sort of. Time to saddle-up. 'You've got a job to do,' said the cat. As it spoke its eyes took on a subtle change of colour. They returned to normal when it had said what it wanted to say.

'A job?' Tom was listening, but not wholly believing. 'What sort of job?' He had just asked a cat about a job! His wheels were definitely coming loose. But then something else kicked in. Tom felt suddenly quite angry. He couldn't quite put his finger on why, perhaps the lap incident, but it was there so why not use it. 'No, scrub that. Who the hell are you?' he demanded. Dream or whatever, he wasn't about to be pushed about in his own shed.

'I am Cat,' replied the cat.

'You don't say,' sniped Tom, who was suddenly willing to play along. It's what you did in a dream. Why hadn't he thought of it before? There was of course a nagging feeling. But that was mostly coming from his groin.

Despite the sarcasm the cat continued undaunted. 'And you are now officially my charge. My job will be to guide you until you fully grasp the situation you now find yourself in. Once there I will avail my services to you.'

'What does that mean?'

'I'm here to train up my new partner, you.'

Chapter 9

It was all too much. But then again it wasn't. As feelings went, or had, during the last ten minutes or so, the one he was having was now was certainly the oddest. He was almost calm, as if he was slipping into something comfortable. 'Train me up for what?' This is unnerving, he thought, mainly because it wasn't in the least. Dream mode, had to be.

The cat gave Tom a look that proclaimed the feline didn't think the man was totally together. 'I think you should come with me,' said the cat. It leapt from the sideboard and landed in one bound at the foot of the door. There it waited for Tom to open it.

After a slight struggle, Tom prised his aching body from the chair. He had decided to play along with his dream; it wasn't as though he had anywhere better to go. He frowned at the rain that was lashing down in buckets outside. 'You want me to go out in that?' he said. 'We'll get soaked.' But maybe not if it is a dream.

'Not if you stay close.'

'Stay clo-' Tom suddenly recalled how dry the cat had been when it had arrived. He had another look out the window, up, above it, craning his neck to see… see what? A giant umbrella? A force field deflecting the rain? Crikey, he thought, cringing, he was beginning to sound like his grandson. But everything was saturated. There was nothing to see. The cat must have crawled as tightly in as it could against the side of the shed. The thing had got lucky with the way the wind must have been blowing. He opened the door.

31

The cat slipped outside. Tom hesitated a second, then popped his head out, which got an instant soaking. His moaning brought the cat back. Tom mopped at his face with his hanky. If this was a dream, it was a bloody good one.

'Sorry about that,' said the cat, 'I thought you were behind me.'

Tom glared at it.

'I said I'm sorry,' said the cat, sitting on the end of the path. The creature was bone dry. The rain appeared to be going round it. 'Now please follow me as closely as you can.'

The cat waited until Tom had stepped out and then proceeded in a straight line along the side of the shed – Tom had been right about that – towards the portable loo. Behind it, Tom, doing as he had been told by keeping close, was wondering how the hell what was happening, was happening. Above him the rain was cascading down, but flowing round him as if he was standing in an invisible tunnel.

The cat stopped when it reached the loo. 'We're here.' Tom, who was mesmerised by the raindrops above him splattering on nothing, almost stepped on the cat's tail. It having the presence of mind to flick it out of harm's way as Tom's boot arrived.

'What!' exclaimed Tom, at the abrupt halt in their journey, 'Where?'

'Here,' said the cat, looking up.

Bemused, Tom also looked up. But all he could see was that damn toilet.

'The time machine.'

It took a second for what the cat had said to register. 'A what machine?'

'A-'

'Save your breath. I heard what you said,' said Tom, shaking his head, 'and now I think it's about time I woke up.' Tom's dream was fast becoming a nightmare he wanted no part of. He had played along, his mind had had its fun, but it was time for the show to no longer go on. Tom closed his eyes and managed a good impression of a constipated man. He flicked an eyelid open and peered down. The cat was still there and he was still where he didn't want to be. He closed his eyes and tried pinching his legs, but all that did was cause him pain. He opened them again and received a surprise. The loo door was wide open. 'Well I'll be…' he said.

The cat stepped inside.

Tom now pinched the back of his hand. It all stayed exactly as it was. This confirmed it. It wasn't a dream; he was going insane. Against his better judgement Tom took a tentative step forward. Another saw him standing in the portable loo. The door slammed shut behind him.

Chapter 10

There was a grubby sort of light filtering in. Tom took a short while to grow accustomed to it.

Gradually his surroundings came into gruesome focus. A grey plastic pipe stood in one corner, a hole smashed into it at its base. The yellowing ceiling was covered in long vacated dusty cobwebs. To his left, the hand wash dispenser hung crooked and empty. He noticed scratches on the wall. There was a smell. Why wouldn't there be? Tom looked down. The toilet seat was broken in half on one side, its lid wedged to one side. Tom ventured a peep into the toilet's bowels and was relieved to find the only thing there was the plastic handle that had once covered the flushing handle. All in all just what you might expect to find in an old disused and derelict bog.

The cat was sat beneath the askew dispenser. 'Bit of a mess, but nothing that can't be put right.' The feline observed.

Tom didn't answer; he was too busy deciding he didn't want to be here anymore. He turned round and started pushing against the door. It wouldn't budge.

'Won't open until it's travelled,' said the cat, sniffing, its features a picture of disdain as the pong assaulted its nose. Bad as that was though, it wasn't as bad as it could have been, seeing that it had been standing like this the past five years. The cat thought back to the last time it had been in here; had definitely used up a life that day. The journey had been a bumpy one.

'The door won't open,' Tom verified, but saying more to himself than the toilet's other occupant. But if it wasn't a dream and he wasn't hallucinating...

The cat rolled its eyes. 'Like I said, it won't open again until we've been somewhere else.'

One last fruitless half-hearted shove saw Tom finally admit defeat. He turned, resignation weighing heavily and leaned with his back against the door. His shoulders sagged and he started to slide down it as far as his old joints would allow. Once there he tipped his head back and closed his eyes – tight. He could feel the pattering of the rain against the outside of the loo through the door. He wished he'd answered that damn phone now. He opened them again and looked at the cat. The cat was sitting, watching him, beside the defunct loo.

'You're real, aren't you?'

The cat appeared almost apologetic. 'Yes.'

'No dream?'

'No.'

'Not even a tad of hallucination?'

The strange smile reappeared on the cat's face. 'No.'

Tom straightened up and put his head in his hands, he rubbed them against his face. Perhaps one last attempt at trying to erase the inevitable. He moved his hands away. He wasn't going to submit quietly. This was his life being messed about with by goodness knows what. 'So, you going to tell me what the hells going on here?'

'Been trying,' said the cat.

Tom tried to get his head around his situation. How did you deal with something like this? He laughed inside; Marc would know. Meet it head on. Sooner the situation was dealt with... Tom then remembered what the cat had said earlier, about them being partners.

'So what are you?'

The cat looked puzzled. 'A cat,' said the cat.

'You're one of them fami... famy...'

'Familiars?' said the cat, helping.

35

'Like witches have,' said Tom, admitting he did have some knowledge of the world of fantasy, 'I've read about those sort of goings on you know.'

'I know.'

'What do you mean, you know?' said Tom, taken slightly aback. Suspicion was quick to surface. 'How?'

'We've been watching you.'

'Who has?' Taken aback now morphed into startled.

'Us, "familiars",' said the cat, who, if bothered, would have raised its front paws and wiggled a couple of claws on each. But it wasn't, so didn't.

The cat's smiling, it really is, thought Tom, I'll be damned. 'So you *are* witches' things,' said Tom, backing away.

'You said that, not me. We're best described as…,' the cat paused for thought, 'a time traveller's best friend.'

There the creature went again with that time travel nonsense. Tom shifted his feet, his right one was going to sleep. Yeah, how crazy was that? About as crazy as the creature talking to him was. In for a penny. 'Time travelling you say?'

'Your Great-Uncle Rufus is one of the best.'

'Rufus was one?' This was getting worse. Tom didn't think his mind could take much more.

'*Is,*' said the cat, carefully studying Tom's face.

The penny didn't have far to drop. Tom's face screwed up as if he was looking into the sun. 'What do you mean *is*?' He turned his good ear to the cat and waited for the reply, knowing the camel's back might just be in danger of exploding.

The cat, sensing the answer might prove to be a major stumbling block, told Tom anyway. 'He's not dead, Tom, he's missing.' He had to know the truth sometime.

'Missing?'

'In time somewhere. We had to cover things up so no one would know.'

Now Tom's mind was in turmoil. He was thinking of the funeral. His inheritance. Talking cats and time travel was one thing but this was... was down right illegal. Grief, he could spend his retirement at her Majesty's pleasure.

The cat though, had known what to expect, what was going through Tom's mind that minute. 'It's all right. You have nothing to worry about. All will be explained in due course, but first we have a job to do.'

Not quite shocked to his boots, but well on the way to the top of his socks, Tom grasped for something to say. He wanted to ask who the "we" were. He wanted to know what the cat really was. He wanted to know what the hell was happening to him.

The cat looked on impassively. It was just a job, it would tell itself. But that didn't always help. It wasn't easy watching the turmoil. But thinking about things didn't either. The cat had learned long hard lessons. It was a professional. The next job was calling and it had to be done. It had to be hard. But... 'Where would you like to go?' It heard itself ask. The cat blinked. Getting soft in my old age, it thought, that smile back again. 'Tom?'

Tom's head had found its way into his hands again. It now rose a little. 'Go?' said Tom, hesitantly.

'Yes, where would you like to go?' repeated the cat.

Tom knew exactly where he wanted to go. Real or not, he had had enough of this nonsense. 'Home,' he said, the hesitation of moments earlier swept away. 'That's where I want to go, home.' Tom turned and started pushing on the door again. Again it stayed firmly shut.

'You have to-'

'Yeah, I know, travel. That's what I'm trying to do. Travel home. Now are you going to let me out or am I going to have to knock the door down?'

With all the will in the world, thought the cat, watching the scrawny old guy still pushing on the door, if we were in a paper bag you'd still have trouble. He needed help.

'The stick,' said the cat, helping.

'What?'

'You need to think where you want to go and pull the handle.'

'The handle?'

Oh good grief, thought the cat, wondering why it was always lumbered with the slow starters. The cat leaned against the toilet flusher.

It then dawned on Tom that perhaps the handle had something to do with the door. Maybe it unlocked it. Against his better judgement, but eager to get out of the place, he decided to humour the furry one. What did he have to lose? He grabbed it, closed his eyes, thought of home and pulled. There was a flushing noise, but no blue liquid swirling in the bowl. He got some weird satisfaction about that without fully knowing why. Toilet flushed, he turned his attention on the door again and pushed. This time it gave way without the slightest resistance and Tom fell out; straight into the hallway of his cottage. The cat trotted past the bewildered, bug-eyed pensioner and disappeared into the kitchen, the next door down.

A couple of seconds later the cat's head reappeared, it was smiling again; at a still spread-eagled Tom. 'You coming?' it asked.

Chapter 11

Because of the deathly pallor exhibited on all of Tom's visible extremities, especially his face, the cat came to the conclusion the mission, for now, however urgent, would have to be put on hold until some explanation had been given regarding the situation and circumstances the pensioner now found himself in. To do otherwise, the cat judged, could well prove to have counterproductive consequences for the mission and all concerned. Put plainly; in the state he was in, the old codger could well bollocks the whole operation.

Still shaken, but now at least able to hold a cup of tea without scolding his hands, Tom listened as the cat – who was called Cat; short for Catranna, as it turned out – gave it to Tom, just exactly how things were.

It transpired that Great-Uncle Rufus was indeed a time traveller and a damn fine one at that, until he got lost that is. And not the first time traveller in the family either. Time travelling was a family thing and passed down the generations. Cat proved a bit reticent when asked how far back that went, but told Tom that Marc was next in line when he attained the coming of travelling age; sixty-five, as he had just done. Tom, tragic accidents aside, will have reached the ripe old age of one hundred and nineteen by then. Cat would not be drawn on the consequences for Tom once his grandson had taken the reins. When Tom had asked why Lucy or Kate weren't next in line, Cat just humphed, admitted it wasn't fair and totally sexist, but she didn't make the rules. She also mumbled something about it being much better before the Victorian era and about outdated values mollycoddled by Victorians; especially the men. Tom didn't push the point.

With that slight grumble out of her system, Cat resumed her tale, explaining who she was, what she was and what the last half hour was all about.

Cat was a Mau, an ancient breed of Egyptian cat; a true breed; one of the very few left in the world and all the scarcer because she was magical.

When Tom baulked at this, sending tea across the table top, and was about too pooh-pooh the idea of it, the whole magic thing, let alone a magic cat, Cat reminded him of the lack of wetness they had encountered on their trip to the portable loo. Tom resumed a disgruntled silence, sipped at his tepid tea and let her continue.

But it wasn't all magic; Cat conceded that there was also a certain amount of science involved, and organisation. Cat, admitting science wasn't really a cat thing, skipped any explanation where that was concerned, but went on to explain what she meant by organisation.

Rufus belonged to a group who existed to protect the world and its past. Here Tom had asked about the present. Cat had told him that without the past there would be no present; or future. Tom finished his cuppa and wanted to know why?

There were people out there, Cat explained, who wanted nothing more than to change the past for their own ends and more often than not without any concern for the consequences of these actions.

At this point Tom was feeling a little calmer so he made himself another cup of tea. He thought he understood most of what he had been told, especially as he was getting that comfortable feeling again. It was beginning to feel as if he belonged. Of course it would all take some getting used to. But there was one question that was nagging at him. Why wasn't the loo bigger on the inside? Cat had rolled her eyes and told him such a thing was impossible.

Tom had batted back with the "lack of wetness" scenario. Cat then countered with the observation that Tom seemed to know a lot more about fantasy than he was letting on. Tom sat with his fresh brew and was happy for Cat to continue.

But as she was about to, Tom had another thought and interrupted her, wanting to know if the loo could travel through space as well as time?

'No,' said Cat, 'it's made of plastic. It would burn up at the slightest hint of re-entry. She then thought she had better come clean about the time thing too. It had all seemed so much easier when she had run the Tom scenario through her head that morning. She hadn't figured on him asking so many questions; had thought things would work out in their own way. That was the problem with humans, so unpredictable. 'It isn't really a time machine either,' she heard herself admitting.

'Aha!' said Tom, becoming animated, certain he had found her out.

'Or rather it is,' said Cat, ignoring his outburst, 'but not a very good one. It's more of a transporter that can take you to any toilet in the world. A portal-loo if you like, as Rufus liked to call it.'

This actually made a modicum of sense to Tom, who was looking through the window at the loo which was still standing where it had always stood. If that thing had landed in the cottage there would have been a hell of a mess to clean up. 'Any toilet?'

Cat nodded.

'But how do we travel in time then?' Tom asked, 'if it's no good at it.'

'That's where I and others like me come into their own,' said Cat, 'where the magic comes in. We have the power of temporal spacial distortion.' Tom's face grew vacant. 'We can open doorways in time.' At least that's what Cat thought it

41

was called; she not being any good at science. Anyway, whatever; she could travel through time.

'Then why the need for the plastic loo?' asked Tom, trying to get his head round the latest news.

'We need to get to the near exact spot in the world before I can open that door in time and the portable toilet is cheaper and quicker than public transport.'

'Makes sense,' agreed Tom, 'but why a portable loo?'

Cat recalled vividly the day Rufus had come up with the idea. It was his little way of having a laugh at the expense of the ageism squad. What better means of transport for a golden oldie than a loo. At least he wouldn't have to stop what he was doing every five minutes to look for one. 'Convenience,' said Cat, with not the slightest hint of her tongue in her furry little cheek.

That was good enough for Tom, who nodded sagely.

'But it's not to everyone's liking,' Cat conceded. She had quite liked the idea Rufus had first put forward – travellers were allowed, if told, to choose the shape of their respective transport. Cat had opted not to divulge this snippet to Tom at this point; perhaps she never would; it wasn't as if there was a definite rule about these things – a nice big comfy wing chair with knobs, whistles etc., that could travel to any chair in the world. But such is life, the idea was determined as being unworkable; too many chairs to land in; not secretive enough.

And that was that as far as the explanation went, as to the whys and wherefores of Tom's new-found role in life.

'So,' said Tom, surprised to find he might be, in some small strange way, looking forward to this time travelling malarkey, 'when do we start looking for Uncle Rufus then?'

Cat looked confused. 'Rufus?'

Tom was washing his cup up, but stopped in mid wipe. 'I

thought that's what all this was about; finding Uncle Rufus.'

Just as she thought she had cracked it. 'He's gone, Tom. We haven't the time to go looking for him now, perhaps later, but matters are pressing. We've more important work at hand. Our mission. We've the worlds to save.'

Not looking for Uncle. Tom put the half washed cup in the sink. And had he heard what he thought he had. He was afraid to ask, but he supposed he had better. 'Did you say world?'

'No,' said Cat. But before Tom had a chance to draw a relieved breath, she added, 'Worlds; Earths to be precise.'

'Earths?' stammered Tom, who would have dropped the cup if he'd still been holding it.

'This one and the parallel ones. They're unstable, drifting apart because the link holding them together has been removed. We've got to find it Tom and put it back before it's too late.'

'We have to find the missing link?' said Tom, wondering if it sounded half as weird as it had in his mind.

'Not just a link,' said Cat, suddenly springing to her feet, her tail and rear frantically wriggling as if happily spraying her territory, 'a sword; *The* sword; Excalibur!'

Chapter 12

What Cat had said didn't instantly sink in; instead it bobbed to and fro like a cork in thin treacle as Tom's thought processes tackled the insanity of it. Excalibur! *Excalibur!*

One minute he had been happily embracing the idea of retirement and all the joy that that brought and the next he was conversing with a magical cat, able to zoom from one toilet to another anywhere in the world in an instant and now, yet more craziness, set to travel back in time to find Excalibur and put it back!

Another cuppa later – this one with sugar in it – Tom was as ready as he was ever going to be. But first they had to visit the shed. Cat had said there was something important in there she had to show him before they set off.

It stopped raining the moment Tom stepped out of the kitchen. He was impressed and told Cat so. She made it clear she had nothing to do with the sudden cessation of precipitation. Sometimes a cigar was just a cigar, she explained. Tom gave her a funny look and wondered, as he wandered down the path, what a cigar had to do with anything.

They reached the shed and Tom's wonderings had turned to what Cat was going to show him. Tom envisaged a suit of some description, one for the discerning time traveller of today. A shiny ensemble perhaps, topped off with mirrored sunglasses, or something chameleon – no lack of imagination there – that would help him to blend in with his surroundings when on his quest in the world of King Arthur. Quest! Tom liked the sound of that. He could see himself now, standing proud, arms folded, one foot pressed firmly on the vanquished foe at his feet. Just who this vanquished foe was and how Tom had come to have him at his feet, him being a giant of a man, encased in shining armour, was a bit of a grey area, but that apart, Tom was starting to wholeheartedly embrace the whole time travelling scenario. In fact, you could say he was on a bit of a high as he opened the shed door. Which explained the throwing open with gusto of it, that slightly damaged one of the hinges.

Cat, who as with all cats, was blessed with an inordinate amount of intuition, especially of not where to be when the shit hit the fan at any given time, slipped smartly out of harm's way and into the shed before the door's inevitable return.

And return it did, with just slightly less force than had been used to throw it open.

Luckily Tom took the brunt of the impact, minimising further damage to the hinges.

'You okay?' asked Cat, grimacing.

'Yeah…yeah,' said Tom, taking a hanky from his pocket. He dabbed at his bleeding nose, which was kind of weird as the door hadn't actually hit him there.

Cat noticed this with some dismay. That's all she needed, a bleeder. Firm in mind now, that travelling with Tom was going to be an altogether different kettle of fish compared to Rufus, she resumed her duties and headed to the back of the shed, leaping from one dustcover to another, until she found what she had come in for. Atop a more than likely antique tallboy, Cat called for Tom to join her.

It wasn't the clearest of pathways from the shed door to the tallboy, but Tom, accompanied by the odd moan and groan, finally got there. Cat told him to open the top drawer. When he did, lifting the dust cover away first, he could hardly believe what he was seeing, he had wanted one, but this was ridiculous. From top to bottom, from corner to corner, the drawer was jam-packed with flat caps of all shapes, colours and designs.

'Blimey,' exclaimed Tom, taking in the sight, 'must be half the caps in the county here. Small wonder I couldn't find one. Are they all Uncle Rufus'?'

'He wouldn't travel anywhere without one. Said it defined who he was. Now they're yours.'

Tom, careful not to get blood on the drawers' contents, delved into it and pulled out a rather natty yellow number that sported a blue pom-pom. He put it on. 'What d'yer think?' he said, casting an eye around for something that would cast a reflection.

Cat said nothing, relying on expression only. She crossed her eyes and pretended to throw up.

Ignoring the offered fashion critique, Tom, after a brief search, spied a small hand mirror. He would rely on his own sense of fashion, thank you very much. He removed a layer of dust from the mirror then held it at arm's length; then a little closer. It would seem the cat was right, he thought, quickly removing the offending titfer.

'Which one then?' said Tom, putting the cap back where it came from.

'Your choice, I'm afraid,' said Cat, managing to look genuinely sad.

Tom pulled another from the drawer, this one grey. It sort of matched the colour of his jacket, yet not so the slightly darker grey of his trousers. This one?' he ventured, not that enthusiastically.

Cat shrugged, she had already overstepped the bounds with her opinion of the yellow one. In her defence, it had been particularly bad. Where Rufus had acquired it was anyone's guess. Cat's personal opinion was from a joke shop somewhere.

The grey cap was tossed back. Then Tom saw it. Over to the side, by where the yellow cap had landed. Silver in colour but matt not shiny, sporty yet understated and with flaps that were bound at its top – surely a boon in cold weather – it was a cap that appeared to have it all. Surely a thing of distinction, thought Tom, plucking it up with the reverence it deserved. He popped it on his bonce and positioned the mirror. 'Voila! I think,' said Tom, attempting a twirl, but only succeeding in denting a kneecap.

Cat gave it and Tom the once over. Could be worse, she felt; seen worse. 'Third time lucky would be my opinion, if I had one,' she said, 'but I do feel obliged to point out you are getting worryingly excited over a flat cap.' She jumped from the tallboy and made for the door.

Tom heard what she was saying, but it wasn't excitement he was feeling, though it was rather natty and to a certain extent chic, if you could use such a word in the same sentence as flat cap, and certain to cut a dash with the ladies, it was anticipation. As smart as it was, and he couldn't believe he was thinking all this, how was it going to help him where he was going? It could only mean there was a time travelling suit somewhere at hand. One that one must surely don if to be protected against the imagined pressure long distance time travel must have on the old bones; and he had plenty of those. Tom wasn't one for dressing up, but mayhap a spacesuit. And what of his disguise? A flat cap and cords were going to stand out like a sore thumb in the court of King Arthur. Surely he was to be provided with cunning apparel that would cast him in anonymity amongst the historical and mythical figures he would be rubbing shoulders with. Tom felt he should broach the subject.

'Where's me clothes?' broached Tom, stumbling along in Cat's wake.

Cat cast a puzzled look behind her. 'You're wearing them?' she ventured, a niggling worry now forming that Tom wasn't perhaps the right man for the job. Sadly there was no one else; or at least no one for another forty odd years or more. Further worries started to form.

'I don't mean these,' said Tom, shaking a lapel, 'I mean the ones I'll be wearing when we travel.'

Cat drew to a halt beside the deckchair and gave Tom another puzzled look.

'My time travelling clothes.'

'Oh,' said Cat, suddenly remembering the first time Rufus had set off on a journey. The portable loo wasn't there then, it had been a plain wooden outside privy. 'Do you mean the clothes that will stop your bones from being crushed by the terrible stresses and strains put on them by time travel?'

'Yes,' said Tom, breathing a sigh of relief.

'You're still wearing them, now come on.' Cat squeezed through the gap provided by the now askew door.

'What? But I…' But no one was listening.

When Tom caught up with Cat she was sitting, waiting for him beside the open door of the portable loo.

'Nothing will break,' she said, standing, 'I promise.' She went in.

That's all well and good for her to say, thought a disgruntled Tom, she's magic. What harm can come to her? He still had one further gripe to get off his chest before he followed though. 'But what about my disguise?'

'That's what I'm here for,' drifted Cat's voice from within. Now come on, the drifting of parallel worlds wait for no man.'

With trepidation remounting, Tom, cap in hand, took one small step for man and then another, bigger one, into the loo.

Chapter 13

Inside, Tom was surprised to find the loo in pristine, if not new, condition. The soap dispenser stood straight and full to brimming. The toilet seat, now with cover and back in one piece revelled in its plastic glory. Even a nice new shiny handle on the flusher and not a single spider web in sight. And more importantly, there was no whiff. The portable loo had undergone a transformation.

'This can't be the same one?' said a bemused Tom, sitting on the toilet and noticing an array of loo rolls on a shelf he hadn't noticed the last time he was in there.

Cat, who had positioned herself on another shelf Tom hadn't noticed earlier, pricked her ears and gave the loo the once over. 'Always does when it's been on a journey,' said Cat, 'but I have to admit, I didn't think it would ever again after the battering it took when Rufus was lost.'

'How's it do it?' asked Tom.

'I don't know,' admitted Cat.

'You don't know?'

'I'm a magic cat,' said Cat, 'not a font of all knowledge.' Cat shifted on her shelf. 'And now, if you've quite finished admiring the décor, I suggest you do what you are here to do so we can get on.'

'About that,' said Tom, 'what am I supposed to do again?'

Cat rolled her eyes. 'Think of where we want to go and hey presto! As simple as that.'

'And where's that exactly?'

Cat stopped short of another roll of the eyes in case it started to become a habit. 'I told you.'

'I know when. I just don't know where.'

Cat realised that in all the excitement, if you could call it that, she'd forgotten to tell him. There was a bit of a blush, but luckily the fur covered it. 'Tintagel,' she said.

'Tintagel,' Tom repeated, running over in his mind and trying to pinpoint just where exactly it was in the world. 'That's Cornwall, isn't it?'

'That's the one,' Cat verified, her patience fraying further.

'Need some sandwiches and a flask then,' said Tom, still not getting it.

Grief! thought Cat, clenching her little paws. 'Just think of it!'

'Okay… okay, no need to get your mittens in a twist.' Tom closed his eyes and once again took on the guise of a constipated man. 'But before I do,' said Tom suddenly, opening his eyes, 'could you turn round a mo, I need a quick one.'

'A quick one?'

'A jimmy.'

'A jimmy?'

'Jimmy Riddle, I need to use the toilet,' said Tom, standing and lifting the lid.'

'Oh for goodness' sake,' groaned Cat.

'Won't be a minute; habit.'

Three minutes and a lot of whistling later, Tom pulled on the flusher, cleaned his hands with the cleanser and reclaimed his seat. 'Nice smell,' said Tom, sniffing his fingers. Cat glared at him. 'Tintagel, you say?'

'Please,' said Cat, staring to the heavens.

The constipated man returned.

'Okay,' said Cat, no more than a thought process later, 'let's go.'

'Already?' said Tom, flicking open an eyelid. He hadn't felt anything. 'You sure?'

'Have a peep,' said Cat.

Tom went to the door and gingerly twisted the catch. He opened it a smidgen. He had a peep. It was a very quick one.

'Well?'

'We're still moving,' said Tom, quickly slamming the door shut. He didn't want to end up like Rufus, lost in the ether.

Cat's eyebrows did some rising. 'We can't be,' she said. More melodramatics from Mister Drama no doubt, she thought, rather unkindly.

'Be my guest,' said Tom, opening the door a crack.

Cat sniffed at the gap, frowned and asked Tom to open the door further so she could get a better look. Tom obliged, but only managed to open it from a small crack to a slightly bigger crack. Cat gave him a look.

'It's as far as it will go,' said Tom, demonstrating the fact by putting a shoulder to it.

'Lift me up,' said Cat.

Foot against the door so it wouldn't close, Tom lifted Cat so she could see what she thought she would see. Cat knew the door wouldn't open until they had arrived at their destination, so had figured that if Tom was right and they were still travelling, they had to be on something moving and judging on the wind speed whistling past her whiskers, they were travelling at about forty miles an hour. The guess was that if she could look down on the portable loo right that moment, she would find it nestling amongst others of the same. And judging by the strap stopping the door from opening, they were on the back of a truck; flatbed no doubt. She asked to be put down.

'We're on the back of a lorry,' said Cat, after Tom had shut the door, 'What were you thinking?'

'Just what you told me to think,' said Tom, quickly on the defensive.

'Tintagel?'

'Tintagel, Cornwall,' said Tom, 'just in case there was another one somewhere we didn't know about.'

'And that's it?' said Cat, suspecting it wasn't, and knowing that if it wasn't it was possibly her fault.

'More or less,' said Tom, beginning to feel guilty, though he didn't know why.

'More or less?'

Or perhaps he did. 'I might have added…' A light suddenly went on somewhere in the recesses of Tom's mind. 'Lorry, you say?' Cat nodded. 'Wouldn't be a flatbed, would it?'

'Yes,' said Cat, pleasantly surprised by Tom's deductions. Things could be looking up. 'Which means you were thinking…?'

'I only wanted the thing to go fast,' said Tom, sitting. 'You kept on saying how urgent things were.'

'You asked it to go flat out to Tintagel, didn't you?'

It was Tom's turn to nod his noggin.

'My fault,' said Cat, owning up. 'I should have pointed out how sensitive the loo is. Explained how careful you have to be with your thoughts. How dangerous it can be with the wrong one.'

'What now?'

'Tintagel.'

'Tintagel it is.'

'Just Tintagel.'

Tom closed his eyes, which wasn't really necessary, and pulled on the flusher. Something else that wasn't necessary. Cat liked her little jokes. Perhaps she would tell him some time, but then again it did help concentrate the mind. Humans, she felt, needed all the help they could get.

'That should do it,' said Cat.

Tom looked from the door to Cat.

'Go on,' Cat encouraged.

Hoping Tintagel *had* been the last thing on his mind and not one of the numerous other thoughts a nervous, nay, scared man might have been thinking, Tom pushed on the door. He was met by a soft light emanating from above.

At his feet Cat gently nudged her way past his legs, but stopped short of leaving the loo. She sniffed the air. To Tom, she appeared to be cautiously casing whatever was on the other side of the door. Eventually she slipped outside. It would appear they had arrived. The Mau has landed, she mused to herself. 'We're here,' she said, squeezing through the gap Tom was reluctantly allowing, 'Come on.'

For whatever the reason, Tom did not want to open the door any further than it already was so also squeezed through the gap, holding the door tight to him. It was quite a feat, not to mention a sight and so totally not needed but he achieved it and stepped cautiously after Cat.

It immediately became obvious to Tom where they were; a toilet somewhere. The lighting was ambient, the walls clean, mirrors in one piece; not a public loo then! He stood for a moment watching Cat cautiously edge to what must be the exit, the giveaway the exit sign above it, then turned to check behind him. The door to the portable loo was still open and as far as he could see, the insides the same, but the outside was now a stall, standing in the middle of a row of five others with normal interiors.

'Won't somebody notice?' whispered a worried Tom.

Cat now stood at the exit. 'It's for our eyes only,' she said, not turning. 'Come on, it's all clear.'

With a last glance behind him, Tom hurried over to where Cat was waiting.

They left the toilets and found themselves standing in a foyer.

'We're in a hotel,' said Tom, stating the obvious.

'Stay close,' said Cat, clearly on her toes. She started

53

across the foyer aiming for a set of double doors, Tom in close attendance.

To their right a staircase and lift, to their left the reception desk. There was no one manning it.

'There's no one about,' said Tom, relieved that there was no one around to witness an old codger in conversation with a cat.

'They wouldn't be able to see you anyway if there were, I've created a glamour to protect us from prying eyes, no one need know we're here,' said Cat, 'but keep your voice down, they can still hear us.'

'Ooh!' whispered Tom, poking forth a finger at thin air to see what would happen, but happening to aim it towards the reception desk where a young lady had just arrived, clutching in her hands a sheaf of brochures.

'They would see that,' said Cat, quickly.

Tom quickly pulled his finger back before there was an embarrassing moment. He wondered what the girl would have made of a dismembered finger floating towards her across the foyer. 'How far does this glamour thing reach?' asked Tom, drawing his arms close to him.

'A bit further than there and a little closer than here,' replied Cat.

Obviously not an exact science then, this magic thingy, thought Tom.

They continued their journey to the double doors, stopping just short of them. Tom went to open the nearest.

'No!' whispered Cat, so suddenly Tom nearly fell from the glamour. 'She'll notice the door opening; lift me up. I only need to see through one of the windows.'

Tom obliged.

A brief scrutiny of the area beyond the doors told Cat all she wanted to know. 'Okay, you can put me down, I know where we are. Let's get back to the loo.'

A quick check to see if the coast back to the toilets was clear and off they went across the foyer; the receptionist, busy placing her brochures on the desk, the only person in sight.

'Quickly now,' said Cat, 'I have a feeling we're no longer alone.'

Puzzled by her comment, Tom pointed at the receptionist again as they reached the middle of the foyer. This time though, the finger didn't go unnoticed. There was a scream, followed quickly by a bump as the young receptionist swooned to the floor. 'Ooo!' said Tom, retracting his incriminating digit.

'Come on, fool,' said Cat, lifting her pace.

Tom was caught in two minds. 'Shouldn't we-'

'No,' said Cat, firmly. 'She'll be alright. Think she's seen a ghost.'

'But-'

'No buts, back to loo now, before we're discovered.'

Feeling a bit of a cad, but what choice did he have? Tom kept pace with Cat. What else could he do? They made it back to the hotel toilet and hurried in.

'Whoa!' whispered Cat, stopping dead.

'What?' said Tom, eyes darting left and right. He couldn't see anything out of the ordinary.

'Someone's using our toilet,' said Cat, keeping her voice low.

Why the hairs on Tom's neck decided to stand up, he didn't know, but he took it as a warning; the old hairs were seldom wrong. 'Who?' said Tom.

'Could be innocent, but I don't want to take any chances,' said Cat, creeping forward.

Could be innocent? thought Tom, as he crept with her. Why wouldn't it be innocent? Perhaps it had something to do with the "we're no longer alone" comment Cat had made in

55

the foyer. Tom was about to ask, but was hushed by Cat.

'They're coming out,' said Cat, as the door to the toilet opened.

There was a rustle followed by a shuffle and then an old lady appeared, rummaging through a large handbag she was carrying.

'It's-'

'Sssch!'

The old lady suddenly stopped her rummaging and stared straight at Tom and Cat. She stood stock still for a moment, squinting behind milk-bottle bottomed glasses.

Tom held his breath. Damn, he thought, we're in the ladies. Pervert, sprang to mind. He'd never hear the last of it down the pub.

The old lady lowered her arms and cocked her head to one side. She spoke. It was a voice with the capability to throw fear into old men everywhere. 'I know you're in here,' she cackled.

Tom gave Cat a questioning look.

'What say we talk?' continued the old lady, whose attention drifted slightly from where Tom and Cat stood as if not quite sure where, who she thought was there, was. 'Come on Catranna, let's chat.'

Tom's eyes were now on stalks. She knew Cat.

The old lady dipped a hand back into her bag. 'Here kitty-kitty,' she said, saying it in a way that drew a spear of cold down Tom's back. 'Come and play with grandma.'

Tom now had the distinct feeling that all was not right with "grandma".

The old lady started to pull something from her bag; something that in no way should have fitted in it.

At first Tom thought it was an umbrella; the telescopic sort, but as it grew longer he caught on to just what it was the old lady was pulling from her bag.

'Bloody-oh!' said Tom, as Cat leapt up a second too late to stop him opening his big mouth.

'Aha!' said the old lady, spinning to face the cut off profanity. 'I knew you were in here. Got a new toy boy have we?' she snarled. She swished what she'd pulled from her bag through the air; it made a whistling sound as it cut through it.

It took a moment for the scared shitless Tom to realise the tapping he was feeling wasn't his knees knocking, but Cat rapping on his ankle. She was gesturing to the exit, but before he could take a step the old lady was standing in their way. She had moved with alarming speed and now stood there, wickedly brandishing a samurai sword.

'Not thinking of cutting out on me, are you?' cackled the old lady, in a way any witch would have been proud of. She started forward, the sword swishing in front of her, ready to slice and dice anything in its way. And that meant Tom and Cat. 'I can't see you Cat, but I can sense the fear dripping from your toy boy.'

Tom automatically, to his embarrassment, grabbed at his groin. Nothing wet there; what was the silly old woman on about? He quickly moved his hand away when he felt Cat looking at him. She nodded to the toilet; their toilet. With a near overwhelming rush of relief, Tom saw that the old woman had made a mistake. They had a way out.

With swishing and whistling filling the air and the room at an increasing rate, as the old lady swung her sword faster and faster, they made a break for it. It was do or die. Tom caught a glimpse of the portable loo inside the stall. Time to run like hell and don't look back.

Time to stop and back away as fast as they could as the old lady, appeared in front of them.

Tom gave Cat a, "what now?" look.

The fur on Cat's tail fluffed and her ears went back.

Cripes, thought Tom, she's going to fight the old lady. But

57

she'll have no chance, magic or no magic; the old lady had to be a demon or something. He looked desperately about for another way out, but there was none and if there was one he suspected the old lady would get there first. His back pressed against something hard; the sinks. It was the end of the road. If he had had time, daresay he would have thought what cruel fate it was to die on the first day of his retirement and at the hands of a demented granny no less, but he didn't and instead grabbed up a cake of soap. At this point he had two choices: throw it at the old lady or towards the exit in the hope of causing a distraction which might give them time to reach the loo. He decided to throw the soap towards the exit.

Now, blame it on old age, a crap attempt, or a bit of good luck, the cake of soap, still wet from its last use, veered from its intended target and found another; the old lady's head; straight between the eyes.

The old lady howled as it crumpled on the bridge of her nose sending soapy fragments into her eyes and her to the floor.

'Bugger!' said Tom, regretting his actions, even though the old lady had been intent on slicing and dicing him. 'We've got to-'

'No we don't,' said Cat, already running for the loo, 'leave her.'

Tom, mightily ruing what he had just done, dithered for a second, but only for a second, as the old lady was getting to her feet and making a sound not unlike a raging bull. He darted after Cat and ducked into the cubicle without a second to spare, slamming the door after him. The door shuddered on its hinges behind him.

'Let's get out of here before she breaks down the door,' said Tom, wild-eyed and wobbly of the knees.

'No need,' said Cat, looking rather cool about it all, 'we're completely safe once in the loo.'

Tom thought of Rufus, but said nothing as a sudden hammering made him jump and scurrying to the toilet where he sat down with heaving chest. Any other time he might have seen the humour in where he was now sitting and what he had nearly done when the hammering started, but there was nothing funny about the situation. Someone, an old lady, had tried to kill him. 'You sure?' said Tom.

'It's banging on the cubicle door, not this one,' explained Cat.

'I hit an old lady on the head with a bar of soap,' said Tom, looking appropriately aggrieved. 'I'm a bad man.'

'No you didn't,' said Cat.

'I did,' said Tom, miserably, 'She went down like a sack of spuds.'

'It's not a she,' said Cat, 'it's a robot.'

Tom's head was set to be claimed by his hands in woeful remorse, but stopped short. 'Robot?' said Tom, turning his face to Cat.

'A ninja robot to be precise,' said Cat. 'Appeared when the latest problem arose. I suspect there are more where she came from.'

Things were now going from bad to surreal. Or had that already happened? thought Tom, feeling he was on the verge of losing whatever it was he had started the day with. 'A robot?'

'In disguise, no one would suspect an old lady.'

Which, to Tom's mind, equated to more confusion. First a talking cat, then a time travelling portable loo – no scrub that – transporter, but not forgetting time travel, oh and an uncle not really dead. And just as he thought he was coming to terms with the whole fantastic idea, a tad quickly when he now thought about it, there comes onto the scene robot ninja grannies. Was this the way for a retired gentleman to spend his time? He didn't think so. One day normality, the next day total fantastical madness. Was this the way of things now? Madness the new normality? Would things get worse? He suspected there was still a lot he didn't know. He shuddered, then shuddered again when thinking this might be how it is for the next fifty years. Did he want that? To be perfectly honest, no, but then again in a strange way, yes. He had never felt more alive than the last couple of hours, but never so close to death. At least he didn't think so. There had been that time with the plastic building block but… He wanted a cuppa. He needed something stronger.

'Can we go home now?' asked Tom, 'and please don't do that.'

Cat stopped her licking and apologised; a cat thing.

'Not yet,' said Cat, stretching, 'I've some tidying to do first.'

The loo looked tidy enough to Tom, besides that was surely something that could be done when they got back. He told Cat.

'Not in here,' said Cat, 'out there.'

'You can't mean?'

'It won't take a moment now you're safely tucked up in here, but keep the door closed until I get back and don't tell it to go anywhere.'

Tom was ashen. 'But…'

'See you in a mo.'

Tom sat in a daze.

'The door please,' said Cat.

'Oh,' said Tom, getting up and reluctantly turning the latch. 'You sure about this?'

Cat left the portable loo. Tom feared he would never see her again.

No more than a thrice later there was a tapping on the door.

'That you?' said Tom, his ear pressed against the door.

'Yes,' said Cat, 'now open the door.'

'How do I know it's you?'

'You're wearing a rather absurd silver cap with flaps on,' came the reply.

Tom opened the door a crack and peered out. Cat was sat patiently waiting at the foot of it. Tom couldn't see any sign of the old la-robot.

Cat stepped in. 'All done and dusted,' she said, licking her lips.

Relieved by her return Tom was able to relax a little. 'What did you do, eat it?' he joked, nervously.

'Black holed it,' said Cat, returning to her shelf.

Tom thought about this, but was as much in the dark as to what she meant as he was to everything else. 'Black holed it?' he repeated.

'Now you see the robot and now you don't. Sucked it in and squished it to oblivion.'

Tom had another peep outside, but couldn't see anything resembling a black hole, a cosmic anomaly that he was aware existed, but in a washroom in Cornwall? Unless Cat had stuffed it down one of the plugholes; they could be grim, but he couldn't see how? The robot had been way too big. 'Do you mean a black hole like they have in space?' asked Tom, plumping for the least believable, but more likely to be the right explanation. ''Cause if you do, where is it now?'

Cat turned her back to Tom and raised her tail.

Tom's eyebrows tucked under the front of his cap. 'And how…' No, he didn't want to know. 'Can we go home *now*?' he almost pleaded, as images he just didn't want to imagine vied for room.

Cat lowered her tail. 'No,' she said, 'we've a mission to complete and sadly it would appear our suspicions are founded, the sword being removed was no accident and someone doesn't want us to put it back.'

61

'About that,' said Tom, sounding completely miffed at not going home, 'shouldn't we tell someone, about the robot. Tell the organisation what's happened? I could have a chat with one of my fellow travellers. Go home, call one up. I mean, say there's more?'

Cat looked suddenly aghast, which was to say her eyes grew wide and the fur on her little face lay flat as if someone was pointing a hairdryer at her. 'That never happens,' she said, becoming visibly agitated, 'unless by accident or the very direst of emergencies. For their own safety all travellers' identities are known by us cats and no one else. To know is to be in danger.'

Tom was taken aback by Cat's response, even cowed a little. He had obviously touched a nerve. He hadn't meant to offend. He was new at all this. 'So what now then?' he asked, happy to change the subject.

Cat's fur returned to normal. 'We continue with our mission,' she said, apparently calm again. 'From what I saw through the hotel window, we won't be too far from Camelot when we go back.'

He wanted to go back home, not back, back. Perhaps he could think home and feign ignorance? No, she'd know. He had a little shudder. Wouldn't want to upset her. Didn't want to end up like the robot, somewhere where the sun don't shine. 'So,' said Tom, 'would I be right in thinking, Camelot here we come?'

'You think it and I'll do the rest,' said Cat.

Tom closed his eyes, laid back and reluctantly thought of England. Then quickly changed it to Camelot, Cornwall. He added the Cornwall so the whole thing wouldn't turn into a lottery.

Chapter 14

The inside of the loo throbbed and thrummed as Tom pulled on the flusher. He chanced a peek at Cat, who appeared quite unperturbed by the new, to Tom, goings on. That was all right then, thought Tom, not convinced. Now there was a rattling. Still Cat lay, undisturbed, on her shelf. Probably turbulence, Tom determined, or whatever you got when travelling in time. He kept a close watch on Cat. Then there came a thump. Not a small one either, more a large one. This time Cat's expression changed; she looked worried. No, thought Tom, more scared. No, thought Tom some more, downright fearful. A sweating came to Tom's palms.

A smile came to Cat's lips. 'Only joking,' she grinned, jumping to the floor, 'We're here.'

Tom let go of the flusher, the one that now had fingernail marks in it and scowled at Cat.

'Oh, lighten up,' said Cat, waiting patiently by the door, 'life's too short. Now, when we leave, remember to stay close and try to keep it together; the first time's always the worst.'

Tom didn't like the sound of that, unless the feckless feline was having another little joke at his expense.

The door started to open on its own. Tom frowned.

'It can do that when it wants to,' said Cat, preparing to alight.

Tom kept his frown. 'Wait!' The door started to close again. 'I can't do this.' It was suddenly hitting home; what was being asked of him. Tom – my life is straight and narrow – Tyme, planted his feet and his backside. 'I can't do it.'

'Do what?' asked Cat, knowing full well what Tom meant. It was always harder the first time. Perhaps she should have kept her big mouth shut.

'Go out there. Step into the past, medieval times, to look for a sword that might or might not really exist. It's not me. I'm not an adventurer. I'm sixty-five for goodness' sake.' Tom was fast losing his cool. 'Knights and swords and bloody magic; dragons next, I wouldn't wonder. You need someone younger. I'm not going.' Tom would have planted himself on the toilet if he hadn't been already doing that. He plumped for aggressive arm folding instead.

Cat remained unfazed by Tom's outburst, but she did wonder where he got the idea that dragons existed; maybe they did, but that was beside the point, which was, she had seen it all before. Tom wasn't unique in the throwing a tantrum stakes. She would just have to play him. Cajole and gently manoeuvre him. 'Sure you won't come?' she said, putting her little plan into action.

Her question was met by a look approaching petulance. He was getting annoyed. He had said no. What was she up to? Whatever it was he still wouldn't take a step outside unless he was back safely in his garden. She couldn't make him.

'Because if you don't I can't guarantee your safety. That's how your uncle disappeared.' A little white lie occasionally never hurt anyone, was Cat's philosophy. 'Dragged his feet and we got separated. Who knows where you might end up without me in the loo.' She threw that in just in case he was thinking of going somewhere when she left, which she had every intention of doing.

She was bluffing; had to be, thought Tom. She was going nowhere. She would see he meant it; they'd go home for a cuppa and work out some other way of getting the sword and putting it back, if it existed. But if she was, she was the owner

64

of one fine poker face. 'I could get killed,' he added, to underline his case.

'You could get killed if you stay,' said Cat, her expression unchanged.

Was that a veiled threat? Was he getting paranoid as well as cold feet? What the hell was he going to do? Tom suddenly stood up. Then, just as suddenly, sat down again. What?

The door had started to open again and Cat was already halfway out.

A knuckle went to Tom's mouth, but he refrained from chewing on it. Cat was almost outside. He stood up again. Bloody cat!

'I've worlds to save,' said Cat, as her tail joined the rest of her outside. 'Just a shame I haven't got opposable thumbs.' A parting shot, aimed at a nerve. ''Bye Tom.'

Darn it! It was invisible to the naked eye, but if capable of X-ray vision someone would have seen Tom's big toe twitch in his shoe. His leg followed suit. He took a step forward. Another. Darn that cat.

Cat was waiting outside, sat, cleaning a paw as if she didn't have a care in the world. Tom knew instantly that he had been duped, but he didn't have time to dwell on it as outside closed in on him, smothering him with its difference; difference to anything he knew.

Travelling sideways would always be familiar. The noises, the smells, the sights, the everyday normality you would associate with living in the twenty-first century. But this was different, almost alien. Of all the things Tom had go through his mind as to what he might expect when travelling back in time, this wasn't it. It was beautiful. It was quiet; not quiet as in Tom's twenty-first century quiet where there is always something going on in the background, but quiet as in silent. Yes the odd bird tweeted somewhere and if you really tried you could hear distant waves crashing on rock, but it didn't seem to break it. And oh, everything was so green, a verdant lush paradise. One Britain hadn't seen in several lifetimes. Tom turned on the spot, trying to take it all in.

'Nice, isn't it,' said Cat.

'Nice!' said Tom, 'Nice! It's bloody wonderful.' He took in a lungful of air and straight away coughed. The air was so clean it was... breathtaking.

'You like?'

'Why didn't you say?'

'It's not always like this. Wait 'til you have to visit the Victorians.'

'Camelot?'

'Down that path,' said Cat, pointing a paw.

'You've been here before, haven't you?'

'A couple of times,' said Cat, wistfully.

'You like it here.'

'You will too if you stay long enough, but not a wise move. This isn't your time, remember that. It's the biggest temptation and the greatest danger for the time traveller, be that man or cat; that and meddling with it.'

It sounded to Tom like sad experience, but didn't press it. Instead he drank in the surroundings again and then nearly choked. 'The loo's gone,' he said, panic in his voice, pointing to where it had been standing not a moment ago.

'No it hasn't,' said Cat, calmly stretching.

Another time Tom might have been in pantomime mood and sounded off an "oh yes it has", but he wasn't. 'Where the bloody hell is it then?' he said, instead.

Cat ambled past the ruffled Tom and walked over to where the portable loo had landed. When she reached the spot, the door opened to expose its toilet in all its glory.

With a severe case of the frowns, Tom went and had a look behind. There was nothing there, unless you counted the grass. 'How?' he asked, scratching at his temple.

'It's still in your garden,' said Cat, causing Tom to undertake further head scratching.

'So it doesn't actually go anywhere?' said Tom.

'Not the shell, no. Transporting or travelling. Well... sometimes, but that's another story.'

There seems to be a lot of stories, thought Tom. He was beginning to believe Cat made it up as she went along.

The door shut again and Tom found he was once again looking out over fields and hills, no loo in sight. He had a question though. 'How do we know where to find it when we want to go home?'

'You have to remember where you left it,' said Cat, her ears suddenly pricking up.

That could be a problem, thought Tom, he being an expert at forgetting why, what and when on oft occasion; where would complete the set. Perhaps he should say.

'Tha-'

'Sssch!' said Cat, 'Someone's coming.'

'What do we do?' whispered Tom. 'Cat?' But Cat had been caught on the hop; caught in the moment just as she had warned could happen and had already high-tailed it to somewhere safe.

A voice thundered from behind Tom, destroying the quiet he had been enjoying; it didn't sound friendly. 'Who goes there?' it demanded. 'You, old man, I'm talking to you.'

Lacking the agility of Cat and the abilities of the chameleon, Tom did the only thing he could think of in the circumstances; he closed his eyes and hoped they would go away. He heard the sound of someone dismounting, at least he thought that's what it was, he not being able to see of course. There was the sound of metalwork jingling, some of which just had to be of the sharp variety.

'I said I'm talking to you, old man. Turn around before I lose my temper and you lose your head,' growled a man,

67

whose voice fairly oozed with excess testosterone.

Tom swallowed hard. Now there was an offer one just couldn't turn one's nose up to, not if you wanted to continue breathing through it. Tom turned to face the angry voice that was much too close for his comfort. Where was that damn cat?

'Open your eyes,' said the man, not missing a trick and instantly seeing through Tom's ruse.

Plan "B" it is then, thought Tom, who wasn't at all confident it would work, but did it anyway. He made a run for it. What he thought he would achieve by this and where he thought he was going was anyone's guess; his included. And it may have worked; who knows? It's just a shame he hadn't opened his eyes first, failing to take in the close vicinity of the growling man and the man's ability to move, which he did with a single sidestep in Tom's path. Tom ran smack bang headlong into the man's chest.

Wallop! It hurt. Chain mail had that effect when smashing your head into it. Tom staggered, bowed his legs, bent his knees and was all set to cede to gravity's demands when a hand, rougher than any pumice Tom had ever used on his feet, reached out and grabbed him by the scruff of the neck. A groaning Tom dangled there, seeing stars.

The man stooped and studied Tom's face. 'Who are you stranger, a traveller mayhap?'

A cattle prod wouldn't have achieved a more sobering effect on Tom. Eyes wide, he stared at the man; a big man with a beard.

'Or a spy?' The man's tone darkened, suspicion spreading across his weather-beaten features. 'Speak man!' The bearded man was growing increasingly angry, his free hand hovering over the handle of his sword.

Things were going badly, Tom could tell, he had a gift for it. Where was that cat? He knew he wouldn't be able to play dumb forever. Sooner or later, and here Tom erred on the side of sooner because of the pain the large hand squeezing the back of his neck was inflicting, he would have to say something, but Tom knew that as soon as he opened his mouth the game would be up. The man wouldn't understand twenty-first century speak. He would probably think he was a foreigner; ergo a spy. Damn it! What did he have to lose? He then had to struggle against the multitude of things that were suddenly coming to mind. It had to be now or never. Before the oaf snapped his neck and it didn't matter what he did.

'Aye,' said Tom, 'a traveller.' Which wasn't a lie. What it was though was a huge surprise – for Tom. Tom knew what he had said, but he hadn't understood any of what had come out of his mouth.

'A Brit, eh?' said the bearded man, 'I had yer down as Saxon scum, but that doesn't mean yer not a spy. Many a man has sold his King's trust for a handful of silver.' The man stroked his beard and appeared to come to a decision. 'I think more questions are needed, old man.' He gave a low whistle and his horse trotted over to him. Tom was hoisted high and over the horse, his belly resting on its back, his head and arms one side, his legs the other. 'I don't think you'll be any trouble, but be warned that my temper is short should you try.' The man took in a deep breath. 'Lucky for you it's a nice evening for a walk.' He tugged at the reins and started leading his horse to wherever it was he was taking Tom.

On the horse's back, Tom turned his head to the clump of trees that stood a short way from where he knew the loo was waiting. Cat had to be hiding in there. Trees, must remember the trees, he thought, trying to drum it into his brain; near a path. Trees, remember the trees. They were oaks. Remember the oaks. A path. Where's that damn cat?

Chapter 15

Smelling of horse, aching in places he didn't know, until now, existed, Tom sat in dusky light bewailing his lot and rueing the day he had laid eyes on that cat.

Thankfully the bearded oaf had thought better of trussing him up like a chicken, not that the man hadn't wanted to; Tom had seen the glint in the man's eyes as he had toyed with the rope, but for whatever reason he hadn't. Perhaps there had been a chance, in the man's mind, that Tom might just be telling the truth; an innocent party.

Rubbing at various parts of his body, Tom got to his feet and took in his surroundings. He guessed he was in a store-room judging by the kegs and sacks lying around, but whatever, it was now his prison. A prison no doubt, that he would rot in for the rest of his days. Unless they thought he was a spy that is and then his stay would be a short one. As he would be, after they'd lopped off his head.

He shuffled over to a window, a hole in the wall with bars, and looked out. The sun was going down, but it was still light enough for Tom to view and weigh up his surroundings. If this was Camelot and Tom had a good idea that it was, due to him having followed the path, which was hard to miss from his position on the horse, from the loo, beside the trees, that Cat had said would lead there, it wasn't like anything he had ever been led to believe it would look like. The films and books had all got it wrong. Not that he had taken a lot of notice of such things, him as he was, not inclined until recently, to be interested in such things of mythological and fantastical nonsense. For one thing and he thought this was important, there was a distinct lack of castle. Had not seen one on the way in and could not see one now. There was the chance it was out of sight, but he assumed a storeroom would be within a castle's walls. And that was another thing, he hadn't seen when arriving; walls, towering stone walls. Tall wooden stakes with a gap for a gate, yes, but no towers with pennants fluttering in the breeze and no maidens with hair flowing to the ground for knights in shining armour to climb up, or was that another story? Tom didn't really know or care. What Tom did care about was getting home. And what he did want to know was where was that blasted cat?

'Tom,' whispered a voice, right on cue.

Tom frowned and peered through the bars.

'It's me, Cat,' whispered Cat.

The frown hardening, Tom turned tail and wandered back to where he had been sitting and resumed the position.

'Tom?' whispered Cat, a smidgeon of concern growing, 'Can you hear me?'

'That depends,' growled Tom, resting his chin on his fists.

There followed a pregnant pause that threatened to go the full term.

'On what?' Cat enquired, carefully.

The pregnant pause proved to be a false alarm and in its stead there now formed a brooding silence as Tom, pondering on his recent misadventures, glowered into the lengthening darkness. He wanted home. He wanted his slippers and a stiff one. He wanted to forget today and wake up tomorrow as if nothing out of the ordinary had happened.

'Tom?'

'Take me home,' said Tom. He was determined. He knew he had had enough. He wanted out, but something inside him niggled. He made an effort to shake the feeling off and succeeded, but he knew it would be back. A growing hunger it was – one for adventure, for more of the same, for it not to stop. For all his aches and pains and misgivings, Tom found he had enjoyed it all. But it wasn't him. He didn't want it. He was a pensioner for goodness' sake. 'Take me home, now.' Before the feeling comes back.

A shadow, fitting Cat's description, appeared between the bars at the window. Cat peered into the room and found Tom sitting against a barrel. The sight wasn't a pretty one and reflected somewhat Tom's mood. Cat didn't think things would improve when she told him her news.

She leapt from the window and landed a couple of feet from where Tom sat. She cautiously sidled up to the old man and mewed a curious meow at him. Tom looked at her. He didn't look as angry as he had sounded. Cat moved a little closer.

Tom watched from the corner of his eye as she approached. He gave a little sigh. It wasn't her fault; she was only doing her job. He reached out a hand. Was he really that afraid of having excitement in his life? Okay – extreme excitement. Excitement that could get one killed. But then he had nearly chocked to death on that peanut the other week. Poor epitaph that, but we all got to go somehow. When it's time, it's time. And what with the pensioner thing? You're as old as the person you feel. He had heard that in the pub, but hadn't quite got it. Well *he* felt fine. Time to throw off the yoke. Meet destiny head on. Tom threw a fist into the air and instantly regretted it. Bloody rheumatics!! This was of course open to conjecture as the only consultation regarding said ailment had been conducted in the pub with a few old mates after supping more than the odd pint. His other hand meanwhile, having found Cat, had but scant time to ruffle the fur on her head before being diverted to give his now aching shoulder a rub.

'I shouldn't have left you,' said Cat, apologising even though there was little she could have done. Magic had to be used sensibly; it wasn't a cure all. There were consequences to be taken into consideration. 'You all right?'

'A few bruises and the odd strain,' said Tom, still rubbing his shoulder, 'nothing a hot bath won't put right.' He stopped his rubbing and looked at Cat. There was something up; he could feel it. 'But that's not going to happen, is it?'

Cat's little forehead creased. 'Well…'

He was sure he would get use to things in the end; he just hoped it wouldn't be his. Cat was doing her job; perhaps he should start doing his. 'It's okay,' said Tom, pushing against the barrel as he got to his feet, 'we've got a job to do, but once we've got the sword and put it back we're outta 'ere 'ombre. I've a stiff drink, a bath and a party to go to in case you'd forgotten.'

Cat waited for Tom to stand before giving him the bad news. Wise move? Maybe she should have told him while he was still sitting. Oh, well. 'It's not here,' she said.

'What's not?' asked Tom.

'Excalibur.'

Tom stopped his rubbing. 'Eh?'

'It's too early.'

'For what?' said Tom, sensing he wasn't going to like what Cat was trying to tell him.

'To put back. It's not out yet.'

Tom raised his hands. 'Whoa now,' he said, trying to make sense of what it was Cat was telling him. 'What's not and what's what? And take a breath before you answer.'

He's right, thought Cat, I'm not making much sense. She took her breath. 'The sword's still in the stone; we're too early.'

Tom took to sitting again. Not that he was in a state of shock by the news, but more in puzzlement. Something had just come to him regarding the Arthurian tales he had happened on during his time. He thought hard for a moment.

73

Had he found a flaw in Cat's plan? Were they on a wild sword chase? Weren't there two of them? The one in the stone and Excalibur; handed to Arthur by a certain lady in a lake. Should he bring this up? Perhaps she doesn't know. Perhaps she had overlooked it as he had. Better now than later. Tom pulled back his shoulders, or at least one of them, and prepared to give Cat the bad news.

Cat in the meantime had taken to looking at Tom in a most querulous way. He was too calm; way too calm.

'I fear I may have bad news for you,' said Tom, looking grave.

Strike that calm rubbish, thought Cat, he's starting to act downright weird.

'I fear it will put you in a quandary,' said Tom, in his best serious voice, but still far from the point. He finally got there. 'I believe you'll find there are two swords; one in the stone and one from the lady in the lake.' He raised his eyebrows and waited for the expected response.

He didn't get it. 'An expert, are you?' said Cat.

'I…' stammered Tom, realising he was not.

'I had you down as a rational man,' said Cat, climbing on a high horse, which in her case would be a Shetland pony. 'For that to be true she would have had to have been a flipping mermaid, wouldn't she!'

'Do they exist?' countered Tom, but wondering why he was bothering.

Cat gave Tom the old slit eyed look; she wasn't going to be drawn on that. 'That's beside the point,' she said, leaving it hanging, 'which is, that there is only one sword and has only ever been one sword, contrary to wayward belief and claims.'

'So you're sure there's just the one sword?' said Tom.

'I'm a magic cat. We just travelled back in time to Camelot. I prove my point I think.'

Tom didn't quite know which point Cat was making, but had to concede, she, if anyone, would probably know best whether there were two swords or not. He started to take on the look of the downcast, but suddenly brightened as another thought came to mind. If there was only one sword and that was still in the stone, then surely job done! Wait, he told himself, think. No, it made sense. A conclusion a rational man might arrive at. He told Cat his thought.

'Job done then,' said Tom, spirits lifting, a smile spreading.

'What?' said Cat, suspecting more nonsense was about to issue from said rational man.

'If the sword is still in the stone it stands to reason all must be well with the world, or worlds, again.'

Cat sat, said nothing and stared at Tom. Tom wilted under the weight of an uneasy feeling.

Cat spoke. 'I think we need to talk some more.' Is what she said, and it was said in the air of someone who had in their care someone who hadn't yet grasped what they were supposed to. 'But first we should make rapid movements back to the loo.' Cat turned, leapt to the window and disappeared through the bars into the near dark beyond.

Tom sat, said nothing and stared at the window. Great, he thought, and just how am *I* supposed to get out? He stood up and turned his attention to the door. Unless Cat has hidden lock-picking skills she hadn't mentioned or there was the magic, perhaps an incarnation, an "open sesame"? 'Cat,' he whispered.

'It's open,' said Cat, from the other side of the door.

'It is?' said Tom, shuffling through the gloom towards it. He made it without falling over anything and gave the door a push. It didn't move.

'Pull it,' Cat instructed.

Tom pulled on the door and outside peeped in. Tom peeped out and cautiously left the building.

'How…'

'They never locked it.'

'They… bugger,' said Tom, feeling a tad foolish at the discovery.

'Come on. This way,' said Cat, leading the way.

Tom, keen as ever to display his depiction of the ever the reluctant hero, reluctantly followed; reluctantly and heroically, darting from one shady-looking shadow to another.

Across patches of green and brown the pair scurried. Cat ever alert; Tom disgusted by Camelot's poor excuse for a courtyard.

The fence came into sight as did the gate. Cat slinked forward, confident in her skills. Tom, blood pressure rising, hoped his captors were as inept in their sentry duties as they were at locking doors.

Chapter 16

The door to the portable toilet slammed shut and Tom made a beeline for the toilet. 'I need this,' said Tom.

'Not again!' whined Cat, closing her eyes and turning her back.

But not a splash was heard as Tom instead, slumped exhausted onto the toilet seat. 'I'm knackered,' sighed Tom, ignoring Cat's remark, his back slumping against the wall.

'I thought you…'

'Yeah, well I'm not, so you can open those beady eyes of yours and relax.' Tom's chest heaved, his pulse raced, but his blood pressure started to steady. There had been no guards, no pursuit, but the adrenalin had risen like Tom had never known before. He still hated the whole idea of it all, but it was all strangely exhilarating. Could it be growing on him?

Another couple of chest heaves and Tom felt ready to comment on his escape. 'Well,' he said, 'that was easy.'

'You think so?' said Cat, ears pricking.

'Don't you?'

'Too easy, I'd say.'

'Too easy?' Tom sat up, doubts now clouding the earlier elation; if you could call it elation. A rather alarming thought was surfacing somewhere in Tom's brain. 'You don't think we-'

'No,' said Cat, 'I know. We were followed. The whole thing was a set up, but I think I lost them in the woods.'

Tom had wondered why they had wandered through the woods when there was a perfectly good path that he knew almost intimately so close at hand. Well, there's no fool like an old fool, he thought, he had been so easily duped. He didn't know what to say, but that didn't stop him. 'How did you know?'

Happy there were no sounds from their pursuers, Cat and her ears relaxed. 'I followed you,' she explained, 'and when the bearded one left you alone without locking you in, I had my suspicions all was not well, so I followed him. They thought you were a traitor and might lead them to others.'

'It wasn't the others then, the grannies and whoever?'

'No,' said Cat, 'it wouldn't have been so easy to lose them.'

'What now?'

Cat leapt onto her shelf. 'Home, James, I think.'

'Home?' said Tom, suddenly beaming.

'We need to assess.'

'Home it is then.' Tom didn't need telling twice.

Tom's hand shook as he filled the kettle. It was the last part of his body to do so. When he had got back and seen the cottage, home again, everything hit him in one big smacker-oony of realisation. He hadn't been able to get up the garden path quick enough. He had thought he was getting his head round things, but obviously he wasn't. Kettle full, he put it on its base, switched it on and then sat to wait for the water to boil.

Cat was sitting on another chair, watching Tom intently. She wasn't sure the old boy was going to cut it, but he had to; he was all she had until Marc came of age and that was much too long to wait, much, much too long. She dreaded to think what the world, worlds, would be like by then. If indeed there were any worlds left to worry about. But now that Tom had finally realised it wasn't a game, that all was real, she would soon find out one way or the other; she hoped he was just a slow learner.

The kettle clicked off as the water came to boil. Tom, who hadn't uttered so much as a moan since getting back, got up and poured the water into a waiting mug with the "World's Best Granddad" written on its side. He stirred the mug's contents and returned to his chair. He held the mug up to his nose and sniffed at the rising steam. This wasn't time for coffee or tea, however sweet. The sweet scent of honey tickled Tom's nose, close on its heels the oaky aroma of whisky. He took a tentative sip. It was hot, but not enough to burn his lips or mouth. He swallowed and felt it warm his cockles. The mug held in both hands, Tom soaked up its heat and looked across at Cat.

Meeting his eyes, but saying nothing, Cat waited. It would be better if Tom started any conversation. She felt she may have done more harm than good with her gung-ho approach. Had perhaps pushed a little hard; no two pupils were the same. He needed to get his breath back and take stock.

Another sip, this one larger as the liquid had cooled a little. Tom shifted his gaze. Cat waited. Tom opened his mouth to say something, but closed it again before he did and instead he stared out of the window. Cat still waited, but was beginning to feel that rational man was now turning into melodramatic man.

At last an utterance from Tom. 'Why did we arrive in the loo in the garden and not my bathroom, like last time?' he said, slightly surprising Cat with such a mundane question.

'Home means its home unless you're already in the garden and then it's your home.'

Tom mulled this over. It made sense. He took a sip from his mug. He had another question; this one a little deeper. 'It's dangerous, isn't it, all this?'

Was this a chink of light trying to break through? Cat asked herself. 'I didn't say it was going to be a bowl of cherries,' she said.

Tom emptied his mug and peered over it at Cat. He had a serious look on. When he spoke it was slow and deliberate. 'What really happened to my uncle?' he asked. The question was quickly followed by another. 'Could it happen to me?'

She knew it would come, the question about his uncle, but how did she answer? Go about the houses? Or did she give it straight? Whatever, it would come round to the same answer, as long as it was the truth. She went for the quick rip of the plaster method, why play it out?

Tom listened intently as Cat described the last time she had seen Rufus. How he had disappeared; his last words sending the loo home. Moments later she had been knocked senseless. She had come round alone and bewildered. How long she had lain there she didn't know, but she was back in the garden; the loo in the condition Tom had first seen it in. She and the others searched high and low, North and South, East and West, the past and present, but nothing. He had disappeared off the face of the Earth. All they could do was to wait, cover their tracks and see if he would return under his own steam and watch and wait and scrutinise his replacement, Tom, if he didn't. And yes, it could happen to him, to any of them. This wasn't like collecting your pension, this was serious.

Cat finished and waited for a response.

Tom fidgeted in his seat. 'It is important,' he said, after a moment.

'What is?' puzzled Cat.

'Collecting your pension.'

Cat frowned, but a smile was crossing Tom's face. He put his empty mug down. He had heard enough. It was dangerous; he'd already sussed that. And it was a serious business. He had sussed that also. But there was something else. Damn it, he thought, he'd enjoyed himself, – had fun. Okay, he had a few bruises and a strained shoulder, but he could have got them in the garden, getting out of bed for goodness' sake. It had been awhile since the old adrenaline had kicked in like that. He doubted he would find anything like it in the garden, or, he thought ruefully, in bed – not these days anyway, but let's not dwell on that, he thought, who knows? He afforded himself an inner chuckle. He had made a decision.

'Okay,' said Tom, 'I think we should start over.'

Cat, who was slightly worried by the different looks on Tom's face the last moment or so, brightened up, she liked the sound of that. She even had a little inner chuckle of her own. She didn't know if Tom realised it, but he was starting to sound a lot like his great-uncle and that wasn't a bad thing. No sirree.

'But firstly,' said Tom, standing.

There's always "a but", thought Cat, fearing it would be one she didn't want to hear.

'How the heck did I know what that bearded oaf was going on about? I might not know a lot about anything, but I'm damned sure I shouldn't have understood a word he'd said and vice versa.'

That smile that only Cat could own returned. She looked up and past Tom's enquiring face to the top of his head and the cap sat upon it.

'What?' Tom reached up and touched the cap. He had forgotten all about it and the fact he was still wearing it.

'Universal translator,' said Cat, 'Past and present.'

'Go on!' said Tom, taking it off and turning it over in his hands. There didn't seem to be any wires or such or anything mechanical about it. He turned it inside out. Had to be magical he decided, but having decided that he changed his mind. There had been some amazing advances lately in the electronics world. But then again...

'Let it go,' said Cat, still smiling, 'Some things don't need explaining.'

'All of them?' asked Tom, remembering the others in the drawer. Surely it would have to be a heck of a coincidence if he had pulled out the only one that did what this one did.

'As far as I know all of them, but they're nothing to do with me. The contents of the shed were your uncle's domain.'

Mysteries upon mysteries were building up around him, some of which lay in the shed, gathering dust. He wondered if Great-Uncle Rufus knew what all of it did. He had the sneaking suspicion he didn't, but he wouldn't know if that was true unless providence or fate lent a helping hand and he found his uncle. Tom started giving thought to the menagerie of weird and wonderful objects sitting in the shed that he hadn't yet been privy to. Would some of them figure in the new future he was looking for-, yes, forward was the right word, looking forward to? He hoped not. Some were well weird; at least what he had seen of them under the dustsheets were, but, he supposed, only time would tell. Laying the universal translator on the kitchen table and his mug on the drainer, Tom resumed his place at the kitchen table.

'So,' said Tom, 'we have to go back again, but not so far?'

'In a nutshell,' said Cat, a fair deal happier now that Tom appeared to be coming on board and on terms.

'Have we a specific time in mind?'

Cat gave this some thought. She had been careless last time, thoughtless. Put the old boy in danger. Time travelling is not easy; she of all cats should know that. They are running low on time, but less haste… 'I think we should aim to get the sword when Arthur loses it during the heat of battle – his last battle. We then put it back in the stone and hide them both.'

Tom, it had to be said, wasn't immediately taken with the idea – battles and all. 'What do you mean loses it? I thought Arthur was supposed to be this big brave knight.'

'Not Arthur, the sword. When Arthur loses the sword,' said

Cat, wrinkling her brow again. She didn't think it would be the last time either; Tom wasn't, from what she had seen so far, one of the world's leading lights.

'Oh,' said Tom, catching up, 'I didn't know he'd lost it.'

Explaining was in order. 'In his last battle,' Cat explained, 'it's said, in legend, the very one you eluded to earlier, that he is said to have ordered, as he lay mortally wounded, one of his knights to throw it back to the lady of the lake.'

'So she was a mermaid.'

'If you'd let me finish.'

'Go on.'

'But we believe it was lost on the battlefield and that's where we'll find it.'

There's that "we" again, thought Tom. 'Battlefield?' He really didn't like the sound of that.

'Yes,' said Cat, 'I don't know why I didn't think of it before.'

Tom wasn't happy with her remembering it now. 'Okay, I'll buy it. When was it lost?'

The look on Cat's face was a study in still life. 'I don't know,' she admitted.

Tom's face was a little more animated as he realised Cat's approach to the sword thing was approaching hit and miss. 'You don't know?'

'I said I don't know everything,' said Cat, defending herself, 'It was Rufus' job – research.'

Tom stood up and then sat down again. He wrung his hands, more for dramatic effect than anything. He stood up again, his mind in flux. Why was he getting so upset? Because the world was going to end, that's why. He sat back down again. But he only had the cat's word for that, but he knew the cat was telling the truth. He wrung his hands again and stood up – which meant everything was dependant on him and Cat. That was a lot to take in. He sat again. Cat had said she would

83

train him, but so far he hadn't had much, unless you counted him now knowing how to stay on a horse without falling off, whilst thrown across its back. That's a talent he could use. Oh yes, he could just see himself in a circus somewhere; come and see Tom Tyme the human saddlebag. Get a grip. Something was up. There was something Cat wasn't telling him.

'What aren't you telling me?' said Tom, standing.

Cat, her head nodding up and down as if engrossed in some futuristic, vertical, tennis match as she followed Tom's every move, lowered her head and closed her eyes. She appeared to be meditating.

'Cat,' said Tom.

Eyelids flicked open and Cat gave Tom such a woeful look he suddenly found himself feeling very guilty about everything and nothing.

'What?' said a worried Tom. Was it something he had said?

'I've let you down... myself down,' said Cat, dodging eye contact. 'You're supposed to be trained. I thought...' Cat's voice trailed off.

This wasn't like Cat. Like the Cat he knew, for all of those couple of long hours. 'Thought what?' said Tom.

'Rufus was supposed to train you, not me. I thought... I thought I could do it. Thought it would be easy, but humans... you're nothing like chimps.' Cat stared out the window at the loo.

Thank goodness for that, thought Tom, who could think of a few who were.

She returned her gaze to Tom. 'But now I realise it's beyond me. 'I'm the assistant, a guide – magical yes, with extremely good manners and poise – granted, and fortitude in spades, but sadly not a trainer. That comes from the line, from the one before – the traveller.' Cat let her sad, furry little head slump sideways.

At this point Tom didn't know whether to laugh or cry. He could feel that his eyes had stupidly welled with tears. Why? Who knows? It was all he could do to stop himself from dashing across the kitchen and giving the little furry one a great big hug. Instead he did what all men did in a crisis, when they had to think, he retired to the smallest room to sit and mull.

Twenty minutes later Cat heard the sound of flushing water. She wondered what he could have been doing all that time, then shuddered and quickly cleared her mind of such things, there were much more tantalising secrets in the universe waiting to be discovered. What, she didn't rightly know, but they had to be better and more alluring than Tom's bathroom habits. Though, what would be interesting where Tom was concerned, would be finding out what he had come up with after his "self imposed" seclusion; whether her plan had been fruitful? They needed help, but it wasn't for her to say so. Wasn't really allowed – not from outside the circle. Tom walked in and Cat once again fell into the persona of one with the weight of the worlds on her tiny, almost nonexistent, shoulders.

'I think we need help,' announced Tom, throwing a well-thumbed newspaper onto the table. It fell open at the cross-word. Cat noticed it had quite a few spaces remaining. She was sure she would be able to help complete it if everything turned out the way she hoped.

'Help?' queried Cat, pathetically.

'Yes,' said Tom, resolutely, 'and I know just the chappie. Come on.' Tom picked up his cap, put it on and headed for the backdoor.

This was better, thought Cat, noticing that the cap was sat on Tom's head at a rather jaunty angle.

85

Chapter 17

'Where are we going,' enquired Cat, as Tom closed the loo door behind them.

'Sssch,' went Tom, closing his eyes, 'I have to concentrate.'

Cat climbed onto her shelf and hoped they were going where she hoped they were. They were treading thin ice by contacting an outsider, but this, and she was sure it constituted as one, was an emergency. Besides, this outsider was different.

Tom stood up as the last of the flush echoed in the bowl and closed a hand around the door handle. 'If I'm right,' he said, 'he should be having a break around now.' He turned the handle and was about to push the door open when he stopped.

'What?' said Cat, giving Tom an enquiring look.

'Thought I heard something,' said Tom, pressing an ear to the door. He listened for a moment longer, then happy there were no further noises, pushed on the door. He carefully popped his head round it. No one about, it looked like he had timed his arrival just right. He looked at his watch. In a couple of minutes the place will be heaving.

'Where are we?' asked Cat, as she popped her head out.

'Marc and Katie's school,' whispered Tom, 'and-'

'Kate.'

'What?' said Tom.

'Nothing.'

Tom scowled at the mysterious feline for a moment and

86

then finished what he was going to say 'And if anyone sees me here, there will be and rightly so, hell to pay. The only adults allowed on the grounds are the teachers and them that does.'

'Them that does?'

'Dinner ladies, school nurse and such.'

'Ah,' said Cat, not up to speed on the workings of a school and to be truthful not that interested either, unless one of the aforementioned turned out to be robotic.

They quickly crossed the floor to the door that led to the main corridor. Tom was familiar with the layout having been to the school on a number of occasions for school plays etcetera. The corridor was clear. Tom and Cat tiptoed into it. Their next target was the double doors at the end that led outside to the games field and the groundsman's hut. From there he should have a clear view of the all-weather playing field where the kids took their breaks.

The only problem was what lay between them and their goal; classrooms – classrooms full of kids and teachers who at any minute would be spilling out for all their worth – this included the teachers – to wherever it was they took their break. Tom had a plan though if he was caught; a plan that involved a doddering old fool that had wandered in by mistake looking for the only friend he had in the world – his cat.

He didn't need it though; they were at the double doors in no time and through them a second later. The hut was to their left by the football pitch. They got there just as a bell started to ring somewhere in the main building. It gave Cat a bit of a start, but Tom calmed her by explaining it was just the signal for controlled bedlam. He then picked her up and dived for the cover of the hut's porch. The door to the hut was locked, but the porch would provide adequate cover unless PE was on the agenda and something from the hut was needed. Tom crossed his fingers and practised his "I was only looking for

me cat Guv'nor" routine. They settled down to wait as children streamed from doors onto the playground – Tom nervous,
and Cat purring with delight that her plan was going so well.

'There,' said Tom, suddenly pointing, 'on that bench.'

Cat looked. Marc and Kate were sat together on a bench.
That could be a problem.

'I've got to attract his attention,' said Tom.

'How?'

Cat's question was answered by Tom as he left the safety
of the porch and then zigzagged across open ground to the
edge of the building they had just left.

Idiot, thought Cat, barely able to look.

Tom flattened himself against a wall and inched round a
corner.

He's been watching far too many old war movies, thought
Cat, cringing. Put in two minds whether to stay put or follow
the silly old codger in his suicide mission, Cat decided to err
on the side of caution and stay put; no point both of them
being apprehended. Thankfully, so far, it hadn't happened and
Cat watched, heart in mouth as Tom waved.

Arriving at the corner of the wall that housed the assembly
hall, Tom thought Marc had looked his way and waved. As
luck would have it Marc had. Tom beckoned for Marc to come
over then melted, so he thought, into the shadows. If anyone
had been bothering to look his way they would have been able
to see, quite plainly, a strange old man with both hands above
his head looking as if he was pretending to be a tree.

On the all-weather pitch Marc was talking to his sister.
Tom thought for a moment they were both going to come
over, but Marc packed up his lunch and started over on his
own. Good boy, thought Tom.

'What are you doing here Granddad?' asked Marc, as he
ambled towards his granddad, 'Are you pretending to be a
tree?'

Silly boy, thought Tom, lowering his hands. He grabbed Marc by the blazer shoulder and pulled him out of view.

'Is there something wrong with Mum?'

'What?' Drat, thought Tom, I've worried him. 'No, I just need your help, that's all.'

Dawning on him that his granddad was perhaps on school grounds without permission, Marc immediately became the conspiratorial schoolboy. 'What with?' he asked, backing against the wall and throwing furtive glances this way and that.

In the porch Cat's ears pricked up. She had quickly warned Tom as Marc had approached as to what he could and could not divulge to his grandson.

'Well,' said Tom, choosing his words carefully, 'as you know I'm totally useless where sky-fi and fantasy things are concerned.'

'Sci-fi,' Marc corrected.

'Yeah and that,' said Tom, 'Well I've entered a competition and I need help with one of the questions.'

Cat was impressed as she listened from her hidey-hole. Tom was thinking on his feet.

'Wow,' said Marc, a little too loudly for Tom's liking.

'Sssch,' hissed Tom, putting a finger to his lips.

'Sorry, what kinda competition?'

'A gardening one,' said Tom, which caused a silent groan within the porch.

Marc gave Tom a long sideways look, but the bait was already taken. 'What's the question?'

Tom bent forward and whispered in Marc's ear. 'I need to know when Arthur's last battle was.'

'Arthur who?'

'King Arthur, the one with the sword.'

'That's not fantasy,' Marc protested, 'that's history.'

'It's a myth actually,' said Tom, getting just a tad tetchy.

'What sort of a moth?'

'What? Not moth – myth – an old-fashioned story.' Tom was getting edgy now as well as tetchy, but he rallied and pulled a master stroke just as communication looked to be breaking down. 'There's a prize,' he said.

Well played, thought Cat.

'I can have a surf,' said Marc, who quickly added when Tom's face went blank, 'On the computer – the internet. I can do it this afternoon when I get home from school.'

Tom hadn't been expecting this. He had figured his strange fantasy–loving, but dear little grandson, would know the answer off the top of his head. This wasn't going to help at all, was it? He gave the porch a confused look. He could just make Cat out amongst the shadows. She was licking a paw as if worlds weren't going to end sometime soon. 'Cat,' he whispered urgently, 'we have a problem.'

Cat nearly choked on her paw. What did he think he was doing? After all she had said to him. Flipping newbie's. She would have to chew grass for a week to recover.

Marc adopted the look of the terminally confused. He always suspected his granddad was AWTF*. This confirmed it. He was talking to an imaginary cat. But, just out of curiosity, he had a quick shufti behind his granddad anyway. To his surprise he found that there was a cat there, emerging from old Groundie's hut. Not that that let his granddad off the hook; he was still talking to a cat as if the thing understood him. He gave the cat closer scrutiny; it appeared to be giving his granddad a pretty stern staring at.

'Granddad?'

Time for Tom to start thinking on his feet again. 'Ha-ha,' laughed Tom, in that awkward way people did when caught with their fingers in the old cookie jar, 'Blooming thing followed me all the way from home so it did.'

---

*Away With The Fairies.

'Whose is it?'

'Just a stray.'

'Can it talk?'

'What!'

'You were talking to it.'

'I wasn't… I was – did I tell you the prize is twenty pounds and a sky-fi thingumajig you put in insoles.'

Cat did worrying eye-crossing.

'Do you mean put in shoes?'

'What? No, in those things you sit in front of the telly with.'

Marc's face creased. Did he mean slippers? Then smoothed again when he caught on to what his old duffer of a granddad was actually trying to say. 'You mean console.' Marc thought on this, then let loose a frown of monumental proportions. 'The gardening quiz is giving away video games?'

'Here kitty,' said Tom, trying to lure Cat closer.

'What games?'

'And twenty British squid.'

It was just enough to get Tom out of the hole he was digging for himself with that spade he might buy with the imaginary twenty quid he was trying to win in the imaginary gardening quiz.

'Will I get some if I help?'

''Course you will,' lied Tom, 'Now-'

'You going to keep him?'

'What?' Grief, thought Tom, I wish I'd stop saying that. 'Who?'

'The cat.'

'Wh- no-yes. He's a she.'

'I could pretend to be ill.'

'Wh- why?'

'I could come home and help you now.'

'Oh, I don't know about that,' said Tom, looking to Cat

91

for some support, moral or otherwise, but she was licking her paw again. He was on his own.

'They'll phone your mum,' said Tom.

'Not if I say she's away. Your number is next on the contact list.'

Tom wasn't adverse to the odd bit of skiving, especially where he himself was concerned, but this was a step too far. Wasn't it? No, he was a responsible adult. He couldn't agree to such a thing – a child missing important educational instruction on a whim. Tut-tut. There was also the welfare of the child to think of, the boy would be home alone. But worse than that, Marc's mother would surely find out about it somehow and he would never hear the last of it.

'What time's lunch?' said Tom, an alternative idea surfacing – one where he wouldn't get it in the neck.

'One,' said Marc, pouting a little as he felt his chance of a skive slipping away, 'why?'

'Can you use the computers?'

'There's a nerd club at half past.'

'Nerd club?'

'Yeah, extra studies if you want it,' Marc explained.

'You shouldn't call them that.'

'What should I call them?'

Tom really didn't have time for this. Cat was glaring at him. 'Ask your teacher. Now, can you use a computer then or not?'

A glum head nodded an affirmative.

'Excellent,' said Tom, brightly, successfully managing to ignore the look his grandson was giving him. 'When you know the answer, give me a call.'

'How am I going to that?' said Marc.

'Use your mobile.'

'You know we're not allowed to use them in school,' said Marc, defensively, slight indignation creeping into his voice at the very idea of such a thing.

'But you do,' said Tom.

The pout grew and the frown of before returned giving Marc the look of the shrew, but he didn't argue the point, especially as Granddad was right. How he knew, Marc didn't know. He wasn't about to ask either, let sleeping dogs lie. How dogs lied in their sleep and why one said it were also mysteries to Marc. One day he might ask, but that wasn't going to be today.

'You won't tell Mum, will you?'

'Um,' said Tom.

'His last battle you say?' said Marc, fully capitulating under the "Um" agreement.

'Where Arthur loses his sword,' Tom reminded.

From nowhere in particular there came the slightest hint of a whisper in the wind. Marc gave Cat a suspicious look. Cat nonchalantly licked at an armpit. Tom emitted a small cough.

'The one where Arthur dies,' added Tom.

'I had better go,' said Marc, remembering where he was, now it was a dead cert he wasn't going anywhere else. His gaze though, stayed on Cat.

'And me,' said Tom, stepping between Marc and Cat, breaking the contact. 'Hear from you later then.'

'What? Oh yeah, see you tonight.'

'Tonight?' said Tom, not able to resist jumping on the word, 'Yer coming to see yer ol' granddad on his birthday then?'

Marc snapped from his self-imposed stupor and glared at Tom. 'Maybe,' he said, quickly correcting his error, 'got that game tonight, remember?'

'Ah yes, the game,' said Tom, trying hard not to smile. 'Later then, maybe?'

'Maybe,' said Marc, hoisting his backpack onto his shoulder. He turned to go with the feeling he'd been played

93

somewhere along the line. A quick goodbye and he scurried on his way.

Halfway back to where he'd been sitting Marc suddenly turned. He didn't know why for certain or what he expected to see, but he'd just had the oddest of feelings crawl all over him. There was something odd about the cat, that he was certain of, but there was nothing to see, Tom and the cat were gone. Marc decided to give it all some serious thought, but luckily for him, before he could do himself any serious injury, one of his gaming buddies caught his attention and the thoughts were like wisps of cloud in the wind – gone.

Hidden from view in the porch, Tom and Cat watched Marc go.

'Do you think he'll remember to do it?' asked Cat, who had decided Marc had a lot of the goldfish way of thinking about him. Training him up will be fun when the time comes, she thought.

'Yeah,' said Tom, emerging from the shadows as Marc's attention was diverted to his friend, 'he won't let us down.'

Chapter 18

Tom and Cat emerged from the bathroom in his cottage and settled down to wait for Marc to get in touch.

A cuppa later found Tom in his usual chair in the kitchen staring into space. He had been looking at the shed and wondering. He now looked at the clock on the wall; still a while before Marc would call – if he called. If he could find what he had asked to find. Tom had heard surfing the cobweb was a bit of a hit and miss affair, like looking for a needle in a scrap yard.

'Penny for them,' said Cat, peeping up at Tom, her chin resting on outstretched paws.

Pulled from his musing, Tom turned to Cat and smiled. 'Just wondering what's in store for me, now I'm a time traveller.'

'Read any books on it?'

'Can't say I have,' Tom admitted.

'Seen any films?'

Tom thought. He couldn't recall doing so, but that didn't mean he hadn't. He played it safe. 'No.'

'Then you won't be disappointed,' said Cat, stretching her legs, 'it's nothing like any of them. This isn't fiction, some far-fetched story of time and space; this is real.' She rose up and yawned. 'But you'll cope, just like your uncle did and those before him. It's in the genes.'

'Don't wear them,' joked Tom, 'must be in the cords.'

'Ha-ha,' said Cat, rolling her eyes.

'You liked him, didn't you?'

If ever a cat could look sad it was then. 'I still do,' she said, her smile fading, 'he was – is a good friend.'

There followed an awkward silence that was mercifully broken by the ringing of the phone.

'Marc?' said Cat, glad of the interruption.

'Can't be,' said Tom, double-checking the time on the clock, 'it's too early. He wouldn't have had lunch yet.'

'Your daughter checking up on you?' said Cat, a wry smile appearing.

'Just how closely have you been watching me?' smiled Tom.

'You going to answer it then?'

'Doubt it will be her. Said she was in a meeting all day – wouldn't want to blow her cover.' Tom winked and tapped the side of his nose with a finger.

The phone continued to ring, its tone insistent, the type you knew would keep on and on. The type Tom would usually ignore and retreat to his shed from.

'It could be important.'

Tom sighed and picked it up. 'Hello?'

'Blah-blah-blah.' Was all Cat could hear from where she sat.

'Yes,' said Tom, 'found one thanks.' He raised his eyebrows at Cat.

More "Blah-blah-blah". Cat thought the voice sounded urgent.

'I can't today. Kinda busy, it's my birthday today, lots to do. I can come tomorrow. Right. Okay, see what I can do. 'Bye. Bye-bye now. 'Bye.' Tom put the phone down.

'Problem?'

'No,' said Tom, fiddling with his earlobe, the one belonging to the ear he had been listening with. It was warm. 'Just old Missus Dewhurst ringing to tell me she'd found a cap after all.'

'You don't need one now.'

'I know. I told her, but she became quite insistent, wanted me to come round right away.'

'That's sweet,' said Cat, grinning, 'I expect she knows it's your birthday and she went out and got one for you.'

'You think?' said Tom, suddenly feeling guilty.

'That or she's got the hots for you.'

'Hots! No.' Tom looked horrified. 'She's got to be at least ninety.'

Cat was enjoying this. 'Age isn't everything,' she teased, 'perhaps she's after a toy boy. If the cap fits?'

'Ha-ha, yes… well,' Tom mumbled, getting just a tad flustered, 'that might well be, but I'm… I'm not available. I didn't even know she knew my number.'

'Phone book?' offered Cat, trying hard not to roll up in a fit of giggles. 'Humour her, go round tomorrow.'

'Suppose, but I kinda promised I might pop round later.'

'I sense a birthday kiss in the offing.'

Tom's jaw dropped and Cat could no longer keep the laughter in. She curled up and nearly fell off the chair she was on.

'Go on, laugh,' said Tom, 'but it's not funny, I'll need some protection.'

This had Cat actually fall off the chair; it was an adult moment.

'Ho-ho-ho,' said Tom, catching on.

After a second or two, Cat managed to compose herself and climb back onto her chair. She had tears in her eyes. Tom was leaning against the sink unit glaring at her.

'Sorry, I'm sorry,' said Cat, still trying hard to keep a titter in, 'but you've got to admit it was funny.' She rested her head and paws on the kitchen table.

'Fine,' said Tom, relenting, 'but you realise I'll never be able to look the woman in the eye again.'

Cat managed to calm down, but a smile remained, though the look in her eye had taken on a more serious look. 'Look Tom,' she said, 'what you said about needing protection.'

'Don't start that again.'

'No, seriously, you should have some.'

'From Missus Dewhurst?'

'From whatever we might encounter on our travels. You need to defend yourself.'

'A weapon?' said Tom, flinching at the idea, 'No one said anything about a weapon.'

'What if we were to become separated for some reason? How long before Marc calls?'

Tom glanced at the clock. 'Half an hour or so, why?'

'Plenty of time. Come with me.'

Capillaries turned blue as Tom's blood ran cold. He couldn't hurt anyone. Would he have to? Cat was waiting patiently by the back door. They were going to the shed. Another secret awaited him. Tom really didn't like the idea of this at all.

When Tom stepped into his shed, the first thing that struck him was that it no longer felt like a sanctuary. It felt alien. Wrong somehow. He had been right; things were never going to be the same again.

Cat leapt onto an old desk, stirring dust in her wake. 'This way,' she said, as she jumped from one tarpaulin to another.

Tom followed, his thoughts filled with all shapes and sizes of weapons imaginable. Had to be a bow or something, he thought, thinking about the task ahead; or a sword, or a dagger. Couldn't be a gun – wrong time. He gave that thought short shrift. There was no right time for a gun – for any weapon.

'Here we are,' announced Cat, stopping on a thing of austere bearing, hidden at the back of the shed.

'It's a chest,' said Tom, thinking he hadn't seen that before, but then he hadn't really ever ventured further than his deck-chair before. And what a chest it was. The finest English oak with heavy leather straps hinging the lid to the bottom through large brass buckles. The escutcheon, a heavy brass affair with fancy etching, was a gaping maw waiting to swallow the key that opened it. It was the sort of chest that would hold the misbegotten treasure of any self-respecting pirate captain.

'Spot on, Einstein,' said Cat, the romance of the thing lost on her.

Tom stared. It was a magnificent sight. 'Is this where Rufus keeps his weapons?'

'Open it and see,' said Cat, somewhat mysteriously.

Tom tried the lid, but it was locked. 'I need the key.'

'Try looking on your key fob.'

Tom's hand went to his pocket. 'My key...?' And quickly withdrew the fob. On it hung, amongst the usual keys, a large heavy-looking one, of the fancy-patterned brass variety. 'How?' he said, staring at the key in his hand.

'It's been in your pocket since this morning. It's what it does. Attaches itself to its new owner as soon as.'

But surely he should have felt something, noticed its weight. But he wouldn't have. As big as the key was, as heavy as it looked, as it lay in his hand, he realised it in fact weighed almost nothing at all. A goose feather would be heavier. Tom scratched at his head. 'What do I do now?'

'You could always open the box,' Cat suggested, jumping clear.

Tom turned the key over in his hand. It didn't feel right – not one little bit. It was as if the thing didn't belong – to this world? He knelt down and placed the key in the lock, it fitted perfectly; why wouldn't it? There he paused. 'Is it safe?' he asked. It was a weapon's locker for goodness' sake.

'Turn it.'

Tom went to turn it and realised his hand was shaking. 'You sure?'

'If I had thumbs I'd do it for you,' said Cat, lifting her front paws to emphasise the point.

Tom turned the key. There was a faint, but satisfying click. Tom waited, then loosened the straps, something he should have perhaps done first. A gap appeared between lid and base. Tom gingerly poked his fingers into it, lifted the lid and peered inside.

'It's empty,' exclaimed Tom, throwing the lid back against the wall and squinting into the chest's inky depths. Any thought of emerging with the odd cutlass was consigned to the scrapheap.

'At the bottom,' said Cat.

'Where?'

'Reach in.'

Tom didn't like it, but he did; he reached in, deeper and deeper; deeper, it felt, than it should have been. It suddenly reminded him of those comedies where someone pulls a ladder and other impossible items out of a hat or something. But there were no ladders or rabbits as his fingers finally scrabbled at the bottom boards. A groping finger touched something. Tom recoiled, pulling his hand out of the chest, whatever was in there felt cold – dead. He glanced at Cat who was apparently taking no notice at all. Some sort of test, sprang into Tom's mind. He gritted his teeth and plunged his hand back in. He'd show her. He wasn't afraid of shadows, or dead thi… He started as his hand found the cold thing almost straight away. He took a deep breath, took hold of it and pulled. It was like the key, almost weightless. Tom staggered back a little with the lack of expected weight. His second surprise came in the size and shape of the object he now held in his hand. In the chest it had felt… different. Wet – no, furry? What the heck *had* it felt like? For the life of him, Tom couldn't remember.

Dumbfounded, he turned to Cat with his find. 'Is this it?' he said, holding it out.

'What did you expect, a ray-gun?'

'You said a weapon; this… this… isn't a weapon.'

'I never said anything about a weapon,' said Cat, 'I said you needed something to defend yourself with.'

Tom looked at the thing in his hand and frowned. She was right, she hadn't, but what was he supposed to do now, with this? Okay, apart from the obvious, how was he supposed to defend himself with a golf club? He couldn't even begin to imagine how he would fare against certain knights of a certain round table should the situation arise. Okay, maybe he could, but it wasn't good – minced Tom with a dash of seven iron. If that was what it was; Tom had less than no knowledge of golf.

'It's a saver,' Cat explained.

Which explained absolutely zilch to Tom. 'So, do I have to open an account or something?' asked Tom, drolly.

Narrowing her eyes slightly, Cat explained further. 'Your uncle used it last and you shouldn't always rely on what your eyes tell you.'

'Still looks like a golf club to me,' said Tom. He twirled it in his fingers, regarding it as one might who wonders at the sanity of chasing a little white ball around some fields and then knocking it into a small hole. He also held it arm's length as one might who was half expecting the thing to explode at any moment.

'What would help you most at this very moment?' asked Cat.

'Pardon?' asked Tom, working hard on his "what's".

'Pretend you're in a situation and need help.'

'I don't need to pretend.'

'Bear with me on this,' said Cat, 'think of something, but not too big.'

As usual Tom didn't like the sound of this, but he gave it a go. Trying very hard not to think of anything that might bring self-harm, Tom brought something to mind. An instant later he felt a slight tickling sensation cross his outstretched palms. He didn't want to look, but he did. 'What the…?' said Tom, lapsing. He stared at the new object that now lay across his hands with a look on his face any goldfish would have been proud of.

A puzzled Cat, asked Tom what the title was.

Tom didn't really have to look, he had an idea he already knew. He turned the front cover to face him and read aloud, 'How to understand your cat.' The title was in gold lettering. Under the lettering was a picture of a rather self-satisfied looking creature that carried a rather uncanny likeness to Cat.

The weirdness of it all would have had a lesser man grovelling for sanctuary, but Tom was past all that. He opened the book and flicked through the pages; they were all blank.

'Well, that's no help,' said Tom, showing Cat the pages.

'The saver's magic, not a miracle maker,' said Cat, tartly; she was not impressed by Tom's choice of help. 'I think you'd find it would be the same for titles such as "How to understand a woman" and "Multitasking for men".

Tom thought of arguing some defence, but opted not to. 'I take it they were titles Uncle Rufus had an interest in?'

Cat nodded.

'So what is it really, this thing?' asked Tom, 'and don't say a book.'

Cat leapt onto the lip of the lid of the chest and keeping her balance, as only a cat can, shifted her weight as she landed, causing it to shut. She now sat on the closed chest. 'It's just what I said it is – a saver. Take care of it and it will take care of you.'

'Question,' said Tom, inspecting the book. 'Why a golf club?'

'Rufus had a rather tricky little shot out of some rough,' said Cat.

'It'll help me?'

'When you need it to, but don't abuse it.'

'Like Rufus?'

'He had an excuse.'

'What excuse?'

'He was eccentric.'

'Why didn't it help him?'

'When?'

'When he got lost,' said Tom, feeling Cat was playing the obtuse card.

'I'd often wondered that myself, but when I saw it just now, still as a golf club, I realised he couldn't have taken it with him that last time.'

Enough said, thought Tom, feeling a little sadness creep in for his feline friend. 'We had better get back. It must be getting close to Marc's dinner break.'

'You're right,' said Cat, 'but just one thing Tom.'

'Yes?'

'Keep it close.'

Chapter 19

A couple of cuppas and the finishing of the crossword later, the phone rang. This time it *was* Marc.

'Granddad, it's Marc,' said Marc.

'Yo-bro!' said Tom, proving he was "with it".

There was a small sigh on the other end of the line. 'Have you been on the medicine again, Granddad?'

Cheeky little so-and-so. 'What have you found out?'

'You owe me big time, Granddad,' said Marc, huffing in a way that spelt trouble, 'it was a bloody minefield out there.' Another saying Marc wasn't completely certain of the context of.

'Mind your language, young man,' snapped Tom.

'You swear.'

'That's different.'

'Well, bloody's in the bible, bloody's in th-'

'You on your mobile?' said Tom, hardly veiling his threat. Silence on the other end. 'Now, what did you find out?'

'No one knows when he died.'

'Nobody knows?' said Tom, frowning at Cat.

'Some don't think he ever existed, in which case he never died.'

Tom couldn't deny the logic in that, but this was getting them nowhere. 'What about those who do?'

'Do what?'

'Think he existed.'

'No one knows.'

Bleeding roundabouts, thought Tom.

'Do they know when his last battle was?'

'If he existed?'

'Marc!'

A deeper sigh, followed quickly by another huff. 'I wasted my entire lunch break doing this for you. My mates think I've gone over.'

'Gone over?'

'Become a nerd. I don't know why I bothered. Is there really a video game as a prize?'

I'm losing him, thought Tom, time for the kid gloves. 'And a bit of extra pocket money.'

'How much?'

Like fishing, thought Tom, smiling inwardly. 'How's a couple of squids sound?'

Marc decided to verify; you could never be too sure with Granddad. 'Two pounds?'

'If you like,' said Tom, put out because he knew where he could get his hands on a couple of the inky critters; would have been a blast to see the look on the kid's face.

'I thought you said there were twenty squids?

'Don't push it.'

This appeared to do the trick. 'You've got three choices.'

'Three!'

'They reckon his last battle was in Cornwall, Wales and Scotland.'

'He couldn't have had his last battle in all of them.'

'Don't shoot the messenger, man,' said Marc, who knew what that meant. 'Like I said, it's a bl- it's hard work surfing the net.'

Tom couldn't even imagine; all this net-surfing nonsense was beyond him, he looked for something to jot a few notes on, but Cat was one step ahead and had already pushed a wad of notelets and a biro his way.

'Thanks,' whispered Tom, putting his hand over the mouth-piece and picking up the biro.

'Right,' said Tom, to Marc, 'what you got?'

Marc reeled off a list of places within the county and countries he had mentioned.

'And that's it?'

'All I had time for.'

'Have to do then. Thanks. See yer. 'Bye.'

'Wait, when do I get my money?' Marc had already earmarked the cash for footy cards.

'Tonight, unless you're gaming that is,' said Tom, remembering his grandson's excuse.'

'Er… maybe, more than likely tomorrow then. Gotta go.'

'Quid it is then.'

'You said two.'

'Oh yeah. Be good. See you later.'

The phone went dead from Marc's end.

''Bye.'

'You're a pretty mean old git, aren't you,' said Cat, pawing at the paper Tom had jotted on so she could see what was written.

'Just funning with him,' said Tom, wondering now he came to think about it, if he hadn't been a little bit too mean. He promised to make it up to the boy – three quid perhaps, maybe two fifty.

'This doesn't help much does it,' said Cat, when finished perusing the notes. 'Camlannis appears to be the name of the final battle, but where?'

'You can read?'

'All languages.'

'Oh. At least we have a date.'

'Two.'

'Must be somewhere in between.'

Cat wasn't so sure. She studied the notes again. Somewhere in between could prove costly, time wise. 'I think we'll have to go on gut instinct.' In the scheme of things, it wasn't much better. 'What do you think?'

Tom picked up his notes. 'Never heard of that Cambodia place, can't be that,' he said.

'It's Camboglanna, but I agree, it does nothing for me either.'

'Didn't he live in Cornwall?'

'So it's said in some quarters.'

'Then it must be the Slaughter place, sounds right – last battle and all.'

'Slaughter Bridge, could be, but a lot of people think he may have been Welsh.'

'The Cader place?'

'There's a Camlann River close by. So stands to good reason and strong chance that Camlann and Camlannis might be connected. Cam means crooked by the way.'

'Does it? I knew a bloke once called Cam. Not far wrong then, I say.'

'So, Cornwall, Wales or Scotland?'

'Which one's the Scottish one?'

'The one you couldn't pronounce.'

'Ah,' said Tom, 'but surely the outsider. Did Arthur travel that far?'

'Some think he was Scottish.'

'Who hasn't claimed him?'

'I don't think the Cambodians have.'

'Fair do's,' said Tom, smiling, 'So which one do you think?'

'To be honest,' said Cat, staring at the notes, 'I haven't got a clue so the best bet to my mind is we use the common denominator in all this and think Camlannis and pick a date.'

'A guess then?'

'I don't think we should be any more specific. Cornwall

for me is the favourite, but I have a feeling that won't go away about the Scottish one. Having said that, who are we to dismiss the Welsh one with any degree of certainty?'

'A guess then?'

'So I think we...' Cat wrinkled her nose as she paused for a moment's thought, 'yes, go with thinking Camlannis, somewhere between AD five hundred and forty-two and AD five-eight-two.'

'A forty year guess then?'

'I know it sounds a long shot, but I'm hoping the loo might help us and home in on the right time.'

'Thought you said we had to be precise with that thing?'

Cat shrugged her shoulders. 'I know, but it's all we got.'

Picking up his saver, which was still in book form, Tom headed for the back door. 'We had better be going then if we're to save the world.'

'Worlds,' Cat corrected, as she leapt to the floor.

'Whatever,' said Tom, placing the universal translator firmly upon his head.

Chapter 20

Camlannis, if it indeed was the right Camlannis, wasn't what you would call an endearing or welcoming place. For a start there was thick fog swirling, which by anyone's standard, was a major spanner in the works when sword hunting. It was also as quiet as the grave. If there was a battle going on, it was being played out in mime. Now there was a new ingredient to throw into the stew of Arthurian myth.

Tom edged slowly from the confines of the loo, then ducked back in, slightly quicker. The fog had unnerved him. The quiet had disturbed him. The thought that it was like the grave had, well, let's just say it was a good job there was a loo at hand.

Cat appeared, shaking her head – humans! She took in her surroundings and sniffed at the mist. When her sniffing told her nothing, as in no sign of battle or any tangible danger other than the chance of getting lost in the pea-souper, she called to Tom. 'You finished in there?' she asked.

'Nature called,' said Tom, offering an excuse for his rather hasty reappearance in the loo. He appeared at the door and peered out. 'Is it safe?' he asked, the saver, still in book form, handy.

'Ready?'

He wasn't and didn't know if he would ever be, but left the loo and closed the door. The loo disappeared from sight. 'Suppose so,' he lied. Tom poked a tentative finger at the empty space where the loo had been standing and felt a little bit better when it touched a solid surface. The loo appeared and then disappeared again when Tom removed his finger. Something else now worried him. 'You sure no one else will find it?'

'Find what?' said Cat, anxious to get going.

'Someone might walk into the loo by accident and find it.'

'I told you, it's not there. Now, come on.' Cat took a couple of steps forward.

'But when I touch it, it appears.'

Cat rolled her eyes. 'It will only appear for you or me, anyone else will just travel straight through it. Now please, come on, we've a sword to find and we don't even know if we're in the right place or time.'

Cat moved on another couple of steps, but Tom hung back. 'I thought of Camlannis. King Arthur's last battle,' said Tom, making sure no blame settled on him, should there be any meted out.

'Site of,' said Cat, 'but that doesn't mean we've arrived at the exact time.' Cat suddenly stopped in mid stride. 'What did you say?'

'Last battle?' said Tom.

'Before that.'

'Camlannis,' said Tom, starting to feel a little uncomfortable. Had he said something wrong?

'After that.'

Oh-oh. What had he said? Tom quickly ran through what he had just said in his mind. Nope, couldn't think of anything wrong. 'King Arthur?'

'Drat.'

'Problem with that?'

'Could be. Depends which side of the fence you belong.'

Tom knew there wasn't one, but he couldn't help himself and looked anyway.

'Figuratively,' said Cat. 'Some people hold the belief that he was nothing more than a warlord.'

Tom thought on this and came up with quite a solid defence. 'But if I hadn't thought King, it could have been any old Arthur's last battle. We could have ended up anywhere. Camlannis is after all, only someone's guess, isn't it?'

A good point conceded Cat. Camlannis, as she saw it, was only supposition agreed on by general consensus, and as she didn't have the faintest idea how the loo worked, decided it was probably the best choice to make. The whole thing was a hit and miss affair at best, especially if you didn't have the full facts at hand to start with.

'Okay,' said Cat, 'let's see what we shall see.' With no preference for direction, Cat set off again, but after only a couple more steps, she once again came to an abrupt stop. 'Can you hear that?' she whispered.

'Hear what?' whispered Tom, clutching his saver all the tighter.

'Nothing,' said Cat, relaxing a little, 'thought I heard something, but if there was, it's gone now.' Cat resumed her forward momentum.

This did nothing to lessen the grip Tom had on his book. Eyeing every direction with the same degree of suspicion, he fell in behind. 'Do you know where you're going?' asked Tom, a couple of yards later.

'What do you think?' said Cat.

'Just asking.'

'Okay,' said Cat, stopping, 'this is how I see it. We have three choices ahead of us.'

'Ahead of us?' said Tom, squinting into the fog they were heading for.

'Again, figuratively,' said Cat. 'We've either arrived before the battle, which makes sense considering the weather,

111

or after the battle, but if so I suspect we would have heard the groans of the dead and wounded.'

Here Tom gripped the book so hard he nearly dislocated a couple of fingers. 'And the third?' he asked, quickly, keen to get off that particular subject.

'We've missed it in any way shape or form you'd care to imagine.'

'Missed it?' said Tom, 'Now there's a shame. Home then?' he suggested.

The look Cat gave him was so sharp it was a small wonder there was no bloodshed. 'What about the worlds, or have you forgotten about them?' Her tongue was just as sharp.

Tom was cut to the quick; again, lucky for Tom, figuratively speaking. 'I was only joking,' he joked, half-heartedly.

'We're all scared,' said Cat, her tone mellowing, 'but if we don't do it who will?'

'I'm not scared,' said Tom, lying through what teeth he possessed.

'Then I suggest we make the best of a bad deal and have a look around. We might turn something up.'

That was one of the things Tom was afraid of.

Cat moved off again and because of her colouring, began to merge with the fog. Because of this, Tom stepped up his pace, he didn't fancy being left alone, lost in the mists of time.

Another few yards were covered before Cat stopped again. She cocked her head to one side, her ears pricked. 'Can you hear that?' she asked.

'Hear what?' said Tom, going through the saver routine again. But this time he could hear something – a clacking noise.

Cat moved stealthily forward, becoming every inch the predator she was. 'I think it's coming from up ahead. Careful.'

Too right he was going to be careful. Tom stood his ground, he wasn't going anywhere, lost or not, it was better than going blindly into the unknown with who knew what lying in wait for them. And there he stayed, for all of five seconds, until all that could be seen of Cat was the tip of her tail. 'Wait,' he whispered, as it disappeared from sight, 'wait for me.'

With each footstep Tom took, the clacking grew steadily louder. And then something, somebody, emerged from the depths of the fog to his left.

'Whoa,' said Tom, coming to a sharp stop. 'Loo… looks like a body.' The observation barely whispered. This was it, thought Tom, the start of the battlefield, the first of the many bodies he would surely have the misfortune to stumble across. Could he handle it? A bead of sweat appeared on his forehead, but a second which had been ready to join it was held in check as the realisation of what that statement meant slowly sunk in. Which would mean the battle was over, but any imme-diate thoughts of joyous relief were swiftly quashed as Tom realised the clacking they had been following was emanating from the corpse in front of him. 'Cat!' he whispered, as loudly as he dared. The second bead of sweat was now set free to join its brother hiding in one of the creases on Tom's furrowed brow.

Cat emerged from the fog and went straight to the body. She sniffed at it. 'It's not human,' she declared.

'Thank goodness for- what?' Conflict was not a descrip-tive enough word to describe the processes going on in Tom's mind at that precise moment.

'It's okay, we're safe enough, the spring's gone,' said Cat. She turned and saw that Tom wasn't looking at all well. 'You okay?'

Tom nodded, but the colour of his face and the whiteness of the knuckles on the hand gripping the saver told a different story. Not human? Spring? Did she say spring?

'Spring?' muttered Tom, not entirely sure he had heard right. Of course I didn't, I'm in shock.

'Looks like it took quite a blow to the cranium,' said Cat, who had clambered onto the body's chest. 'Nasty gash – sword I'd say.'

One heave away from a vomit, Tom inched closer. He could see the body clearly now, it was an elderly woman. Half her head was missing. 'Is… is she…' Of course she is.

'Yes,' Cat confirmed, 'a robot. They know we're here.'

Tom just managed to stop his stomach from sharing its contents with the past. Hands resting on knees, bottom jaw hanging slack, he looked at Cat. 'Did you say…?'

'Yes,' said Cat, jumping down from its chest, 'another ninja granny.'

'But… I thought.'

'Thought what?' said Cat.

'I... I… never mind.' Tom slowly righted himself. He chanced a half glance in the direction of the body. There was a fair amount of metalwork showing. Why hadn't he noticed that before? Because he only saw what he wanted to see. Only heard what he wanted to hear. Perhaps he was in shock. 'Did you mention something about a spring?'

'Yes,' said Cat, back to sniffing at the fog. 'Once the spring goes they're just so much scrap metal.'

'Spring?'

Cat ceased her sniffing and gave Tom the old once over. 'You sure you're all right?'

There was still a certain amount of cold sweat about Tom, but he was feeling better – a lot better, but he was puzzled. 'Do robots have springs? I thought they were all hydraulics and servo's.'

'Not these. They're clockwork. Victorian you see.'

Tom didn't. 'But they're ninja.'

'I think you'll find they had ninjas in Victorian times.'

114

'But clockwork robot ones?'

'They had clocks.'

King Arthur, time travel, missing uncles, presumed dead, swords, savers and now Victorian clockwork robot ninja grannies. It was all piling up like a psychiatrist's dossier. The Tom of old would surely have capitulated under the weight of it all, but the Tom of now was fast becoming a fellow made of sterner stuff, though the whimpering sound he was making was doing little to reinforce that. He just needed a moment or two to catch his breath, that was all.

'You sure you're okay?' asked a concerned Cat.

'Yeah, fine.'

'Only, I thought for a moment back there you were thinking the robot was a real granny.'

'What? Me? Nooo.'

'Glad to hear it,' said Cat. 'Now... let's see what else we can find. We're getting close, I can feel it in my water.' Cat cocked her little head. 'Speaking of, do you want to...?'

'No... no, I'll be fine,' said Tom.

'Shall we go then?'

'Why not?' Tom straightened his cap cum translator and set his jaw. 'Lead on Catranna.'

This brought a smile to Cat's face. It really was in the genes.

Together as one, man and cat strode boldly into the fog and the waiting unknown – Cat afire with steely determination concerning the saving of worlds – Tom wondering if maybe he should have gone one more time before they'd left.

'One thing,' said Tom, as the robot corpse was swallowed by the swirling mist behind them, 'how did it know we were here?'

'That, my friend, is a good question.'

Chapter 21

The journey into the foggy unknown lasted for roughly five more minutes before anything else of significance happened. This time it was the body of a man, a real man, lying bedraggled on the ground. A sword lay broken in his hand. They approached with caution, Cat to the fore.

'I believe we're here,' whispered a grim Cat, judging the man to be dead and the first of many they were now likely to find.

'Well I'll be,' said Tom, recognising the man as the one who had imprisoned him in Camelot. The man had aged some sixty years, his beard now the same grey as Tom's jacket, but Tom would have known him anywhere. Tom couldn't get over how old the man was and still bearing arms. 'Grief,' said Tom, 'how old do you have to be before you retire here?'

'They didn't have the luxury, not in these days,' said Cat, sidestepping the man. 'Besides, he's not done so badly. I'd say he's lived way beyond the norm for these times.' She moved away, back in predator mode. 'Come on, we're getting near. I can almost smell it.'

Tom shuddered as he pulled his gaze away from the dead man. Thankfully he hadn't noticed any visible wounds. In truth, he hadn't looked that hard, he was no rubbernecker. He quickly turned his mind back to the job at hand and leaving the man behind, tried to prepare himself for what lay ahead.

More bodies appeared out of the mist, strewn at ever decreasing intervals. While Cat sniffed this way and that, Tom kept eyes strictly front.

'There!' said Cat, so suddenly Tom nearly jumped clear of his skin.

Instinctively crouching, Tom tried to see what it was Cat had seen. It was difficult though, as he had put himself in a position that blinkered his already "straight and narrow looking ahead only" approach to the battlefield they were now deep within. 'What?' said Tom, trying to peep over without actually looking at the surrounding bodies.

'Movement, a little to our right,' said Cat, joining Tom in his crouching. 'I suggest we proceed with caution.'

Tom as usual didn't need telling twice where danger was concerned. He started to sidle away to his left.

'Where're you going?' hissed Cat.

'You said there was movement to our right,' whispered Tom.

'Yes,' said Cat, 'and that's where we're heading.'

'Whoa,' said Tom, in a no-nonsense, scared shitless kind of way, 'is that wise? Could be dangerous.'

'We have to find the sword.'

'We can search the bodies,' suggested Tom, erring on the side of a less dangerous, but not necessarily pleasanter idea.

'Have you?'

'Have I what?'

'Been searching the bodies?'

'No,' said Tom, disturbed and disgusted by the very idea, even though it was his.

'Well I have,' said Cat, wrinkling her nose.

Tom grimaced. 'You have?'

'And it's got us nowhere thus far. What if the myth is true about Arthur surviving the actual battle and asks for it to be thrown into the lake for the lady? Follow the living I say.'

'Thought you didn't believe in mermaids?'

'It's not what I think that counts.'

'But at least we'll know where it is if he does.'

117

'Ever used an aqualung? 'Cause I don't do water.'

'What if they're armed?'

'I'm going to follow them, not ask for directions.'

'What should I do?'

'Be careful and wait for me here.' With that Cat bounded off before Tom could react, leaving him alone on the battle-field. Well, not actually alone, there were the dead.

'Well I...' Tom crouched indecisively for a moment or two then cautiously stood up and surveyed the immediate surrounding area. Because of the fog there wasn't much of it. A silly thought came to mind. Perhaps he should kick one of the bodies closest to him just to check it wasn't going to get up any time soon, but thought better of it. It was a silly idea; what if it was playing possum and waiting for just that situation? Waiting to rise and attack the enemy who had left him for dead? What if they were all playing possum? Waiting to rise and attack him? Maybe the dead would rise and take revenge? The saver was grasped with both hands to Tom's rapidly beating chest as his imagination and eyes darted hither and tither.

By the time Cat returned with news, Tom was in quite a lather. 'Tom?'

'Yah!' yelled Tom, assuming a defensive position. He had gotten so wound up with the idea of facing legions of the dead, it was a wonder he hadn't corkscrewed himself into the ground at Cat's arrival. Instead, he faced Cat with the saver, now in a confused mix of spade and crossbow, pointing it at her head – if she was six foot tall that is.

'Tom?'

Tom looked down, the saver went with him.

'Hey!' said Cat, taking evasive action, 'it's me.'

'It is you,' said Tom.

'Who were you expecting?'

Tom shouldered his spade and said nothing. If he had had

118

a serial number and rank he might have mentioned them, but he was keeping shtum about the possum-playing knights and legions of the dead.

'Tom?'

'Could have been anyone creeping up on me.'

'What's with the shovel and-?'

'It's a spade.'

'Okay... what's with the spade and crossbow?'

'I...er... I don't actually know,' said Tom, examining it. 'It was still a book just before you arrived.'

'What were you thinking of?' asked an intrigued Cat, putting aside her news for the moment, exciting as it was.

He really didn't want to go there, but if it helped explain the nature of the beast – the saver, he thought he had better. 'Two things really,' he said, 'what would happen with all the dead and...'

'And?'

Tom swallowed. 'And... what to do if they attacked?'

Cat had heard it all now. Time for more eyeball rolling.

'I know... I know,' said Tom, starting to feel exceedingly foolish, 'the dead don't walk.'

'Damn right they don't,' said Cat, 'not here.'

His eyes widened, but he just wasn't going to ask.

Cat strolled over and inspected the saver. The crossbow was actually part of the spade. 'I think the saver got a little confused by your thoughts,' she said, 'looks like it couldn't make up its mind whether you wanted to bury or shoot them.' Cat looked up with a smile on her face. 'A case I think, of its new master being a little wayward in the thought processing department.'

'Will it change back?'

'I believe that's up to you. Try it, go on, have a little think.' Cat said this without the slightest glint of humour, but kept her smile.

119

'Maybe I should wait a while. Clear my head.'

'You have to carry it.'

She was right; it wasn't the lightest of spades, or cross-bows. He decided to give it a go. The saver instantly changed into a whistle, which Tom almost dropped.

'What the heck were you thinking of this time?' asked an astounded Cat.

'How I was going to get out of this situation,' said a very puzzled Tom.

'Judging by the state of your mind at the moment, I expect it thought you were all at sea.'

'Sea?'

'Never mind,' said Cat, now eager to relay what she had found out. 'Now listen, I've found Arthur.'

Cat explained as they travelled, that Arthur was alive and conscious, but suffering with a wound that needed attention. She didn't know how serious it was, but didn't think it that bad.

'How do we get the sword then?' Tom enquired, not liking the sound of things. Not that he wanted Arthur dead, but it seemed to him that procuring a sword from someone who didn't have a use for it any more was the easier option. Unconscious would have been fine. To make things worse, the fog was clearing.

Stepping carefully, Cat led Tom to a piece of land that rose quite sharply to form a small ridge. They climbed to the top and peered over. Arthur was some thirty to forty yards to their left, propped against a rocky outcrop, his sword by his side and surrounded by a small group of men aimlessly milling about. The fog was now nothing more than a thinning mist as a swirling breeze started to build.

'Okay, so what's the plan?' whispered Tom, having to squint as the sun had decided it too wanted to see what was going on.

The answer was straight, but didn't fill Tom with a happy glow. 'You go and get the sword,' said Cat.

Turning on his side and hunkering out of sight of those below, a flabbergasted Tom asked Cat the question he couldn't wait to hear the answer to. 'Me? *How?*' He had also wanted to add, "Are you out of your tiny little mind?" but decided he would wait until after Cat had explained to ask that.

'You go over to where he's sitting, pick up the sword and ask him if you can look after it until help arrives.'

There's no time like the present. 'Are you out of your tiny little mind?' said Tom.

Unfazed by Tom's response, Cat explained. 'He's dazed and tired, his men the same, some in deeper shock. It's been a hard-fought battle against people they once called friends. A confident voice will be heeded with favour.'

Tom made a play of looking around. 'Nope,' he said, after a moment, 'can't see anyone confident, and the man doesn't know me from Adam, why's he going to give Excalibur to me? I could be anyone.'

'Rufus-'

'I'm not Uncle Rufus,' snapped Tom.

A frosty atmosphere now descended on the pair, but Cat was above this; she was a professional, a fully paid-up member of TAG (Travellers' Aide Guild), and though other guilds accused them of not taking the whole guild thing seriously – it was widely thought that they treated everything as a game – she was proud to be part of its number. Besides, she knew she was right. Her mistake as far as she could see was coming straight out with it and not manoeuvring it so Tom thought the idea was his. Time to manoeuvre.

'So,' said Cat, manoeuvring, 'how do you think we should go about it?'

'Wait,' said Tom. 'Wait and see what happens?'

'And just how long do you suggest we do that for? Until someone sees us?'

'Something will turn up.'

Yeah, thought Cat, a regiment of angry knights…. she had an idea. 'Did you see that?'

'What?' said Tom.

'No, panic over, thought I saw that soldier over there move.'

'Which soldier?'

'Doesn't matter, my mistake.'

'Are you messing with me?' said Tom, nervously eyeing the numerous bodies littering the ground.

'No,' said Cat, her voice sharp, indignant. 'A girl can make a mistake can't she?'

Tom didn't think Cat made mistakes which meant… 'Which one moved?'

'Good grief Tom,' said Cat, thoroughly warming to the task, 'you're getting paranoid.' She huffed annoyance and pointed to a space on the ground. 'That one.'

'Which one?' said Tom, scanning the space Cat was pointing to.

'Oh for goodness' sake, that one, the- oh! Where's he gone?'

Tom drew his feet up beneath him. She was winding him up, wasn't she? 'He can't have gone,' said Tom.

'You're right, must have been that one I saw.' Cat pointed to another body a few feet away. 'I think.'

Winding him up or not, it was enough for Tom to want to take up sticks and get out of there. 'How dazed is he?' said Tom.

'Who?'

'Arthur.'

'Doubt he would recognise his own mother if it came down to it.'

'Could you create a diversion – draw off some of his men?'

'Could try,' said Cat, looking slightly interested. 'So what are you saying? You go down and grab the sword while I get the others to chase me?'

'Something like that,' said Tom.

'Great idea,' extolled Cat. 'I'll wait for you to get within twenty or so feet and then I'll stir something up.'

'But what about my clothes, won't he notice them if you're not around?'

'No worries, you leave that to me.' Cat gave Tom a huge smile that did nothing to calm the unease he was feeling.

'Okay,' said Tom, getting to his knees, 'I can do this.'

'See you back here,' said Cat, 'Good luck.'

Tom stood and hovered on the brow of the hill like a non-swimmer having to trust a life jacket for the first time. He was leaping into deep water and he wasn't sure he would come up again.

'Ready?'

He was as ready as he was ever going to be. Something he felt he was going to feel quite a few times in the near and distant future. He felt for the whistle. It's presence reassuring him. 'Ready,' said Tom.

'See you when I see you then.'

Tom watched for a moment as Cat headed away to wher-ever it was she was headed then took a step forward. This was followed by another. He was doing it.

Chapter 22

It was going to be a close-run thing. What would give out first, his courage, his luck, or his heart?

Edging ever closer to where Arthur lay, Tom, chest tightening with every step, had the sudden ridiculous notion to indulge in a bit of nonchalant whistling. What was he thinking? He quickly quashed the thought, afraid of drawing the unwanted attention it might bring and continued in as much silence as he could manage. Thankfully the milling men had moved away, but were still hanging around on the peripheral.

As Tom reached spitting distance of Arthur, he could see, contrary to what Cat had said, that the man wasn't faring that well. Tom could hear the man's groans and wheezes as each laboured breath caused him pain. What now? Tom glanced at the men. Some had wondered off but two of them still lingered as if waiting for something. Where had that Cat got to?

Away from prying eyes, Cat watched Tom's progression across the battlefield. She was ready to pounce, create a diversion, but for the moment she was going to sit tight and see what unfolded. Her plan: let Tom sidle up beside Arthur under his own steam. Cat knew she was putting her head on the block by doing so and if things were to go wrong she was prepared to take the flack, but she deemed it necessary. Tom needed that little bit of confidence to set him on his way. He would still need a bit of polishing here and there to become the finished article – the time traveller, but if he could do this by himself...

His mind on Cat, Tom unwittingly ventured closer to Arthur than he had intended. His attention to this little detail was swiftly brought to bear by a tired, but commanding voice. "Who goes there?" is how Tom's translator translated it.

A few moments ago Tom had been wondering what would give out first. Luckily for him it appeared it was his luck. The startled pensioner mused on the irony of this for a split second before looking down and meeting the searching stare of Arthur who was sitting only a sword thrust from him.

'Well?' said Arthur, pointing his sword at Tom.

What did he do? What did he say? He was going to be found out for sure. Tom peered down at the sword pointed at his groin and gulped.

'I said, who goes there?' demanded an impatient Arthur, the tip of the sword wavering dangerously close to Tom's flies.

Cripes, thought Tom or words to that effect. He tried to think. Something came. In for a penny, he decided. 'A loyal subject, Sire,' said Tom, behind him his fingers were crossed every way possible. He thought he remembered someone talking like that in an episode of Robin Hood once. 'Bout the same period, give or take?

The sword wavered for a moment more then dropped to the ground. Arthur was growing weaker by the second. 'Step closer man so that I might see you better.'

A relieved Tom shuffled closer.

'I do not recognise you. Give me your name.'

'Tom, Sire,' said Tom, trembling a little about the knees.

'Tom?'

'Er... Thomas, Sire,' said Tom, quickly, just in case his name didn't exist in Arthur's time and then added, pressured perhaps by the stern, albeit groggy stare of Arthur, 'I work in the kitchen.' Tom couldn't think why else he would have said it and had no idea which kitchen where.

Arthur looked a little puzzled and after a sudden fit of coughing, that didn't sound too encouraging where good health was concerned, questioned Tom on it. 'This is a place for warriors not for kitchen help. Why are you here?'

Tom didn't like the look of Arthur, he was definitely on a down turn. That said, whether Arthur survived was neither here or there, it wasn't his business. He wasn't here to help. He was here to get the sword. All he needed of Arthur was for him to stay conscious long enough to identify Excalibur. It could be the one that had been pointed at his privates, but Tom had to be sure. He didn't want to be popping back and as Tom had, for once in his life tapped his dormant imagination, why stop now.

'As soon as we heard-'

'We?'

'The other kitchen staff and me,' said Tom.

Arthur waved for him to continue.

'When we heard you had been hurt, we came to help.'

'And where are these others?' asked Arthur.

Cripes, thought Tom. Think man, think. He thought. 'Lost I'm afraid,' said Tom.

Arthur coughed and seemed to sink into himself. A cloud of sorrow swept across his old face. 'It has been a sad day for us all and many good men have fallen, but,' he said, his demeanour now brightening a little, as far as the pain would allow, 'I feel the day has been won and won well if you and men like you, common men, rally with their heart to my banner. Fear not, good Thomas, they shall be remembered and those that live rewarded.'

Tom frowned, then realised Arthur thought they had been killed. He had meant as lost, meandering in the fog... still.

Raising his body slightly, Arthur spoke again. 'Come forth common man and kneel before me.'

A rather hesitant Tom did as he was bid, but not before

casting a nervous glance for any sign of Cat. He was disappointed.

Arthur now raised another sword, from where, Tom hadn't seen, him being too busy scanning for a certain feline, and this one, as Tom's eyes fell on it, needed no introduction – Excalibur. It rose like a silver bird and shone like a torch of flame in the sun's gaze. It rose above Tom's head and then, rather unsteadily in Arthur's ailing hands, lowered towards him.

Had Tom not been paralysed with fear, admiration or awe, he may well have fainted or made a break for it and suffered the consequences, shorter by ten inches being one of them, but he didn't and the sword eventually alighted gently onto first one shoulder and then the next.

'You may rise, Sir Thomas,' said Arthur, releasing his grip on the sword as the weight of it became too much. It slid to the ground and lay there shining in the sun. 'Now go find me my physicians so that I may survive and celebrate this day.'

A flummoxed Tom stood up. What now? The answer came in the shape of a moan and cough as Arthur finally succumbed to unconsciousness.

'Well I'll be,' said Tom, pushing back his cap, 'wait 'til Cat hears about this.'

'Cat did,' said Cat, causing Tom to start and nearly trip over Arthur's legs, 'and I still don't believe my ears, or eyes. Now grab it and let's get out of here before someone comes.'

'Grab?' said Tom, still in flummox.

'The sword,' said Cat.

It was like watching something played in slow motion, but Tom managed to rouse himself and grab Excalibur. 'Crikey!' he said, managing to get its handle in the air, 'It weighs a flipping ton.'

'Good job he's such a strong fellow then, isn't it?' said Cat, referring to Tom's impromptu knighthood, 'or.' She chopped at the back of her neck with her paw.

Tom grimaced as he tried to pick the sword from the ground. It was a no go. Straining, he had another attempt, but twinges in various parts of his back gave way to the idea of dragging it instead. He had only got a couple of feet when the sound of worried and urgent shouts reached his ears.

'Keep moving,' hissed Cat, 'but stay close.'

'They'll see us,' groaned Tom.

'They won't.'

Of course they won't, thought Tom, remembering the escapade in the hotel, but it still didn't fill him with an abundance of confidence.

The men belonging to the voices appeared and headed towards Arthur, their leader coming within a hair's breadth of running into Tom. Cat pulled at Tom's trouser leg and made keep still motions with her paws.

The first man to Arthur, the leader, looked grim and knelt by his side. He beckoned the others over and told some of them to hoist Arthur above their shoulders. 'Take him to his tent – quickly,' ordered the man. They moved off, again coming close to where Tom and Cat stood.

Tom held his breath as they drew near. It was touch and go, but they passed without incident. This left the leader and two others standing where Arthur had lain; they appeared to be looking for something. The leader was scuffing the ground with his foot.

'Find it,' said the leader after he had moved a couple of yards in Tom and Cat's direction. 'And don't come back without it. I'm going to Arthur's side.' The two men nodded and he left.

'Why us?' asked one of the men, when he felt it was safe to do so.

'Because you're too slow-witted to move when I tell you to,' growled the other, under his breath.

'It's not here.'

'It had better be or we're in trouble.'

'Why us,' whined the first man, repeating himself.

As the men argued, Cat tugged on Tom's trousers and gave him the nod to move. Off they went, Tom struggling with the sword, Cat keeping a wary eye open for trouble. They were still in earshot though, when the search behind them came to an inconclusive end.

'It's not here,' concluded the whiner.

'It'll be our heads if we go back without it,' said the other.

The whiner's face drained of colour. 'What if we say someone ran off with it?' he said.

'And we chased after him,' said the other, getting in the spirit of it.

'And killed him,' said whiner, a ghastly grin appearing.

'But we still won't have the sword,' said the other, realising the glaring flaw in their plan.

All fell quiet, then, after a moment or two, the whiner's grin made a tentative return. 'What if we said he threw it in the lake?'

'Good idea,' said the other, 'but they'll ask us why we didn't go in after it? It wouldn't go far.'

But the whiner wasn't about to be beaten. 'But what if we say a magical hand rose up from the water and dragged it into its depths?'

The other one looked at the whiner with murder in his heart. The man was a fool, but he heard himself ask… 'Do you think it will work?' It was desperate times.

'If we both keep to the same story it could.' There was more hope than conviction in his words.

'We better chop off a head then,' said the other one, warming to the idea as one adrift in a shark infested sea might warm to a passing plank. It's something. 'They'll want proof.'

'Good idea,' said whiner, drawing his sword, 'now, which one is one of theirs?'

By the time Tom and Cat reached the relative safety of the ridge, Tom was feeling decidedly rough.

'They cut off someone's head,' groaned Tom, as he hauled Excalibur up and over.

'The man was dead,' said Cat, matter of fact.

'And that doesn't matter?' said Tom. 'It was nasty – horrible.'

'Better him than you.'

Fielding a sickly grimace, Tom had to agree, but it didn't make him feel a whole lot better. 'Do you think they'll believe them?'

'Believe a story about a magical hand appearing from the lake and grasping the sword?'

'Yes,' said Tom, struggling behind.

'What do you think?' said Cat.

'Well… oh,' said Tom.

'But if for some reason they don't, we had better move it. We're leaving them a nice trail to follow.'

Tom looked behind him. The sword had dug a nice clear furrow all the way from where he had got it. 'Drat!' He doubled his efforts, but didn't double the speed they were travelling.

Not long after, he had had enough. 'That's it, I'm done in. I can't pull it another inch,' he announced, leaning on the sword's hilt.

'It's not far,' encouraged Cat.

'I'm too old for this.' Tom dipped into a jacket pocket and took out a hanky. He mopped his brow with it.

'But you're a knight,' said Cat, thinking it might somehow motivate the old boy.

'Yeah,' said Tom, puffing, a tired, wry smile creasing his cheeks, 'a "good night all" at ten o'clock with a cup of cocoa kind.'

Cat saw she was going to have to get a certain someone in better shape.

Raised voices suddenly erupted somewhere back from where they had come.

'Grief,' said Tom, tucking away his hanky, 'do you think they've discovered the rut?'

'Who knows,' said Cat, peering past Tom to see if she could see anyone, 'but I don't think it'll be a wise move waiting to see if they have.'

Grasping the sword with both hands, Tom started to drag it, but it really was no good, he managed nothing more than a couple of feet before having to stop again. 'I can't do it.' Behind him, the voices were growing louder.

'The saver,' said Cat, urgently.

He didn't know how it could help, but Tom took the whistle from his pocket and closed his eyes. He opened them to find he now had a scabbard for the sword. It didn't help.

'What did you think of?' said Cat, a tad anxious as she glanced back at the ridge.

'Something to put it in,' said Tom.

'Try again,' said Cat, 'but this time, think on.' She wanted to hurry him, but she knew it might make him nervous and matters worse.

Tom closed his eyes again.

No one had appeared as yet over the ridge and Cat was safe in the knowledge that even if they did they wouldn't be able to see her or Tom, but if they had found the rut the sword had made and were following that, that would be a different story, she knew where the butt would end – right at Tom's feet. And then all it would take was some clever clogs to start swinging his sword and... Cat didn't want to think about it. Of course she could help, but dare she? What if something she did changed the course of history? Again Cat decided not to

131

think about it. As she did, or didn't as was the case, Tom let out a low, long, whistle.

Tom was now holding, and it was still as light as a feather, a pretty nifty-looking sack truck. It had it all, straps, pneumatic tyres as standard...

'Tom.'

'What?

Cat gave him the hurry up.

'Right,' said Tom. As quick as his tired old arms would allow, Tom fastened Excalibur to the truck and started to push. After a couple of feet he changed his mind and started to pull it. It was much easier. With Cat loping beside him and the voices not getting any closer – perhaps they hadn't been following after all, Tom started to whistle the little ditty he had thought better of as he had approached Arthur.

'What is that?' asked Cat.

'Just a little ditty about someone showing me the way home,' smiled Tom.

Chapter 23

OAP jokes aside Tom was never so happy to see a toilet in all his life. He pulled the trolley and sword inside and slammed the door shut behind him. Cat had already climbed onto her shelf.

'Job done,' said Tom, who, although puffing like a steam train, was smiling from ear to ear. He flopped onto the toilet seat exhausted, but happy.

'Not quite,' said Cat, 'we still have to get it to the stone and put it back.'

But this reminder of the work still to be done failed to put little more than a residue dampener on Tom's rising spirits. 'A cuppa first though,' said he, confidence perhaps not brimming, but a lot higher than it had been half an hour ago. 'A man can't do much good on fresh air alone.'

It wasn't an ideal suggestion, Cat wanted the sword back in situ as soon as possible, but while spirits were high, perhaps it wasn't such a bad idea. Keep the old boy happy. A small reward for services thus rendered. 'Home it is then,' agreed Cat.

Tom closed his eyes and thought of that cup of tea.

'It wasn't my fault,' argued Tom, backing out of the portable loo, 'this thing's far too sensitive.'

'It was,' said Cat, unhappy with the unscheduled stop and the trouble it had caused. 'I thought the bearded lady was going to flatten you when you barred her way.'

'I thought that was the strong man,' said Tom, stopping what he was doing, 'those muscles were huge.'

'Just keep it simple,' said Cat, 'Complicate things and that's when trouble happens.'

'But a funfair? How the heck did it mistake me wanting a cuppa for a funfair?'

'Because you couldn't just think of home, you had to think of "that good old-fashioned cuppa" you wanted.'

'I still don't get it,' said Tom, moving the truck round so that he could push it now they were on the path.

'They had a theme going. A Victorian one where you could get a good old-fashioned cup of tea just like your grandparents would have had. That's why. The thing has got a mind of its own, so bear that in mind next time and *keep it simple.*' Having gone on ahead with the truck, Cat couldn't see the faces Tom was pulling as he trundled it along. 'And I think it would have made better sense to leave the sword in the loo – much safer in there.'

'You could have said earlier. What about the saver?'

'It isn't going anywhere.'

Tom snorted and returned the sword and saver to the loo.

Home at last, a light snack as well as a well-earned cuppa was prepared.

'We'll have to get you in some cat food,' said Tom, rummaging through a cupboard for something to give Cat.

'I prefer chicken,' said Cat, disturbed by the thought of some processed concoction being lumped out in front of her.

'Wouldn't we all,' said Tom, standing on tiptoes. 'Ah!' He found something he may or may not have been looking for and removed it from the cupboard. He was sure Cat would look on it with disdain, but beggars... He opened the tin he had found and placed its contents on a saucer. He then placed the saucer on the floor.

Cat, who was sitting at the table, waiting, humphed her displeasure at its placement and reluctantly jumped to the floor. Things would have to certainly change – her own plate at the table for one. She sniffed at the concoction laid before her. 'What is this?'

'A mixture of pork, ham and spices,' said Tom, reading the side of the tin. 'Do you like spices?' He gathered together his snack of tea and biscuits. 'Only it's all I've got 'til I go shopping.'

Tightwad or frugal? thought Cat, who had noticed most of the cupboards were bare.

Tom sat in the chair Cat had vacated and wiggled his backside. 'Cor,' he said, 'seat's nice and warm.' He took a biscuit from the packet and proceeded to dunk it in his tea.

Yes, thought Cat, turning her stubby little nose into the up position, standards have most definitely slipped.

'So,' said Tom, wetting a finger for crumb gathering, 'what's next on the agenda?'

On the floor, Cat was gingerly patting the meat with her paw. This just wouldn't do. She took a small bite and prepared herself for the worst. Astonishingly, she discovered it wasn't as bad as she thought it was going to be. It was quite delicious actually – a little garnish perhaps but...

'Good eh?' said Tom, who had been observing Cat's approach to her lunch with curious amusement. 'I fry it up in a bit of batter, goes down grand with some chips and some of yer old petits pois.'

Cat would have preferred a nice sauce, but each to his own. She took another mouthful and relished the meaty yet spicy taste.

'So,' Tom repeated, having dunked his last biscuit, 'what's next?'

Next? Cat removed her face from her plate. As good as it was this really wasn't the time for self-indulgence. She licked her lips. There had been much too much pussy-footing around already. She ceased her licking. Had she really just thought that? Surely time to go. 'Camelot, and I think we should be on our way.' Cat, somewhat reluctantly, it has to be said, pushed her saucer away and headed for the door. 'Tom?'

Tom was still sat at the table. 'But I've still got some tea left.'

'Leave it.'

Tom's unfinished tea was barely cold when Hope End's back gate swung cautiously open. A moment later a face appeared at the kitchen window and peered in. It was a face Tom would have recognised had he still been there. It searched this way and that for signs of life, but soon realised it was too late, the place was empty. The face scowled its displeasure and twisted by contempt turned to the shed and portable loo. The owner of the face had mischief in mind – the destructive, permanent kind.

Chapter 24

'You sure this is the right place?' asked Tom, peeping from the confines of the loo, 'It looks much the same as the last one, but with less fog.'

'As long as you kept it simple, we shouldn't be far from where the tournament was held.'

Tom had, the experience with the bearded lady was one he didn't want to repeat in a hurry.

'Come on,' said Cat, who had assumed the role of lookout, 'it looks all clear.'

Tom trundled the sack truck with Excalibur firmly ensconced on it past Cat and towards a path she was pointing to. They warily followed this until it came to a crossroads.

'Which way?' said Tom, resting on the truck's handles.

'Left,' said Cat, indicating thus, 'and keep it down, you don't know who might be within earshot.'

'Sorry,' whispered Tom, sinking his head into hunched shoulders. He kept forgetting that while no one could see them, there was every chance someone might hear them. He wheeled the truck onto a less worn path.

They hadn't gone far before Tom whispered to Cat, wondering how much further they had to go.

Cat called a halt. 'If my memory serves me right, it's being held in a meadow about half a mile further on.'

'You have trouble with the old memory as well eh?' said Tom. 'You know, I went upstairs the other day and when I got to the top, I was darned if I could remember what I'd gone up there for.'

'No,' said Cat, and with a determination not to get embroiled in more idle chit-chat, put her best paw forward.

'Hang on,' said Tom, caught on the hop, 'wait for me.'

Quarter of a mile on Cat called another stop. 'Someone's coming,' she hissed, 'quick, get off the track.'

Tom did as he was told and steered the truck into the shadows of a small copse, but wanted to know why. 'Why? They won't be able to see us.'

'I'm not taking any chances now we're this close,' said Cat, stretching her neck to see if she could see who was coming, 'they're bound to be watching.'

Tom was about to ask who that might be exactly when Cat hushed him.

Two men had appeared. One a small man, quite old, a little stooped. The other, younger, tall, broad-shouldered with a full beard.

'And you have the gold?' asked the bearded one.

'You'll get it as promised, when the job is done.'

'How do I know I can trust you?' The two men stopped walking as the bearded man put a hand on the old one's shoulder, the other on the sword hanging by his side.

The smaller man smiled. 'You worry too much. You'll have your gold as soon as I have the sword.'

This seemed to pacify the bigger man. He released his grip. 'You say Merlin has it?'

'He aims to place it in the stone I showed you. Get it before he does.' The old man unclipped a small bag from his waist-band and removed something from it. 'Here, take this as a gesture of good faith.'

The bearded man took what he was offered, examined it closely then put it between his teeth. He bit on it. 'It's real,' he said. A smile appeared, splitting his beard. 'And there will be a hundred more like this when the job is done?'

'Ninety-nine more actually,' said the old man.

'As soon as you have the sword?'

'Would I lie to you?'

The smile wavered, then disappeared completely as the bearded man thought about what the older man had said. 'Just you try,' he snarled.

'We have an understanding then?'

The bearded man nodded and then he and the older one walked on.

Huddled low to the ground, within the long grass and shadows of the copse, Tom raised his head to have a better look at the men as they approached along the path. Cat immediately waved him back down again.

'What you trying to do,' hissed Cat, through clenched teeth, 'lose your head? Those swords they're carrying aren't props you know.'

'But-'

'Ssssch!'

'I wan-'

'Sssch-sssch-sssch!' hissed Cat. 'You want them to hear you?'

On the path, Cat's fears were about to be realised.

The two men stopped.

'Did you hear that?' whispered the bearded man, drawing his sword and holding the older man back.

'Hear what?' said the old man. But instead of drawing his sword as his companion had, the old man pulled something from an inside pocket which momentarily glinted in the sun. He quickly covered it from view.

'Talking – it came from there,' said the bearded man, pointing to the copse.

'Oh-oh,' said Cat, as the bearded man took a step in her and Tom's direction. 'Stay here.'

From his face down in the grass position, Tom could see nothing. He had wanted to tell Cat something, but that could now wait. 'Where're you going?' he whispered, but Cat didn't have time to explain as the bearded man was now advancing on the copse, sword held steady.

'Woof!' woofed Cat, who, to the eyes of the advancing men, appeared as no more than a mangy cur on the scavenge. Behind her, Tom, if he hadn't been keeping his head down, would have seen no difference, but he was wondering where the dog he could hear had come from. Cat added another woof, this time in such a way that if at first heard at a distance could be misconstrued as human speech.

'It's nothing but a mutt,' said the old man, on seeing the disguised Cat, 'you're getting jumpy.'

The bearded man curled his top lip and snarled. He didn't like being made a fool of, even if it was his own doing. 'I hate dogs,' he said, picking up a stone and hurling it Cat's way.

It was easily dodged, but Cat wasn't in the mood for fetch. She threw a growl in the man's direction then, remembering to curl her tail between her legs, legged it back into the copse.

The bearded man thought about throwing another stone to see the dog on its way, but decided the mutt wasn't worth the effort. As he did the older man took the opportunity to return whatever it was he had taken, back to his inside pocket.

'Tomorrow you say?' said the bearded man, casting one last suspicious glance towards the copse.

'Before he puts it in the stone.'

'Then let us go before someone does see us talking.'

The old man smiled. 'After you.'

In the copse, an anxious Tom was beginning to fret. Should he get up? Where was Cat? Is this grass damp? Where did the dog come from? Were a few of the many worries building. Luckily, Cat returned before matters came to a head.

'You okay?' asked Cat, appearing as if from nowhere by Tom's face.

'Where were you?'

'I've only been gone a minute,' said Cat.

'Feels like a lot longer.'

'Did you miss me?'

Tom did eye narrowing. 'Have they gone?'

'Yes, but I think we might have a problem.'

Tom stood up, brushed grass from his clothes and tutted at the grass stains on his knees. 'That's going to be a devil to get out, that.' He spat on his fingers and began to rub at a patch.

'Did you hear what I said?'

'Yeah, a problem,' said Tom. He stopped rubbing the knee of his cords and looked at Cat. 'What problem? Is it the dog?' Tom started looking around for it.

'That was me.'

'The dog?'

'More glamour.'

'Ah, so what is the problem?'

'I think we're too early.'

'Again?'

'By a day by my reckoning, but lucky we did.'

Tom couldn't see anything lucky about it. 'We'll just have to come back tomorrow then,' he said, returning to his stains. 'Gives me a chance to soak these.'

'You don't understand,' said Cat, 'that's not the problem.'

'It will be if you don't get them into soak as soon as,' said Tom, half listening again.

'I'm talking about the sword, not your trousers. We have a problem with the sword.'

'But we've got the sword, haven't we?' Tom checked and yes, Excalibur was still on the truck.'

'Not with that one,' said Cat, 'the one that Merlin is going to put in the stone tomorrow.'

Tom's brow wrinkled. 'Am I missing something?' he asked.

A lesser being may have stepped in here with a witty retort, but Cat wasn't in a laughing mood. 'I think those two men we saw are planning to stop Merlin from placing the sword in the stone.'

'You saw,' Tom corrected.

'Sorry?'

'I didn't see them. I was face down in cow lunch if you remember. Why I don't know, they couldn't see me.'

'They might have done when I went to confront them, but that's neither here or there now, like I said, I think those men will try to stop Merlin putting the sword in the stone.' Cat was getting just a tad exasperated.

'Job done then,' said Tom, missing the point by a country mile. 'If it was never in the stone it won't be taken out so we don't have to replace it. I could do with a cuppa.'

Cat said nothing; she just sat, staring at Tom, her thoughts kept to herself. A near silence now fell on the copse, only a low whistling wind keeping it from being perfect. If a tumble weed had tumbled past, the scene would have been complete. It lasted a full ten seconds.

'Oh,' said Tom, at last, leaving his knees alone.

'You with it now?'

'What do we do?'

'We'll have to stop them somehow. If Merlin doesn't put the sword in place, I dread to think what might happen.'

Cogs were whirring and they belonged to Tom. 'But we've got this one,' he said, gesturing to the Excalibur they had. 'Can't we give it to Merlin? Make up some story about finding it or something? No one will be the wiser and job done!'

For a moment, for a split second, it actually sounded a bona fide solution to their problem, but then Cat realised the men, whoever they were, would not be, could not be, satisfied with just stealing Excalibur. For their plan to be able to work, if they wanted the worlds to drift apart for good, it would have to be destroyed, which meant, as the Excalibur they meant to

142

steal was the first one, all others would cease to exist. Cat told Tom her worry.

This would take some considerable head-getting-round, thought Tom, trying to understand; so he didn't bother. Time to get with the program. 'We have to warn Merlin then.'

Cat, who had been thinking along the same lines, actually took a step back on hearing the idea spoken aloud. It wasn't ideal. It would mean dabbling with the past, but what other choice did they have? It was dangerous and it was going to get a little – no – very complicated, but wasn't it always? One step at a time then, she decided. That would be the best policy.

'Okay, I doubt he's far away, but first things first, we should return our sword to the loo. Too many swords might spoil the broth.'

Tom readily agreed, feeling a slight relief that they were going back to the loo even if they weren't going home. He supposed because it was home to a certain extent. He began to walk, trundling the truck before him. It was as they were returning to the loo that Tom remembered what it was he was trying to tell Cat as he lay hidden in the copse.

'You know,' he said, frowning, 'I'm sure I recognised a voice back there.'

'You would have,' said Cat, 'one of them was the bearded oaf who imprisoned you.'

'The dead one?'

'He wasn't back there.'

'It's a bit spooky that,' observed Tom, 'the same man every time.'

'Happens,' said Cat, 'Rufus called it an anomaly.'

'Strange though,' said Tom, his frown deepening, 'how his voice changed over the years. You'd have thought he would have sounded younger here, not older, or am I getting my times mixed up?'

'I thought it sounded the same,' said Cat, 'apart from when he was dead, there isn't a lot of time between this and the first time we saw him, a matter of days I suspect.'

'Then why did he sound so old?'

'He didn't.' Cat stopped walking as a warning light flashed in her head.

'What's wrong?' asked Tom, pulling up.

'I don't think you did recognise his voice.'

'I didn't?'

'No... I think you recognised the voice that belonged to the old man.'

'How could I,' said Tom, 'I've never seen him before.' Come to think about it, thought Tom, he hadn't seen the man at all.

'This is a worrying development,' said Cat. She started walking again, her pace quicker. She had to think – try and recall who Tom had spoken to on their travels. There had only been four people; the bearded man, Arthur and the two men who had been searching for the sword after Arthur had been taken away. No, there had been more, there were the men who had been milling about and those that arrived to collect Arthur, but she had been in earshot of all of them. None had sounded like the old man, besides, she doubted he would be still living; the bearded man had been an old man at the end. It could only mean one thing then; the voice and its owner didn't belong to the past. It had to be someone who knew Tom, perhaps even Rufus. This was serious. It also strengthened the idea that it was no accident the sword was removed from the stone and that there did indeed appear to be a conspiracy afoot to stop it even getting there.

Cat called another halt. 'Tom,' she said, sounding very serious, deliberate, as if talking to a child, 'I want you to think very carefully about this, where have you heard that voice before?'

'I'm not five,' said Tom, indignantly.

'Sorry, I know, but this is important.'

Tom leant on the truck, stuck out his bottom lip and had a long hard think. 'Nope,' he announced after a few seconds, 'can't say I do.'

'Good grief, Tom,' groaned Cat, 'you must have an inkling – you only heard the man five minutes ago.'

'Sorry Cat,' said Tom, straightening up, 'but you've got the wrong man if it's memory games you want to play. I have trouble remembering something I was told five minutes ago, and no jokes about my age – I've always had a bad memory.'

Great, thought Cat.

'But it'll come to me in the end, it always does. Usually when I least expect it. Though then I can't always remember why I was thinking it in the first place.'

Double great! thought Cat, angrily. Why she was so angry, with herself as well as Tom, she didn't rightly know. She didn't speak again until they arrived back at the loo.

'Put the sword inside, but bring the saver with you, you might need it,' said Cat, a grave expression clouding her sweet little face.

Not liking the sound of that one little bit, Tom wheeled the truck inside and unclipped the sword. After a bit of a struggle, he managed to prop it in the corner by the pipe. He pulled the truck out again and closed the door.

Chapter 25

'Why couldn't we stay in the loo?' moaned Tom, trying to arrange what was at hand into something approaching comfortable. He was in a small, low, ramshackle shack that Cat had assured him was a seventh century version of a safe house.

'As I've told you,' said Cat, wondering what she had done in another life to deserve her latest responsibility, 'it will save us travel time. We have to try and protect Merlin the best we can, as soon as we can.'

At last finding a position that he felt wouldn't cripple him for the rest of his life, Tom did his best to settle. 'So,' he said, 'you going to tell me what's worrying you?'

'I think the old man you heard talking back there is a traveller.'

'A gypsy?' Tom couldn't see why Cat would be worrying about a gypsy.

'A time traveller.'

Tom sat up, bumped his head on the end of a low beam and sat back down again. 'Like me?' he said, rubbing his scalp.

Nobody's like you, thought Cat. 'Yes,' she said, 'like you.'

'Shouldn't we talk to him then?'

'I doubt that would be wise,' said Cat, 'he's not one of ours.'

Not one of ours. It sank in, got chewed up and then was finally spat out. 'A baddy do you mean?' said Tom, aghast.

Cat couldn't help her smile. 'If you like.'

'Good grief. Do you think he's one of the bounders that got Rufus lost in time?'

'Perhaps, perhaps not, but he's working against us. He doesn't want the sword anywhere near the stone.'

The bump hadn't been remotely bad, but Tom was reeling all the same. 'But,' he said, 'surely the sword gets in the stone or how else does Arthur get it?'

Cat shrugged her little shoulders.

I can do this, thought Tom. 'So, and correct me if I'm wrong, this baddy wants to stop the sword from being put in the stone. But surely if Arthur pulls it out it's what they want?'

'Yes, but we've got the sword now, haven't we? And we're going to put it back, which negates what they've done. See? So their plan now I assume, now that they know we're onto them is to destroy the sword so it can never go in. Getting Arthur to take the sword may well have been a temporary measure until they found a way of destroying it. It was also a good way to send us on a wild goose chase and buy them time.'

'But what about Arthur? What happens if he's not king?'

'I don't know,' admitted Cat.

'So what was the point of the sword in the stone in the first place? I know it's there to hold the worlds together, but couldn't something else have been used – something a little more discreet?'

'It kept with the ethos of the time and besides it had an aura of invisibility put on it. It seemed a better idea than the last link.'

Tom now had questions coming out of his ears and was feeling pretty pleased with himself for keeping up so far. 'Okay,' he said, gearing up to ask some, 'if it was invisible, how did they find it? And is Merlin one of us, a traveller or helper of some sort?'

'I don't know, but when they did they did a rather good paint job on it before luring Arthur to pull it out.'

'And Merlin?'

'A second-rate, slight of hand magician and would-be alchemist who happened to be in the right place at the right time.'

'Didn't he ask questions?'

'Thought he was doing it himself, all we had to do was feed him with ideas and the odd nudge. Rufus called him a brilliant enigma. There are different views on this.'

'That doesn't sound right.'

'We do what we have to.'

'So what was it before it was a sword, the link?'

'A button.'

'A button? Like a "don't press me" sort of button?'

'No, a coat button.'

'Who thought that was a good idea?'

'It was a good idea, until it got lost that is. It was found of course, but it was felt something substantial should replace it.'

'And was there something else before the button?'

'There are tales.'

'What I don't understand though,' said Tom, 'is why they want to destroy Earth; won't they come a cropper too?' Tom shifted position – his left leg was going to sleep.

Cat sighed. 'They don't usually want anything destroyed. They just do these things to give us the run-around while they change the little things they really want changing. Usually for power or a financial gain, it's never-ending. This time though I think it's different. This time I think whoever's behind it wants the planets to drift; the worlds to crash about our ears.'

The shack fell silent. Tom didn't really know what to think any more, nothing made sense. Except... and this suddenly came to him as he thought about tomorrow's coming events.

'What about my party?' said Tom, 'I'm going to miss it and probably be reported missing.'

'No you won't,' said Cat, a sparkle in her eyes, 'you forget – you're a time traveller. We can get back before you even left if you want.'

This in a way didn't help, but if true, why couldn't they just go home, rest there and come back just before Merlin travelled to the stone? It would make more sense, wouldn't it? Just a little more confusion to add to Tom's already befuddled mind, but he wouldn't ask, there had been enough questions for one day. Had it been a day? He was tired and tomorrow might be an even longer day than this one.

'I think we should sleep now,' said Cat, noticing Tom's drooping eyelids, 'tomorrow could be a long day.'

Had she read my mind? may have crossed Tom's mind had he not been succumbing to sleep. His eyelids had even fluttered for a second when she said it, but nothing was going to stand in sleep's way. Tom lay back and closed his eyes; not long after, he was sound asleep.

About five minutes later, after checking to see if Tom was in deep sleep, she too, drifted off. But not to sleep, Cat had other plans. She left the shack and disappeared into the night.

Chapter 26

The sun had just put in an appearance when Cat arrived back at the shack. She was agitated, even excited as she entered.

'Where the hell have you been?' demanded Tom, as Cat's nose popped through the entrance. He was crouched in a corner.

This caught Cat on the hop as she had expected to find Tom still asleep; it was only just past six o'clock.

'Well?' said Tom, face like thunder.

'I…' She stopped; there was no point lying. It would only make things worse. 'I've been to see Merlin.'

'And you couldn't tell me? Why?' Tom's anger had started with puzzlement three hours earlier when he had woken and wanted to take a leak. The puzzlement because when he had tried to leave the shack, he found he couldn't; something invisible was keeping him in. Fear followed when he went to tell Cat what was happening and found she wasn't in the shack. Then the anger when he realised the barrier had to be of Cat's doing. This anger was compounded with the embarrassment of having to relieve himself in the corner. 'You didn't trust me, did you?'

'I had my reasons for what I did,' said Cat.

Anger rising further Tom, this time with presence of mind to miss the beam, got up and in a stooped position sidled to the door. 'So job done then? I take it we can leave now.'

Cat hadn't wanted to say what she was about to say, at least not yet, but she felt she no longer had a choice. 'He's your uncle.' It was going to complicate things.

Tom was halfway through the door and determined to go back to the loo in silence, but curiosity dictated otherwise. 'Who is?' he asked, reluctantly.

'Merlin, but you can't meet him,' said Cat, doubting anything she said was going to help, 'because this Rufus isn't from your time; it's a blood thing.'

Standing outside, Tom was finding this hard to understand.

'Tom?' There was no answer. Cat left the shack. Tom was leaning against it. He still looked angry, but it was now fused with confusion. 'I'm sorry. Truly I am, but I couldn't take you with me. I thought I'd get back before you woke.' She thought for a moment then added. 'You were totally safe.'

She just didn't understand. It wasn't about safe; it was about trust but... He was starting to cool down a bit. There was no point hitting the roof – again. He touched the spot on his head where he had bumped it yesterday and smiled. The anger was starting to pass. 'Why couldn't you tell me where you were going?'

'Because you would have wanted to come along and it wasn't possible and you wouldn't have understood.'

Tom's anger subsided. The cat was right; he would have wanted to go; would have wanted to say hello to his uncle; would have caused problems. 'So, Uncle Rufus is Merlin?' said Tom, with no sign of surprise. Why would there be with what has gone on? Go with the flow boy, go with the flow and see where it takes you. Treat it as a holiday. It had been a while since he had had one of those. Tom had a little trip down memory lane. Mexico was the last holiday; covered with itchy spots the first week and a jab in the backside; the second week – full of cocktails. Perhaps this adventure was going the same way. He hoped so – the second part anyway.

'Tom?'

'What? Sorry, where were we?'

151

'You were asking me about Rufus.'

'Oh yes, is he?'

'Yes and no,' said Cat, looking awkward.

'He is or he isn't,' said Tom.

'He wasn't always and this is Rufus from the past not the lost version, does that make sense?'

That was a good question. Go with the flow. 'I suppose so,' said Tom, 'Did he say anything?'

'About?'

'Me?'

'Not really.'

'Oh.'

'Wanted to know how you were coping of course,' lied Cat, Rufus wasn't much for chit-chat – tunnel vision when on the job.

'And?'

'And?'

'What did you say?'

'Not bad for a novice,' she lied again. She consoled herself with the notion that it was only a white lie and that it was what she would have said if asked – maybe.

'Um,' said Tom, a slight glow of pride spreading. 'So, did you warn him about the men?'

'Yes.'

'What's he going to do?'

'We've already put the original sword in the stone and hidden them and he's going to carry a decoy sword this morning.'

'Won't he get hurt?' said Tom, looking worried.

'You ever seen your uncle run – like the wind. He'll drop it and scarper.'

'Then all's well that ends well then,' said Tom. 'What time shall we aim to get home? When we left or just before the party? I'm quite hungry you know. A nice bit of cake would go down quite nicely.'

'Not quite,' said Cat, quietly.

'Sorry?'

'Not quite,' said Cat, 'It would seem we have to guide Arthur to the sword.'

Was he hearing right? 'But… we… I… what?' Flow boy – flow. 'Why?'

'Continuity, according to your uncle.'

'Continuity?' Tom felt he was beginning to sound like a parrot, but he had to ask.

'It happened so it's got to happen again. If the legend of the sword no longer exists who knows what might happen in the future. All those theories lost – all that goes with it, livelihoods and the like – gone. Your uncle feels we can't take the chance.'

Resigning himself to this new twist of fate with an ease that surprised him, Tom asked Cat what the plan was.

'We guide Arthur to the sword, get him to take it out, all's well with the legend and when he's gone we replace it with ours. And before you ask – yes, we can then go home to your party.'

'Just like that?' said Tom, erring on the side of caution; he'd been here before.

'Juss like that,' said Cat, pushing her paws out in front of her in true Cooper style. 'One of the greats,' she sighed.

From what Cat figured to be a safe distance – enough so the two time lines didn't touch, she and Tom watched, waiting for events to unfold.

'Won't they find out?' said Tom, referring to the false Excalibur.

'Of course they will, but it will be too late by then. Look.' Cat motioned to their right; Merlin had appeared. He was just how Tom remembered him – Rufus that is… Cat now motioned left to a group of men; the bearded one leading them.

'What's he doing?' said Tom, when he noticed Merlin was still walking towards them, 'I thought he was supposed to run?'

'So did I,' said Cat.

Anxiety built. 'Perhaps there's something wrong?' said Tom. Beside him, he could feel Cat tensing up. 'What you going to do?'

'Nothing yet, but I want to be prepared if I'm needed.'

Merlin/Rufus finally stopped a couple of yards from the men. Words were exchanged. Merlin chanted something that sounded like an incarnation. From somewhere in the group of men a shout of "doddery old fool" was heard. Swords were drawn. One was dropped. A tad of profanity was thrown in by both sides. And then it was all over. Merlin hitched up his robes, threatened all with the promise of future tadpole parentage and ran. Not quite like the wind, but with enough gusto to leave his armoured foes in his dust-laden wake.

'Did he-'

'Yes,' said Cat, 'always ready with the one-fingered salute our Rufus.'

'But he aimed it our way.'

'Just his idea of wit,' assured Cat. 'Come on, time for us to move; we've a date with destiny.'

Chapter 27

The face Tom would have recognised left the kitchen window and headed down the garden path, grabbing a garden fork on the way from a half-turned flower bed. The shed would be the first to feel its wrath. Then the loo – no one would be coming back that way when it was finished with.

Stopping just short of the shed door, the fork was thrust with might and malicious purpose, but the expected splintering didn't materialise. Instead, fork and face that Tom knew, were thrown backwards across the garden.

The fork was broken, the face furious. It cursed and swore. 'Damned cat,' it spat. 'Damned magic,' it cursed, rising. It now eyed the portable loo. 'That too no doubt,' growled the face. It now knew it was a waste of time bothering with further assaults. It looked back at the cottage. 'That as well I'll be bound; damned cat with her damned protection spells.' But the face had other ideas in mind. When dealing with the cat it was best to have a few contingency plans; plans where she would perhaps think twice before using her magic.

It was to one of those that the face now headed.

Chapter 28

'What's going on?' said Tom, peeping from the shadows of a derelict building.

'There's a tournament going on, remember?'

'Oh yeah, so where're the knights in shining armour then?'

'There,' said Cat.

'Where?'

'In the square.' Cat gave Tom a look. 'You sure you don't need glasses?'

'Them?' The only people in the square were a group of men of varying ages dressed in what looked like sackcloth under chain mail.

'Yes, sadly more mud than majesty about them I'm afraid, but that's myth for you – rose-coloured glasses.'

'Which one's Arthur then?'

'He's not with them; he's only a lowly squire. He'll be sharpening an axe or sword for someone somewhere round back.'

As Tom watched, the old grey cells in his brainbox took up full-time employment. 'Didn't the others all have a go before Arthur? That could be a problem.' Cat was impressed. And as Tom could tell, he confessed. 'Saw it in a film.'

'It's true, but this time Arthur's going to get there first and then Merlin will show his impertinent self to all and announce him the king.'

'Don't you mean imperious?'

'I know what I said.'

'He's going to con them.'

'Just cut the faff.'

Their discussion left at that, they scanned the square as it had fallen quiet.

'Where did they all go?' said Tom.

'Must have opened the beer tent or something,' said Cat.

'Shouldn't that be mead tent?'

'Whatever,' said Cat, more intent on the empty square than the tipple of the time. All appeared very quiet – ideally so. 'Let's go find ourselves a king.'

They scurried across the square as quick as Tom could go, keeping backs to the shadows, ears to the ground and eyes front. Not as easy as it sounds. They reached the other side without incident and hid by a barn.

'How we going to do this?' asked Tom, getting his breath back.

'That's your job, 'said Cat, 'Me magic cat – you time-travelling meddler.'

The look Tom gave Cat was sharp, but she was smiling. 'Don't worry, I have a plan.'

Finding their quarry wasn't as hard as Tom thought it was going to be. All they had to do was come across a gaggle of giggling young women and hey presto! standing in the midst of them – Arthur. It appeared the heir apparent was quite the ladies' man. There now posed a problem though...

'How are we going to get him on his own?' posed Tom.

'That's what they're thinking,' smiled Cat.

'You're not helping.'

'You know I told you I had a plan.'

'Yes,' said Tom, slowly, wondering if he was going to like whatever it was. If his water was anything to go on, the feeling was no.

'Well, I've changed it.'

'Go on.'

'I won't do it,' wailed Tom, just short of stamping his feet, quietly.

'It's a good plan,' said Cat, trying not to grin. It was a good plan and she was sure Tom would come round to her way of thinking in the end, but grinning wouldn't help.

'For you it is,' said Tom, not at all amused by Cat's idea.

'Well, I'm open to any suggestions, got one?'

'I need to think.'

'Well don't take too long, we're on a deadline here. Besides, it's a good idea and you know it.'

It was a good idea; a brilliant one in all truth, but that didn't mean Tom liked it. To tell the truth, he hated it, but begrudgingly, when nothing came to mind – the old grey matter downing tools – he had to admit it was all they had, unless they carried Arthur bodily to the stone, but one glance at the man's rippling muscles told Tom that was a no go. Cat's plan it was then, whether it left him open to future ridicule or not.

'Okay, I'll do it, if it means I can get home sooner than later,' said Tom, 'but pray tell, where are we going to get a dress from?'

'You still haven't got the gist of things, have you?'

Blank look.

'Where do you think we're going to get enough make-up to turn you into a pretty young girl?'

'I… where…?'

'We're not, are we? It would be impossible. There isn't enough in the whole wide world for-'

''Ere, hang about.'

'I'll project the impression.'

'You will?'

'I'll cover you with a glamour, he'll never know the difference – not unless he gets up close and personal that is. Have you shaved?'

'What?'

'You'll just have to use your womanly wiles.'

She was taking the mickey now. 'I'll do it, but the first sign he's getting wily, you do something.'

'Agreed.'

'Job done then,' smiled a relieved Tom. He hadn't been looking forward to wearing a dress; it wouldn't be right.

'But I can't do everything; you'll have to do the actions.'

'What actions?' Tom's world of relief had taken a sudden nosedive, his smile with it.

'You know. The fluttering of eyelashes, pouting of lips, the old "come on malarkey".' Cat had to admit, she was perhaps enjoying watching Tom squirm just a tad too much.

It had been quite a little while since Tom had been on the receiving end of such activities. The thought filled him with sudden dread. How could he, a man, hope to emulate women's natural talents such as those? He decided he couldn't. 'I can't do that,' he said.

'Well I'm afraid you'll have to, he's seen you and he's on his way.' Cat made with the haste and disappeared from sight.

The colour drained from a flustered Tom's face as he turned to see hunk Arthur heading his way with all the purpose of a shark with the promise of a free lunch.

'Well hello,' said Arthur, on arriving at Tom's side. Exuding sex appeal in buckets he stepped up, his chest beating assault on the beauty standing before him. 'Where have you been all my life? Surely heaven is missing an angel?'

Surely I am about to be sick, thought Tom, but he had a job to do. 'Hello,' he said, fluttering his eyelashes as if there was no tomorrow. He decided he should totter a little in the high-heels he thought he should be wearing, even though they had not been invented yet.

It was all Cat could do to keep the glamour going as the sniggers came to call.

Arthur meanwhile took Tom's tottering as a sign the young lady had been drinking a little too much. He moved in closer.

Tom tried to back away, but found his escape blocked by a fence. He decided to attempt the tried and trusted line of attack is the best line of defence. 'Oh,' he said, in his lady voice – which he didn't much like. He thought it made him sound like some upper class hooray Henrietta; he would have preferred something a little more on the husky side. What was he thinking? Grief. Mind on job boy – mind on job. 'What's a nice boy like you doing in a place like this?' Tom waved a petite hand in the general direction of somewhere. At the same time he was wondering what the hell he was playing at saying something like that? And was that Cat laughing he could hear? Oh woe was he.

'Funny you should ask,' said Arthur, who was running his fingers through golden ringlets that for some reason, which he couldn't put his finger on, didn't feel quite right. With it came the feeling that he was taking on something with a little more than he could handle. Come Arthur, he told himself, this wench, this merry strumpet from some farm or kitchen was no match for his charms. She was just a chicken waiting to be plucked and he was the man for the job. 'I'm training to be a knight,' he lied, flashing teeth that could do severe damage to the optic nerve if looking directly at them, 'To rescue beauteous damsels like you in times of distress.' His voice now grew deep and husky. 'Are you in distress?' he asked, pouting manly lips, his hands beginning to wander.

Too bloody right I am, thought Tom, trying to wriggle from Arthur's advances. With some effort he managed to halt the wanderings of Arthur and flashed him a smile accompanied by more of the eyelash fluttering. He even added a giggle, but instantly regretted it as it sounded a cross between the cry of a mad seagull and the bray from a disturbed donkey. Sadly, for some bizarre reason this appeared to only strengthen Arthur's ardour.

'Because if you are I will be more than happy to rescue you from, say, yonder hayloft.' Arthur's features changed from that of boyish rogue to wolfish fervour. Arthur winked at Tom. It was wicked. It was delicious.

What am I thinking? 'Ha-ha-ha,' laughed Tom, as he attempted to pull his hand from Arthur's grip. If he didn't do something quick the game would be up and then the future had better watch out; Arthur would never be the same – he doubted he would either. 'I… er,' said Tom, trying to multi-task, 'I know of a better hayloft. Somewhere more private.' He waved his petite little mauler again, this time in the direction of the "other" girls.

It worked and bought Tom some time. He quickly scanned the square to see if he could see Cat while Arthur dispersed his admirers. She wasn't to be seen. Where is she?

'Off you go, ladies,' said Arthur, 'Nothing to see here, but plenty for all later, if you're good.' He winked that wink again and the ladies scurried away giggling and perhaps wishing it was they heading to the hayloft. 'So,' said Arthur, wasting no time in turning back to the prey in his clutches, 'what, pray tell, is your name, my sweet?' Arthur's huge chestnut-brown eyes bored into Tom's.

He was doing this. This is it – luring time. Tom gulped a small gulp, conscious of his Adam's apple even though he doubted its bobbing would be noticed. 'Tom,' said Tom, not altogether doing it after all.

'Tom?' said Arthur, taking a step back, his ardour wilting.

Whoops! But at least Tom had succeeded in giving himself some space. 'But you can call me Tomasina,' corrected Tom, eyelashes fluttering madly. Somewhere a certain cat was giving Tom due acknowledgement for his quick thinking amidst heavy fire.

'Ah,' said Arthur, 'a pretty name.' This though, was said with a lot less conviction than previously shown.

I'm losing him, thought Tom, got to do something. Think man. Tom thought and then… 'What about this hayloft then?' he asked, folding his arms under where he thought his breasts were and raising them.

The ardour came flooding back. Arthur, eyes literally popping, wriggled his eyebrows – a passing caterpillar would surely have fallen in love at the sight – and drawled, 'A very pretty name, from where does it hail?'

'It's Welsh,' said Tom.

'It's not like any Welsh name I've heard,' said Arthur, a quizzical look raising his caterpillar beguilers to new heights.

'My mother knew a Roman.'

'Ah,' said Arthur, his face becoming a pool of living sex appeal, 'a touch of Latin fire eh?' He winked again. Somewhere a caterpillar swooned.

Not what I'd call it, thought Tom, and still thinking on his feet.., 'Perhaps we should give the old hay a miss then, you know how flammable it can be.'

'You enchantress,' said Arthur, a heavily dimpled smile spreading across his manly features. 'Come.' With one swift, fluid movement, Tom was no longer standing on the square but in Arthur's mighty arms. 'You are heavier than you look,' he said, after nearly overbalancing, 'but no matter, I prefer my women with a little meat on them.' He now greedily eyed Tom's wares in a way that had Tom vowing never to eat meat again.

'It's all the pasta,' said Tom, feeling a little light-headed after his sudden going up in the world. He tried to wriggle free, but Arthur was as strong as he looked.

'You like to fight eh?' said Arthur, enjoying the struggle Tom was putting up, 'and so we shall.' With another swift movement he threw Tom over a shoulder and playfully smacked his bottom. 'Now, my buxom beauty, where is this hayloft of yours?'

Enough was enough! Queen and country and all that malarkey was fine sentiment indeed, but this was way beyond the call of duty. Tom yelled at the top of his Henrietta voice, 'Caaaat!'

'Where?' said Arthur, peering past Tom's posterior and down between his feet.

Cat appeared from behind the fence.

Tom spread his arms in desperate appeal. 'Do something,' he hissed.

'Did you say something, my love?' said Arthur, still looking for this cat his Tomasina had warned him about.

Cat motioned to the right. Arthur and Tom were heading to the left. 'You're going the wrong way, my dear,' said Tom, 'The hayloft I mentioned is to the right.'

Arthur continued on a left hand route. 'But this one is so much closer and as we are now all alone, private – just like you wanted it...' He gave Tom another playful smack on his bottom.

Tom glared at Cat. He didn't fancy his chances should they reach the hayloft and Arthur discover that Tom's charms weren't what he was expecting.

Cat for her part was more worried about the plan going awry. They had to get Arthur to that stone before the others realised they had a copy. She had an idea. She darted forward and between Arthur's feet.

'Cat?' said Tom, as Cat approached.

'There is no cat, my little one,' said Arthur, laughing. 'I think you may have drunk a little too much.'

But this time there was and Arthur and all came tumbling down. Tom luckily landed on Arthur, knocking the wind from his sails for a moment, giving him the time to break free and scramble to his feet.

'What happened?' groaned a dazed Arthur.

'It's my puddy tat,' purred Tom, back to the eyelash fluttering, 'she wants me to take her home. There's a goose down quilt and Mama and Papa are at the tournament and won't be back 'til nightfall.'

Arthur was beginning to have his doubts; it was all becoming too much like hard work.

Then Tom pulled a master stroke. 'My sister will be there.'

Doubts suddenly blown to the four corners of the Earth, Arthur was up like a shot. 'Sister?'

'Twin,' said Tom.

Cat was in awe, she would have to make him some sort of medal for this.

'Lead on, fair maiden,' said Arthur, grinning so hard the top of his head was in danger of coming off, 'would be a shame to keep the poor girl waiting.'

He really didn't want to, but Tom held out a hand and giggled his best girly giggle. Arthur snatched it in his paws and kissed each of its fingers in turn. Tom snatched it back.

'Now kind sir, let us be on our way,' said Tom, rubbing the defiled digits against his trousers, 'my pussy awaits.'

'Hur-hur-hur,' sniggered Arthur.

Oh good grief, thought Tom, grabbing Arthur by his hand again and pulling him along before he could get those lips anywhere near his fingers. 'This way.'

Arthur, still sniggering, was willingly led along the path Cat was leading him up.

The sword and stone weren't all that far away, hidden in woods far enough away from any drunken soul from the tournament to unwittingly fall over, but close enough for the milling knights of the tournament to be at hand when the great moment came.

'Is it much further?' asked Arthur, after a couple of minutes; suspicion not yet strong enough to find a chink in his testosterone armour.

'Not far,' smiled Tom, his squeaky attempt at coyness bringing a look from Cat, which he returned with a glower. Too far, thought Tom, wishing he was rid of the youth's sweaty hand.

And then they were there. Something glinted in the bushes to their left. It caught Arthur's attention and he let go of Tom's hand; a dagger appeared as if from nowhere. 'Who goes there,' demanded Arthur, in the same way the future Arthur would speak to Tom.

Tom took a step sideways and peeped into the bushes. 'Why,' he said, feigning surprise, 'there's no one there, just some old sword stuck in a rock.'

Suspicion now usurping his manly wants, Arthur stepped towards the bushes, but before he pushed his way through them, he grabbed Tom by the shoulder and threatened him. 'If this is some sort of trickery girl, you'll wish you never got up this morn.'

With Arthur's mind now on other things, Cat took the opportunity to skedaddle. It was going to be difficult to keep Tom and Rufus' paths from crossing, but she would have to deal with that as things started to unfold.

With Tom stumbling by his side, Arthur pushed through the bushes. The sight that met his eyes when he got through caused an instant amnesiac effect on him where Tom was concerned. Pushing the "wench" aside, Arthur strode forward, sheathing his dagger, his eyes never leaving the magnificent weapon embedded in the rock; something he could only dream of owning. The craftsmanship was superb – even exquisite.

Tom saw his chance and took it, making a hasty exit for the rendezvous point he and Cat had agreed on earlier. At the back of his mind the consequences should he and Rufus meet.

Cat hadn't gone into detail, but the gist of it wasn't good. The other reason for making a swift escape was because he had forgotten to ask Cat the range of the glamour she had put on him. The last thing he wanted to do was have to explain his appearance in the spot where moments before a wench had been standing.

Arthur meanwhile, oblivious to Tom's rapid departure, was inspecting the sword and carefully running a finger down its length; he could swear it sang as he did. It was indeed a fine sword. The problem he had, as Arthur saw it, was how did he get the sword from the rock? He would need a smithy's hammer to chip the stone away. He could always give it a tug and see if it came out that way, but Arthur wasn't stupid; it had taken some force to put it in there so common sense dictated it would need equal, if not more force to pull it out. But being the lad he was, Arthur tried anyway – or at least attempted to. As he climbed onto the rock he was disturbed by a sudden kafuffle coming from behind him.

'And whoever pulls the sword from the stone will be King,' boomed a voice.

Such was the suddenness of this voice, Arthur started to lose his balance. Desperate not to fall he grabbed at the sword's hilt as he leaned backwards.

As he did this Merlin/Rufus made his way through the bushes, a score or more knights at his heel. 'Ah,' he said, on seeing Arthur,' you are here already, Arthur.'

'Ye-aargh!' said Arthur, falling backwards, Excalibur coming with him.

'Hail the King,' hailed Merlin/Rufus, rousing those around him, 'Hail King Arthur.'

'Hail King Arthur!' roared the crowd, who grasped him and hauled him above their shoulders. 'Hail the new King!'

The crowd began to make their way towards the square, taking Arthur with them, who had now quite forgotten the wench and her pussy. 'Hail me,' he shouted. There would now follow much lauding and carousing and backslapping and probably more of each interspersed with the odd moment of womanising thrown in for good measure.

Behind them, in different locations, a peeping Tom, a peering Cat and a spying Merlin/Rufus watched them go.

'Job done,' said Merlin, removing his pointy hat to reveal Rufus in all his eccentric glory. Eccentric-looking as in what one might expect of your common or garden mad professor type.

'Job done,' agreed Cat.

That's my line, thought Tom, who was still in earshot, but shouldn't have been. He quickly upped sticks and made haste to where he should be.

'Now I should go,' said Rufus, 'Things to do, people to impress, but before I do, what does destiny hold for me?'

'You know I can't tell you that,' said Cat, 'but I will say this, if you see yourself coming, it might not be your reflection – beware.'

Rufus smiled and tapped the side of his ample nose. 'Nuff said, old girl.' He made to go, but lingered a moment. 'Oh, and give my best to the boy, will you?'

'I will,' promised Cat.

'Tally-ho then, see you again no doubt. Have safe journeys. 'Bye.' And Rufus was gone, through the bushes and away.

'I'll try,' said Cat, a sadness settling on her, 'Take care.'

Cat found Tom sitting beside the safeshack; he was feeling slightly downcast, but perked up a little when he saw Cat approaching.

'All done,' said Cat, 'Your uncle sends his best.' She noticed Tom's cloudy demeanour. 'You okay?'

'Funnily enough, no, I was actually feeling a little sad that our adventure was coming to an end – silly really.'

'There'll be plenty more.'

But the end of the adventure wasn't the only thing on Tom's mind. 'He'll be all right, won't he?'

'This one will be.'

'And the real one? I mean the lost Rufus.'

'He'll be our next adventure, I promise,' said Cat, claws crossed.

Tom brightened further. 'Shall we finish this then? I've a party to go to and a cuppa and a nice slab of birthday cake would go down just dandy.'

'Excalibur then cake it is,' said Cat.

Chapter 29

It should have been the end of the story. Tom should have been home, grumpily enjoying his sixty-fifth birthday party, a cuppa in one hand, a piece of cake in the other.

Cat would have been introduced as the newest member of the family; a stray that had adopted Tom. She should have been snoozing, happily sleeping off that chicken dinner in the cottage's most comfortable chair.

But things are never that easy. Fate has a habit of guffawing rather loudly when hearing talk of the best laid plans. Fate likes to refer to these as works and just so happens to be adept at spanner throwing; everyone has a party piece.

And so it was with Tom and Cat's simple "all we have to do is... and off we go" plan. Get Excalibur. Return with Excalibur. Place Excalibur. Job done. Nothing could be easier. They never heard the spanner coming.

'It won't go in,' groaned Tom, bowing and sweating under the weight of Excalibur's bulk. He was determined not to drop it – again.

'You can't be doing it right,' said foreperson Cat, who was growing increasingly impatient with every failed attempt.

'I am,' snapped Tom, as once again Excalibur's tip slipped into the slot in the stone, only for it to slip out again and land on the ground. 'Perhaps if madam would care to lend a hand instead of standing there giving orders?'

Cat rolled on her back and waggled her paws in the air. 'Look, no thumbs.' It wasn't helpful.

'I meant your magic,' said Tom, trying again, but to no avail, the sword didn't even reach the slot this time before returning to the ground. As it slid across the stone a shower of sparks sprayed skyward, one of which found its way between Tom's neck and collar.

'Ow-ow-ow!' yelled Tom, pulling at his collar and performing a dance that would surely bring on rain. 'It's impossible,' he moaned.

Resuming an upright position, Cat mused on the current dilemma. She had noticed, while in her reverse position, something she hadn't noticed when standing. The stone appeared to be, or the sword appeared to be, or both appeared to be, repelling the other, thus making any effort by Tom redundant. Perhaps it wasn't Tom's fault after all. These thoughts led her to another – one that boded serious problems if what she was thinking was right. She needed help and there was only one person she knew, who might be able to.

'But I don't wanna sit in here,' wailed Tom, more petulant child than OAP, 'you could be gone for ages. What am I going to do while you're off gallivanting?' He had noted earlier the lack of reading material in the loo. How he now wished he had seen fit to stack the spare shelf – Cat's – because he was in a bad mood, with the odd magazine. A popular geographic or something the reader could digest.

'He won't have gone far,' said Cat, knowing exactly where he had gone, 'I'll be back in a trice.' She paused and took on a more serious demeanour. 'Until I do, keep the door locked and don't open it under any circumstances.'

Tom *did not* like the sound of that. *Did not* like being locked in the lavatory, especially with nowt to read. And most definitely *did not* like the fact the adventure had taken a turn for the nasty just as he was coming to terms with going home to tea and cake.

'How will I know it's you?' said Tom, his top lip packed with sullenness yet to dribble forth.

'I'll meow twice,' said Cat, not altogether seriously.

'There *are* other cats out there, you know,' said Tom.

Yes, thought Cat, but I'm the only one that will be meowing at an invisible loo – but to appease, 'I'll bark as well then.'

'Okay,' said Tom, sounding not at sure about it all.

'Good grief, Tom, how many cats do you know that bark?' Come to think about it, she thought, how many cats did he know that would tap on the invisible loo he was sitting in and ask him to open it? She gave herself a mental shake down; she wasn't going there with him; she didn't have time for his games.

'Suppose,' said Tom, the sullenness starting to drip.

'I'll see you in a while then.'

'Suppose.'

Should have gone straight to the grandson and cut out the middleman, thought Cat, wondering if there might be a loophole somewhere. She left the loo and a sulking Tom behind and for a good while thought seriously about the pros, cons and whether-there-could-be-a-ways of having the first pre-pensioner in the ranks.

With Excalibur playing silly beggars, Cat had decided it best to hide the sword and seek out the help of the only one she felt qualified to be able to do that – Merlin. And as never the twain should meet, she thought it wise to leave Tom somewhere she knew he would be safe. It wasn't the only reason though. As well as Tom had performed so far, tantrum's aside, he was still only a novice and until she knew what she was up against, she felt it better he was out of harm's and her way.

By the time Cat reached the square and tournament area, all was quiet. It wasn't every day one had themselves a new king so the excuse for imbibing copious amounts of alcohol had been duly seized upon as the only right way of celebrating the sudden rising of a royal in their midst.

Moving stealthily through the lengthening shadows of the surrounding buildings, the use of magic to shield her advance out of the question as she suspected Merlin's old sword shuffle would certainly have come to light by now and any sign of its use would be looked for, especially if it had been noticed that a mysterious cat had been seen aiding and abetting, she headed to where Merlin would be. She just hoped he was keeping his wits about him.

Rufus, a great fan of alchemy and an even greater fan of Merlin, had been, in the words of the younger generation "made up big time" when he discovered the next mission he would be on would be taking him back and forth to the time of Arthur. Sadly the joy was short-lived as during only the third re-entry to the time, the loo was caught in a serious flux storm which severely damaged the guidance system, whereupon the loo itself was sucked from Rufus's garden to land as a solid entity, culminating in the sad demise of a poor old duffer who happened to be standing in the spot where it landed. The poor old duffer just happened to be none other than Merlin.

A meeting of travellers was hurriedly convened and it was decided the Merlin myth should continue, but who should step into the sorcerer's flattened shoes? Rufus put himself forward and it was agreed. A few trips back before the accident to study Merlin, and Rufus was ready to assume the role alongside any missions that came his way – which rather explains the sketchy comings and goings of Merlin during that time.

Merlin's place wasn't far from town, but far enough away from the casual prying eye. Merlin had taken the line that if someone wanted to make it their business to spy on you, there was nothing you could do about it – unless you managed to catch them that is.

A crouching Cat, hidden amongst foliage on a low branch, was now a member of the prying eye club as she looked down a slight incline to Merlin's abode. All was still – good. And better still, all was quiet – very good. Not a whisper of a click was to be heard. She leapt to the ground and moved closer.

Back at the loo, a restless Tom was in the process of squatting. He had a dodgy knee, you see and it was part, the only part he could remember, of the physiotherapy exercises he was supposed to do.

'Down-one-two,' said Tom, back against the wall, knees bending, 'up-one-two,' legs now straightening and so it went on for a full minute and a half. Tom slumped onto the toilet seat, exhausted. It was a record. He glanced at his watch; Cat had been gone over an hour. Surely she should have been back by now? He started strumming his fingers against the plastic casing, a little something about showing him the way to go home – very limited music selection in Tom's head. He glanced at his watch again; just over an hour and another couple of minutes now. He stood up and gave the inside of his plastic cell a good look over. Handle still there – check. Shelves still there – check. Soap dispenser with, Tom lifted the lid, full compliment of liquid soap – check. Door – check. Tom yawned and then grimaced; his knee was beginning to ache. He needed to stretch it otherwise it would seize. He tried, but there wasn't enough room in the loo. He looked at the door again. Surely it wouldn't hurt to have a small potter about outside? What could happen if he stayed close? He had his saver – which was no longer a sack truck – which was just as well as he had it in his pocket. But nothing would; he was sure of it. But he dithered; he had promised Cat he would stay put. He scanned the loo again. Nope, it was no good – there was only so much time one could spend in the confines of a toilet, barren of the mandatory reading matter. He pushed the door open and peeped outside.

What wasn't good was the door to Merlin's home standing slightly ajar. That wasn't Rufus. Security for a traveller visiting a different time was paramount; your life might depend on it. This was sloppy and that was a word that just wasn't in Rufus' vocabulary. Cat smelt a rat or two. Skirting the building she headed for a discreet recce round back.

With trees for cover, Cat arrived and saw a dim light burning from within. Someone or something was at home. Cat moved cautiously towards the window the light was emanating from.

It was still light outside, but it was that grey sort, where you would have to switch lights on to see what you were doing inside. Tom looked at his watch again. It said four o'clock on the button, but that didn't mean it was that time here. Cat had tried to explain, but it had fallen on deaf ears. It could be six o'clock. His head hurt just thinking about it. Or midnight, but that wasn't right, it was still light. Unless, you were in the arctic where… was that right? Enough, Tom told himself – it wasn't helping. Cat had tried to drum it into him not to think about things, "Just take it as it comes" she had said, "sometimes nothing makes sense". Wasn't that the truth? Time to stop thinking; time for action; he stepped outside.

The distance from ground to window wasn't far, but Cat wasn't going to make things easy for anyone who might be waiting inside with mischief on their minds. She had decided her point of entry would be unexpected – the chimney. If there was anything going on untoward inside she wanted the element of surprise.

The chimney bugged her. She wasn't totally certain, but she felt sure she had read somewhere that in the seventh century they only had strategically placed holes in the roof to let the smoke escape. Then again Merlin was supposed to be innovative. But didn't he live in a cave somewhere? Note to self, thought Cat, read up on one's history cum myths before visiting them.

As she passed by the window, curiosity, the bane of the magic cat as well as your more common or garden moggy, took control and she just had to have a look. Lucky for her there appeared to be no one around to catch her peeping. Inside was in shadow, apart from the source of the light she had seen from the outside; a small oil lamp, turned low; the daylight finding it hard to penetrate the surrounding woods this late in the afternoon, but she saw that the chimney led into it. Cat moved on.

The sun was getting lower in the sky. Tom glanced for the hundredth time at his watch and went back in. He had been nervously stepping in and out of the loo for over half an hour now, and each time he had stepped back in and come out again so the day had moved on. This he had worked out by himself. It meant Cat had been away a lot longer than Tom had been waiting in the loo. There it went again, his brain hurting. But it was worrying. What could it mean? Was she in trouble or was she enjoying a shot of catnip as she chatted over old times with Uncle Rufus? Tom couldn't believe that and took his tally to one hundred and one glances at his watch, which managed to infuriate him. He had never been a clock-watcher, but here he was... But this was different. He didn't know why, but he had a feeling in his gut that Cat was in trouble. Only one thing to do then. Problem was, he didn't know where Merlin lived and if he did find it, how could he ask for help if he couldn't be in close contact with the man? Tackle that when the time comes then, old chap. He opened the loo door again and stepped outside for the umpteenth time, making sure it was closed behind him. Can't be too careful, he thought, just as a weighted net entangled him.

Peering down the chimney, Cat thought she heard a sound from the room below. Was that clacking she could hear? She strained her ears. If it had been, it had now stopped – unless it had just been her imagination running away with her. She clambered onto the pot and climbed inside.

When she reached the bottom of the chimney the room was dark. The oil lamp was no longer burning. Cat didn't like it, the hairs on her neck stood on end, as did those on her head, legs, body and tail, something was seriously wrong. She lingered there for a moment, deciding what to do next. She made a decision. Then, as she prepared to jump, she saw something below her she hadn't noticed before.

Scrabbling from flue to inglenook in the most inelegant, un-cat like fashion, Cat, instincts taking over, tried to stop her descent as the large pot of water standing on a trivet directly below loomed large. She lost her grip, fell past it, and arrived, rolling in an untidy ball, at the edge of the hearth.

Cat quickly regained her wits and sprang to her feet, but the element of surprise was now lost and the lamp flickered to life. She looked up into the muzzle of a gun, disguised as a dagger. She knew it was a gun as the dagger was gun-shaped. Someone had a severe lack of imagination, but it was no consolation; the thing still looked pretty lethal. Cat froze – questions on her lips.

'Get off me, you oafs!' shouted Tom, as he was gathered up and then lifted a couple of feet from the ground, the net having been skewered by a heavy oak pole. On either end of this pole

176

stood a good-for-nothing-ask-no-questions rogue, doing it for the money. 'My solicitor will hear of this, mark my words. Now, unhand me this instant. Help! POLICE!'

But Tom's threats and wailings fell on deaf ears, or to be correct, ones that didn't understand a word he was saying.

Without Cat to shield him, Tom was as naked as any twenty-first century guy in the seventh century could be and to cap* it all, his cap no longer seemed to be working – which was a bit of a problem.

''E sounds funny,' said the bearer at the back.

'A foreign village idiot I'll bet,' said the bearer holding up the front of the pole, 'A Dane or summit I reckons.'

'Not like any Dane I ever saw,' said the back bearer, peering in through the netting at the struggling Tom, ''e ain't wearing one of those funny pointy 'ats they be always wearing.'

'He is,' said the front bearer, bringing proceedings to a halt and pointing at Tom's head, 'but it's not like any I saw before.'

'Yer right,' observed the back bearer, 'it's flat. I thought it were 'is 'air. Same colour.'

'It's not,' argued front bearer, 'His hair's white, see, it's poking out underneath his hat what's a silvery colour.'

'So it is,' said back bearer, 'Must 'ave been the light playing tricks on me ol' eyes.'

'Let me out of here!!!'

The owner of the gun, an elderly man, was recognised by Cat as the man whose voice Tom thought he had recognized. The man, his eyes not leaving Cat for a moment, reached across and lit the oil lamp. It flickered into life illuminating the room in which they stood – kitchen cum living area. It was sparsely furnished. There was a great oak table on which the lamp stood, a rocking chair and an ordinary one, again both made

---

* Sorry! S.J

177

of oak. It was the ordinary chair that got Cat's attention. Tied to it was a bound and gagged Rufus.

'Gnaff-ger-gar,' garbled Rufus, when he saw Cat.

The cat version of hackles rising was observed.

'Careful,' said the old man, aiming the threat at Cat, 'or Rufus gets it. All I want is the sword.'

The old man had her covered, but what was the threat to Rufus, thought Cat, who knew the old man knew he wouldn't have the time to carry out his threat once he took his eye off her.

And just like that her question was answered. Movement in the far corner caught Cat's eye as something detached itself from the shadows. It was a granny, in its hand a vicious-looking knitting needle. Cat felt surprise, but not because she hadn't seen it; the corner was hardly touched by the light from the lamp – through design, thought Cat, but because she hadn't heard it.

The old man was smiling now. 'If you don't play nice, he gets it – in the neck probably. Show her!'

The granny stepped forward and placed the sharp end against Rufus's throat.

'Ah,' said the old man, who had noticed the look in Cat's eyes when the granny appeared, 'you haven't met, have you? Let me introduce you to the latest, improved, silent-running model – my idea – the battery-run granny.' The old man fair beamed with pride.

The granny actually took a bow.

Grief, thought a horrified Cat, silent grannies.

'And now, if you please,' demanded the old man, 'the sword.'

'Mayhap he's a Roman,' said back bearer.

'Naw,' said front bearer, shaking his head, 'they buggered off ages ago.'

'A Welshie then?'

'Dunno what they look like, could be.'

'What about a Saxon?'

There came sudden halting as the front bearer suddenly dug his heels in bringing the bearing to an abrupt halt. He turned to the back bearer, a wary look in his eye. 'Them are dangerous ain't they?' He doubted he was being paid enough to carry a Saxon.

The back bearer, who was rubbing his shoulder where the pole had chaffed against his sackcloth jerkin due to the sudden stop, gave Tom the once over. ''E don't look dangerous.' Tom stared back at him and scowled. This didn't enamour him with the back bearer who came up with a suggestion that might wipe the look right off the Saxon's face. 'Give 'im a poke wit yer sharp stick.'

The front bearer obliged, prompting from Tom growled disdain and a series of expletives that wouldn't see the inside of a dictionary for many a year to come – some of the worse ones never would. The front bearer quickly withdrew his stick as Tom made a grab for it, he proffered wisdom. 'Mayhap he's only dangerous when you poke him.'

The back bearer likewise proffered wise words. 'Better not do that again then,' said he.

'Better not,' agreed front bearer.

The two bearers, happy with their new-found wisdom, shouldered their load and at the trot, with a snarling and growling Tom swinging between them, continued on their way.

Cat wasn't about to give away the sword's location whatever the cost, but perhaps she could still get them out of this. The trouble was the old man wasn't acting like your normal trouble making in and out Traveller. For one thing it was rare you saw one, they weren't interested in confrontation; something big was going on. She had to think, play for time; find a weakness she could exploit. It came to her in a flash. The way the old man had grinned when introducing his obvious pride and joy – *pride*. It always came before a fall, but how to use it? A bit of buttering up? Flattery to knock him off his guard?

Here goes, she thought. 'What's does a great traveller like you need with the sword? Surely it's just a tool for mischief so why bother with it. You must have far more important things to do?' she said, but had to admit it didn't sound all that convincing.

It wasn't. 'You don't know me, cat,' spat the old man, 'but I know you. You're trying to play me for a fool, you all are. Think you can trick me into telling you my plans.' He glared at Cat. 'This is your last chance, where's the sword?'

That's strange, thought Cat, the man's acting as if it's personal. She needed to get him talking some more – unbalance him. If it is personal she might be able to tip the situation her way.

She decided to stand her ground and throw some pressure his way. 'I can't do that,' she said, 'because if I do you'll kill Rufus.' She didn't think he would; it was a feeling, 'and try to kill me. You'll have no use for us.' She stared the old man down as hard as she could. 'But I won't be so easy to kill as an old man tied to a chair.' She saw hesitation in his eyes.

'You don't understand,' said the old man, appearing to waver, 'I need the sword.'

She was getting to him, she was sure of it. 'But you'll destroy the Earth, all the Earths. Think about it.'

But just as Cat thought she was on the verge of a breakthrough...

'Not all,' said the old man, his voice becoming thicker, deeper. He motioned to the granny who drew a trickle of blood from Rufus' neck. 'Now,' said the old man, his demeanour changing – darkening, 'I won't ask again.'

Cat suddenly found herself wishing Tom was there, or at least his saver was.

'There it is,' said the front bearer, as Merlin's home came into sight.

'I 'ope we've got the right one,' said back bearer, growing nervous. He held no truck with magic and he had heard the rumours. A shiver ran down his spine as he imagined living out the rest of his life as a frog.

'The old man said we were to wait for a strangely dressed idiot to appear out of nowhere, it's got to be him.'

'About that,' said back bearer, 'don't yer fink it a bit odd? 'im showing up like that out of fin air like.' He gave the net a shake.

The front bearer laughed. 'They do it with mirrors, ain't nothing magic about it.'

'Ain't there?' said the back bearer, 'I never saw no mirrors.'

'That's where they're clever,' said the front bearer, tapping the side of his nose.

Clever or not, something smelled of magic and it made his skin crawl. The back bearer wanted to be on his way as soon as he was able. 'Gold 'e said, didn't 'e?' said back bearer trying to take his mind off the ways of wizards.

'Two pieces each,' confirmed front bearer.

It was no good though, back bearer's mind was stuck in a loop. Could frogs spend gold? He didn't think so. Frogs didn't do much but sit around on lily-pads and croak. He took a second to spit on the ground. There was a word he didn't much like the sound off – croak. 'Can't we jus' knock an' run an' leave the Saxon on the step like?' he asked, not wanting to be around when the door opened. He did, after all, have a wife and fourteen kids to think about.

'And what about the gold?' said front bearer, stopping.

''Twas only a thought,' said back bearer, rubbing at his shoulder.

Front bearer noticed the still open, front door. 'That's strange,' he whispered.

Back bearer broke into a cold sweat. 'What's strange?' he whispered back, not noticing the door was open as Tom was in the way.

'The door's open,' said front bearer, voice still low.

Back bearer's legs were beginning to feel like jelly. He had a phobia about open doors.

Front bearer tried to peer through the gap, 'Perhaps we should go in and wait.'

Perhaps we should just bugger off home, thought back bearer, eyeing the gap with trepidation.

'Oh well,' said front bearer, in a cheery voice that you just knew was courting disaster, 'in for a penny'. He then threw the door wide and barged in.

Who says wishes don't come true?

Front bearer entered Merlin's house, closely followed by Tom and the back bearer who sank to his knees as he crossed the threshold.

'What the-?' said the old man, thrown by the sudden intrusion.

Front bearer, unfazed by the scene before him, lowered his end of the pole to the floor. 'One idiot as ordered mister,' said he, removing his hat. The other end of the pole clattered as it and back bearer hit the floor.

The old man wavered, but managed to hold his weapon aimed at Cat. 'What the hell are you talking about?' he said, his voice rising.

'It's Merlin's friend,' said front bearer, feeling the onset of mild puzzlement. 'You said to bring him here if he made an appearance.'

The old man had started to shake. 'I said to take care of him and then report back to me when it was done,' he shrilled, 'and can't you bloody knock?'

'Oh,' said front bearer, feeling a tad foolish. 'Shall we do it now?' he asked. 'I mean, get rid of him.'

Back bearer was crawling for it, he had heard enough. He didn't want to be a frog. There were tears.

As the old man whistled like a kettle coming to the boil, Cat saw her chance. With a single bound that would have cleared a model building with ease, she sent the gun cum dagger cum gun-shaped dagger out of the old man's hand. It landed heavily on the floor causing it to go off. A bullet whizzed over the shoulder of the front bearer causing his earlobe to sway in the breeze it caused and embedded itself in the door jamb.

Front bearer was off in a flash. Loud noises and holes magically appearing in solid oak caused by a dagger was not in the job description. If he had had time to reflect, neither was bringing Tom to the house, but time was short and the distance he wanted to put between himself and the mad old man – as much as he could – was a while away. He hurdled the back bearer, who was still crawling for all he was worth. The back bearer hadn't seen the hole appear or seen the flash, but the loud bang…

Twenty yards later the back bearer, who was now hopping on all fours, passed the front bearer who had not seen the tree he had run into. Sadly the front bearer would lose his memory and spend the last of his days as a knife-fearing, wandering, whistling minstrel. Happily neither event affected the future. Unless someone somewhere has a family trait that is either amphibian in nature or takes in the irrational fear of exploding cutlery!

Meanwhile, in the house:

The old man span round and as luck would have it, retrieved the gun before Cat could disentangle her claws from the net,

183

where she had landed. The gun was once again aimed at her.

Cursing her luck, Cat loosed a last claw and backed away.

'Get out of there,' yelled the old man, at Tom, who was struggling to get free. The old man motioned for the granny to help. She removed a vicious, curve-bladed knife from the pocket in her pinafore and slashed at the rope netting, freeing the cowering Tom.

'Frisk him,' ordered the old man.

Robot granny grabbed Tom by the ankles and gave him a good shake. Not much fell from his pockets, but enough to satisfy the old man who, with gun trained on Cat, bent and picked something up.

'Not very original, are you?' he said, smiling at Tom, 'But then you are only a novice.' The smile was replaced by a snarl. 'Tie him up.'

The granny carried Tom by his ankles to the vacant chair, righted him and bound him to it.

'Now,' said the old man, who was now looking fairly pleased with himself, 'where was I? Oh yes, the sword, where is it?'

Cat growled. 'I told you, I'm not saying.'

Tom, who was a little dazed and a tad disorientated by his ordeal, heard what was said and thought he would help. 'I know where it is,' he said, blundering in.

Rufus, who was beside him, was now beside himself. 'Ger-na-ger,' he protested.

Cat glared – dumbstruck.

But Tom, poor dazed Tom, wouldn't be deterred. 'Me and Cat... I mean Cat and I, hid it.'

'Aha!' said the old man, in the tradition of baddies every-where, an evil sparkle gleaming in his eye, 'and whereabouts would that be?' An "Arr... Tom lad" surely wouldn't be far away.

'No,' said Cat, finding her voice, but harbouring a

moderate confidence that Tom wouldn't remember where it was hidden.

'I have a map,' said Tom.

'A map!' said the old man and Cat in unison.

'Show me,' continued the old man.

Tom wriggled in his chair. 'Right hand jacket pocket,' he said, pointing with his chin.

The old man told the granny to do the honours. She retrieved a piece of paper and handed it to the old man.

'NO!' shouted Cat, on the verge of doing something someone would regret.

'No, yourself,' said the old man, clicking his fingers. The granny resumed her position beside Rufus, which had been between both chairs and so was now standing between both bound men. She produced a pair of knitting needles and held them at their necks. The old man greedily unfolded the piece of paper, but delight soon turned to bewilderment and then to anger. 'What's this?' he demanded and then read out what was written on it. 'Surprise?'

This instantly made Tom the only one in the room not mystified. He closed his eyes and the note morphed.

'Whaa!' shrieked the old man, as the note changed from a piece of paper to a super-size magnet of the horseshoe shaped persuasion.

Its attraction soon became obvious as the robot granny suddenly veered towards it. Inside her, her insides were no longer running like clockwork or as was the case with this particular granny, no longer juiced up. Sparks began to fly and what parts that could fall limp, did.

The old man's anger turned to fury; outwitted by a halfwit. He spat as he vented his fury at Tom. 'You think you're so clever, don't you… you meddling busybody travellers?' He started to wave the gun about in a somewhat reckless fashion. 'Well you're not going to stop me. I'm going to get that damn

185

sword and when I do, me and the wife will rule the only Earth left in existence.' The gun stopped its waving and pointed at Rufus. 'And you are going to help me.'

'Neger,' growled Rufus, furiously shaking his head.

'And don't think there'll be any bargaining, because the cat and that fool there,' he now swung the gun at Tom, which caused Tom to lean back which in turn, caused the rocker he was sitting in to start a rocking, 'wouldn't be around much longer anyway, once the worlds started to fall about. Why, I'll be doing them a favour, at least this will be quick.' The gun steadied in his hand as he took aim.

It's now or never, thought Cat, realising the old man had put her out of his mind for the moment. She leapt at the back facing her and landed squarely between its shoulders, her claws digging deep.

The old man screamed in pain as Cat's claws did their worst, but the gun still fired. The loosed round flew straight and true at its intended target – Tom, but missed. Luckily Tom was still rocking and was leaning backwards as it whistled past him. There was a ting as it struck metal; it ricocheted and found a new target – the oil lamp, which burst into flames as it hit home.

Frantically grabbing at his back, desperately trying to dislodge Cat whose claws were gripping like four sets of tiny grappling hooks, the old man stumbled forward and tripped over Tom's feet. Cat, seeing where things were heading, leapt clear as the old man, unable to halt his downward momentum, tumbled face first into the small inferno that had been the oil lamp. He screamed again, rolled clear and managed to stagger to his feet. Gun dropped and forgotten, hands covering his face, he turned and fled past the horrified onlookers and through the door.

Cat went to give chase, but stopped in the doorway as two grannies, summoned by the old man as he fled outside, came running to his aid. She lingered for a moment, deciding whether or not to follow as the grannies led him away in the direction of the woods. She could handle two, but what was to say there weren't more, hidden, waiting to attack. Instead she closed the door shut on the outside and went to help Rufus with his bonds.

Free, Rufus produced a fire extinguisher and doused the flames. A couple of minutes later after congratulations were passed to Tom on his clever thinking and having made sure the coast was clear, Cat, Tom and Rufus headed for Excalibur. There were questions to be asked, answers to be found, but first they needed to put the sword in the stone and make it disappear.

Chapter 30

'Did you see his face?' said Tom, grimacing as he walked beside Rufus, 'It looked as if it had melted.'

'It had,' said Rufus, grimly, 'it was a mask.'

'A mask?'

'Obviously didn't want to be recognised,' said Rufus.

'Tom thought he recognised his voice,' said Cat, chipping in, but her mind was on something else, something that would soon need resolving; she just needed the right moment.

'But he wasn't counting on young Tom here turning up, so it must be one of us, Cat.'

'I saw his face earlier, but I didn't recognise him,' said Cat, deliberately falling behind, 'so that leaves you.'

'Tom and me, as he recognised his voice, but the mask was for my benefit, as like I said, he wasn't expecting Tom,' said Rufus, thoughtfully.

'He said he had a wife,' said Tom, thinking it might be a clue.

'Could be anyone,' said Rufus, slapping it away.

On they continued, Tom now leading the way, he and Rufus surmising on the identity of the masked man until Tom had to call a halt and admit he didn't have a clue where he was going. Behind them, Cat was relieved to hear she had been right about something.

'Well, Cat,' said Rufus, assuming his renowned explorer stance – foot on handy rock, hands on hips – 'where is this bally sword of yours? It seems my young nephew here still retains a head like a sieve.'

Young, thought Tom, haven't been called that in a while and was about to say so when he noticed the storm brewing in Cat's eyes; she appeared to be glaring at Rufus. He took a step away. Something was wrong; he hadn't seen her looking this intense before. It was as if she were looking through Rufus' skin to the organs beneath. It fair shook him.

'Well,' said Rufus, oblivious to the way Cat was looking at him, 'let's be doing this, I've a pile of lead that needs turning to gold.' It was just a joke, but it was the catalyst for what followed. And it happened so quickly Tom, for a moment, could hardly believe what he saw.

Cat, happy her magic could go unnoticed now they were deep in the woods, flew through the air and landed on Rufus' shoulder, twisting him round and pushing him to the ground. A light emanating from somewhere, Tom couldn't tell where, appeared to be holding him there.

'Cat,' shouted Tom, now tending to believe what he was seeing, 'what the heck are you doing?'

On the ground a struggling Rufus was getting nowhere fast as he tried to get up. His mouth though appeared unaffected. 'What's the meaning of this, Catranna?' he bellowed, in a tone most schoolchildren caught doing something they shouldn't, would recognise in an instant – that of authority. 'Get off me at once!'

Cat ignored the plea or order or whatever it was and, standing on his chest stared him in the face. It was her turn to make a demand. 'Who are you?' she growled, menacingly.

Rufus frowned, as did Tom.

'Rufus,' said Rufus.

'It's Rufus,' said Tom, then remembering the look in her eyes, 'isn't he?'

'I think not,' said Cat. She looked up at Tom. 'Think about it Tom, what did I say about you two never being allowed to meet?'

The frown became deeper as Tom thought about it.

Cat gave him a nudge. 'You can kiss your whatever goodbye,' she reminded him.

A light went on in Tom's head – a red one, flashing alarm. He backed away, almost tripping on a tree root.

'Don't worry,' said Cat, glaring at the man below her, 'if this was Rufus we wouldn't be having this conversation, it would have all ended back at the house.'

'But who is he then?' said Tom.

'That is what we are about to find out,' said Cat. 'Who are you,' snarled Cat, 'and what have you done with Rufus? And don't try to lie; I'll know if you do.' Her eyes changed hue as they bored into the man's eyes.

'It's me, Rufus but…'

Cat probed the man's mind. Not all of it, she wasn't that kind of cat, just the bit that would reveal if he was lying or telling the truth.

'What are you doing?' said Tom.

'A bit of lie-detecting,' said Cat. A second later it was done.

'Well?' asked an anxious Tom.

For a moment Cat seemed to stagger. The light disappeared and she climbed from the man's chest.

'Well?' repeated Tom.

'He's telling the truth,' said Cat, her voice lacking the sparkle you might have expected.

Tom was puzzled. 'But that's good isn't it?'

Depends which way you look at it,' said Cat, acting strangely subdued. She looked at Rufus. Was that a touch of disdain in her eyes?

Rufus raised himself up onto an elbow and, eyes lowered, spoke. 'Sorry, Cat.'

'Will someone please tell me what is going on?' begged Tom, totally bewildered, puzzled and perplexed by it all.

'It's me,' said Rufus, who was now sitting upright. This didn't help Tom one iota. 'The real me.' This did – sort of.

Rufus was now standing, his robe in his hand, brushing bracken and dirt from it. Cat was standing a short distance away, her back to him, her stance not a happy one.

Tom's expression hadn't changed much from the bewildered one he had been carrying the last few moments because the handle he thought he had on things wasn't making an awful lot of sense. He was looking at Cat. If this was the real Rufus, the Rufus that was lost, why was she sulking? Surely she should be over the moon? They had found him. He looked on in a daze.

Replacing his robe, Rufus went to say something, opened his mouth, but closed it again. There was really no way of dodging the issue. He tried again. 'I'm sorry, Cat, for deceiving you.' In his favour, he did look extremely sorry.

Cat shuffled her feet a little, but said nothing.

'I know I should have told you, but how could I? We're bound to an oath of non-interference, you know that. You would have tried to stop me.'

Tom was now getting the feeling he was standing in the middle of some sort of domestic upheaval. Then it clicked why Cat was behaving the way she was. He rounded on Rufus. 'You were never lost,' said Tom, aghast at the idea.

'I'm sorry, Tom, but I had no choice.'

Full understanding now awash, Tom pointed at Cat. 'I don't think it's me you should be explaining yourself to.'

'I know, I'm trying.'

'Not hard enough.'

Rufus took a step towards Cat who kept her back to him, her tail disapprovingly down. He didn't move any closer. 'I know.' Rufus lowered his voice. 'It was all the to-ing and fro-ing. It wasn't fair on you, Cat. My mind was constantly on

191

being Merlin. I was continually putting you and our missions in jeopardy. It's why I went.'

Cat's stance changed a little – softened slightly, she turned. 'You could have told me.'

'You would have stopped me.'

'I would have tried, yes. We searched – the others and me. We hardly rested. We must have even spoken to you in your guise. Why couldn't we tell?'

'That depends on which moment in time you visited, but yes, we have spoken and as for why you couldn't tell it was me, well, the real Merlin wasn't a complete charlatan; he did know a thing or two. I adapted one of his spells. Now you see me, now you don't. A little bit like the glamour spell you use.'

In her mind Cat couldn't really blame him, she knew how travelling could take you. Had she not stumbled, hesitated a little, when a mission took them back to ancient Egypt and it was time to go back. She had pined for at least a week afterwards. The situation was different; she could see that, but how different? For her it had been like going home. For Rufus it was like starting that new life, which up until his disappearance, was one he had only been able to flirt with. It had got in his blood. Cat softened further; she couldn't really blame him, well, just a little perhaps.

'I wanted to tell you. I missed you.' There was genuine sadness in them there tones.

Cat's tail began to rise a little. There really was no reason to cry over spilt milk and anyway it was partly her fault, the way she felt, hadn't she been warned not to grow too attached to her human – their short lifespan. She turned and ran towards Rufus, but didn't stop at the hand that reached down to stroke her.

'Cat?' said Rufus.

She stopped. She was going to have to be tough. 'You made your choices, Rufus. What's done is done. The world goes on – for the moment. Tom and I have a job to do. I'm his familiar now.' Cat caught the shadow of hurt that passed across Rufus' face. She did have a job to do, but perhaps she was being a smidgeon harsh. Humans were, when all said and done, only human. 'But we do need your help.'

The shadow passed. Rufus knew he was in the wrong; this was his chance to atone for some of it. 'Lead on then,' said Rufus, waving an arm, a smile on his lips, 'together we shall solve the problem of the sword.'

Tom, who had been keeping his distance, now stepped forward, his hand held out. 'Nice to see you again Uncle,' he said.

But Rufus was having none of it, he pushed Tom's outstretched hand aside and grasped him in a hug that would have brought tears to that of a bear. 'Good to see you too, nephew,' he said, his eyes glistening, 'but enough,' he released Tom from his killer embrace, 'we have a mission and Catranna is waiting.'

Excalibur was well hidden, partly by the local flora, mostly by the invisibility spell Cat had put on it and the stone. She made a noise, which Tom thought at first to be a sneeze, and the sword appeared.

'So,' said Rufus, rolling up his sleeves, which immediately rolled down again, 'the sword won't go in.' He picked up the sword and started examining it.

'It's the real thing,' said Cat.

'Caused sparks,' said Tom, carefully touching the spot on his neck where one had landed.

'Should go in,' said Rufus, holding the sword aloft. The feat readily belying his skinny frame and frail appearance.

Tom looked on in admiration. Maybe travellers got stronger the longer they went on?

Rufus slammed the sword towards the stone with all his might. It went straight and true.

Cat, who was secretly harbouring a view as to why the sword wouldn't go in, but was saying nothing until Rufus had had his try, retreated to a safe place, just in case. Perhaps Rufus would solve the problem, but if she was right in her assumptions, he wouldn't.

He didn't. The sword and Rufus flew back in a hail of sparks and mild cursing. He and sword landed in a pile. Tom, pulling his collar tight to his neck hurried to his uncle's aid.

'I'm fine, fine,' said Rufus, waving away Tom's attempt to help him, 'Must have put it in at the wrong angle, that's all. No fuss now, no fuss.' Rufus stood up and tried again.

The third attempt saw Rufus achieve an ambition that had eluded him as a child – a perfect cartwheel. Luckily, the sword didn't go with him, preferring to shake Tom's nerves by landing with a twang between his feet.

'Enough,' said Cat, now certain she knew the reason why the sword wouldn't cooperate.

'One more go,' said Rufus, determined not to be beaten, but looking that way as he lay spread-eagled beneath a spreading chestnut tree. 'I think I nearly had it then.'

'You're telling me,' said Tom, leaving the sword where it had landed, 'one more go and I think you will have. I think we should listen to Cat.'

Managing to get into a sitting position that didn't remind him he had an ache in every joint – just some, Rufus accepted defeat. 'All is lost then I fear,' he sighed, 'and I feel it's my fault – if I hadn't left Cat in the lurch.'

If it was the good old days and the price of butter hadn't gone up, yakkity-yak,' said Cat, somewhat caustically.

Rufus and Tom exchanged puzzled glances. Had Cat taken a knock to the head they hadn't noticed?

'What I mean,' said Cat, frowning on those looks, 'is that it doesn't matter how many times you try to return the sword or what excuses we come up with, the result will always be the same – failure. We need Arthur.'

'Arthur!' exclaimed Tom.

'Arthur!' echoed Rufus, a fraction of a second later. He was still seeing the odd star.

'Yes,' said Cat, looking serious, 'and not just any old Arthur either. I think you'll find we need the services of the original Arthur, the one that pulled the original sword, our sword,' she nodded to Excalibur, 'from the stone.'

Chapter 31

Preparations were in full flow. Paper cups, plates, serviettes and plastic cutlery had been sorted and placed in a box. Sandwiches and rolls were being filled and sliced – cling film and trays were at the ready. Vol-au-vents, things on sticks, sausage rolls and small fancies were like soldiers on parade waiting for their orders. The cake, covered by a multitude of candles, sat on the kitchen table surrounded by an array of ridiculous hats, bleepers, honkers and party-poppers.

'What time are we going to Granddad's?' asked Marc, secreting about his person one of the fancies – a French one.

Lucy sensed there was an ulterior motive lurking somewhere behind her son's seemingly innocuous question. 'Don't tell me,' she said, feigning exasperation, 'you need to go on the internet; the world needs you.'

'No,' said Marc, caught out by his mother, but playing the looking hurt card for all he was worth. 'I just want to see him, that's all.'

You know, thought Lucy, as she sliced a ham sandwich in four, I almost believe him – almost. He's up to something. Should I ask? Possibly. Do I want to know? Possibly not. She decided to play the play along card. 'Oh,' she said, 'in that case, as soon as Mister Smokowski arrives with your granddad's present and card.'

'When will that be?'

'About six thirty,' she looked up at the kitchen clock, 'a couple of hours yet, but we'll give Mister Smokowski a few minutes head start so he can get Granddad out of the way. That okay for you?'

'Yeah,' said Marc, narrowing his eyes. He knew when his mother suspected something, but he also suspected she played him somehow when she did. At times like this it was best to keep one's head low. 'I'm going to my room,' he pouted, drawing on an old favourite in times of uncertainty. He had learned at an early age that parents were always more than happy to have their kids disappear to their rooms. One, it meant they knew where their kids were and two, it kept them from under their feet.

'Okay, darling,' said Lucy, playing the game. The food preparation was almost done anyway. She ruffled his hair as he turned to go.

'Ah, Mum!'

'But mind you're washed and back down here pronto when you hear Mister Smokowski arrive.' Which meant in mum language, don't play your games too loudly.

Marc knew exactly what she meant, but she was wrong for once. Marc really did want to see Granddad. He wanted to know how he had got on in the competition. Find out how much was coming his way if he had won. One up to me, he thought, trying not to show it. 'I will,' he groaned, and went to the bottom of the stairs.

As he reached them there came a tap-tap-tapping at the front door.

Chapter 32

The portable toilet was a bit crowded, but as it wasn't going anywhere it was only a minor inconvenience. The occupants were in deep discussion.

'But we don't know where they took him,' said Tom, referring to Arthur, the one that had knighted him. A fact that when made known, had Rufus beaming with pride and saw him congratulating Tom with a round of hearty backslaps.

'And if we did,' said Cat, idly licking a paw, 'it would be very doubtful he would be fit enough to travel, if indeed he survived.'

'And what if we did and he didn't want to go?' said Tom, 'I wouldn't fancy our chances.'

'That wouldn't be so much of a problem,' said Cat, meaning the arsenal of magic she had at her disposal, 'but I doubt it would work if he were coerced into doing it. I have the feeling he will have to do it under his own free will.'

Listening intently, but not saying much, Rufus gave the situation a lot of serious thought. He knew how badly Arthur's wounds had been, but not because of what Cat and Tom had said, but because he had been there. This was causing him a bit of a quandary. There were things he knew, but did he say anything? He had a secret that only he and one other knew about. Perhaps as a last resort, but he knew they were already way down that road. He would wait, something might come up; but in his heart of hearts he knew he might soon have to break a promise.

'What if we turned up before he got injured?' said Tom, clutching at that well known straw.

'And how do we explain the fact we have his sword which he just so happens to have as well?' said Cat.

'Good point,' said Tom, wishing Rufus would vacate the loo seat so he could sit down. It was his.

'It would appear we have come to an impasse,' said Cat.

'There are other days,' said Rufus, grabbing at Tom's straw, but for differing reasons, 'Perhaps we could catch him at a moment when he was sword-less, said ours was his and persuade him to pop it back in.'

'And you really think that is a viable idea?' said Cat, 'There are thousands of days for us to choose from. No, I'm certain it has to be the sword we have and the man we took it from – the full circle. We have to find the injured Arthur and hope he's well enough and willing to put it back.'

Rufus stood up.

Tom seized his chance and sat down.

Rufus tried to pace, but there wasn't room to swing a… Cat wasn't going to be happy when he tells her what he's done, but what else *could* he have done? How did he know what would happen? Maybe he wouldn't have to.

Cat, who had started on another paw, looked up. She thought she felt Rufus looking at her. His eyes darted from hers. She stopped her cleaning; there was something he wasn't telling her – again.

'By the way,' said Rufus, attempting to divert the attention Cat was giving him in another direction, 'nice trick with the saver, Tom; really thought for a moment it had been the penknife.'

'So you said,' said Tom, giving Rufus a quizzical up and down.

He's trying to cover himself, thought Cat.

Rufus clamped his hands together. 'So I did, so I did. Now,

which day shall we plump for? I reckon we wouldn't go far wrong turning up on his birthday – always had a skin full – usually unconscious by ten, what.' He chanced a peep Cat's way; she was still looking at him in that suspicious way of hers. Damn!

'What aren't you telling us, Rufus?' said Cat, hoping she was wrong, but in her heart knowing she wasn't.

'Whatever do you mean?' said Rufus, suddenly defensive.

He was definitely hiding something. Cat had known the man long enough to know when he was being evasive. Only, before today, it had usually been something small he had been trying to get away with – the smuggling of a hipflask aboard, alcohol for personal consumption was not allowed – or the odd relic, which was doubly taboo. It was roguish behaviour, nothing more; she often turned a blind eye to the lesser transgressions, but she felt this wasn't one of the lesser ones. This time she was worrying that it might be on a par with his Merlin caper. 'Come on Rufus, I know you too well for us to make a song and dance out of the question,' she said.

'Uncle?' said Tom.

The game was up. Cat knew him too well. Rufus took a deep breath and prepared for the worst. 'All right... all right,' he said, wishing he didn't have to say what he was about to, 'I know something about Arthur, but it's a secret, a matter of trust.'

'And you don't trust us with it, friends and family?' said Cat, all four paws set firmly on her shelf.

'No, it's nothing like that. I made a promise which I see now I am now going to have to break, but it's not an easy thing to do. I will be letting down an old friend.'

'You're talking about Arthur aren't you?' said Cat.

Rufus nodded.

'You are?' said Tom, astonished.

Rufus nudged Tom along and perched on the edge of the loo's surround. 'Remember when you took the sword from Arthur; men arrived to carry him away? Well one of those men was me disguised as one of his court.'

'You were there?' gasped Tom.

'Yes, and I managed to cover your tracks for a short distance so you weren't discovered.'

'I had wondered about that,' said Cat, 'but I figured the men looking for the sword were idiots when they didn't follow.'

'They were, that's why I chose them, but even they wouldn't have failed to notice that furrow you were leaving in the ground.'

'But what has all that got to do with your secret?' asked Tom.

Cat thought she knew. She was right.

'The quacks that were calling themselves physicians back there could do nothing for him. He was going to die. I had to do something.'

'You looked after him yourself?' said Tom, not quite on the right track.

'No, I took him to a hospital. A private one that I know, that seldom asks questions.'

Tom was puzzled, he hadn't realised there were private hospitals back in Arthur's time.

Cat on the other hand wasn't. 'And just where is this hospital?' She also thought she knew the answer to that question as well – the gall of the man. It did leave other, intriguing questions unanswered though.

'You know damn well, Cat,' said Rufus, readying himself for those intriguing questions.

'Where?' asked Tom, feeling completely out of the loop.

'Home, Tom,' said Cat.

'Home?'

'He took Arthur to our time.'

It took a second or so for it to sink in. It took another second or two for a question to bubble forth from the maelstrom of thoughts that were running through Tom's mind. 'How?'

'Yes,' said Cat, her brow wrinkling, 'how?'

'I've built my own time machine,' Rufus confessed. 'It wasn't easy, but I improvised and with a little magic-'

'Magic!?'

'As I said, Merlin had his moments and lucky for me he wrote them all down, but the machine is pure science.'

'I take it you built it before you staged your disappearance act?' said Cat, unable to believe the man – wondering if she really knew him. The planning must have gone on for months. How hadn't she noticed? He would have needed numerous things – would have needed to smuggle them on board the loo. She had underestimated him, but she couldn't help but feel a little admiration. She decided she did know him, only not as well as she had thought.

'Yes,' Rufus admitted.

'So you can travel through time like the loo?' said Tom, not knowing what to think of Rufus' admissions, except, perhaps, that his uncle was a bit of a cad.

'Sadly, no,' said Rufus, 'It has tunnel vision where travelling is concerned. Here to home and back again is about its limit, but with stops along the way of course. It was meant to be an emergency backup really, an escape pod if you like.'

The time machine revelation had managed to overshadow the Arthur saga, but Cat dragged it back into the limelight. 'And where is Arthur now?' she asked.

Rufus looked at Tom and Cat in turn; he couldn't evade the reality of what he had done any longer. 'Still in our time.'

Tom's eyes bulged for a second. 'You mean…' it took a moment, 'two thousand and nine… now?'

'When he recovered, Arthur decided he was getting a bit long in the tooth for the gallivanting expected of him in his own time so asked if he could stay.'

'And you let him?' said Cat.

'Not right away.'

'Go on.'

'Well, it was difficult at first; took him a while to accept who I was and where he was but, with the odd sedation here and there – he was mightily strong even at his age you know...' Cat gave him a look. 'Sorry, I digress. To cut a long story short – once he was recovered and what had happened had sunk in he decided he didn't want to go back so I took him home.'

'Home-home?' said Tom, catching up gradually.

'Before you moved there,' said Rufus, nodding. But there was more to his tale. 'There was still a lot to be done – a certain amount of duplicity to be performed, especially at Arthur's end. Stories had to be fabricated – spread. It wasn't enough to just say "hey the King is dead, long live the King, but we haven't got a body", it wouldn't wash. There had to be more – something beyond the ken of men – something magical.'

'*You* started the Arthur legend?' said Tom, awestruck.

'Not I as such,' said Rufus, 'but I did kindle a few ideas. Man it appears has an inordinate amount of imagination waiting to be tapped and, how shall I put it, manipulated. One supplies the match – what they do with the fire is up to them.'

And once again Cat wonders if she really knows the man, it sounded all so callous. 'Where is he now?' said Cat, suddenly wanting to be away and doing.

'It stays between the three of us.'

'Don't worry, you can *trust* us,' said Cat.

The accentuation on trust was not lost on Rufus, but he said nothing, he knew he deserved it. He ushered them into a huddle, then, keeping his voice low, told them.

'Bloody hell!' said Tom.

'Language,' said Rufus.

Chapter 33

'I'll get it,' shouted Kate, emerging from the lounge. She automatically flicked the hall light on even though it was still light outside; something mum was always going on at her about.

Lucy sighed and did an about turn, heading back into the kitchen. 'If they're selling something, tell them we don't want it,' she called, throwing the tea towel she had been using to wipe her hands over her shoulder, 'If it's a pair of helping hands, send them through.'

Kate opened the door.

The caller smiled, she had nothing to sell, but neither was she there to lend a helping hand. Neither were her companions.

Chapter 34

The bombshell Rufus had dropped as to Arthur's twenty-first century whereabouts was digested and absorbed – Tom had needed to take an antacid tablet – the three got down to business. Number one on the agenda: how were they going to go about it?

'We could tie him up,' suggested Tom, not totally happy with having to see the man who had knighted him face to face again; he might take umbrage and attack him. Worse still, he might annul the title. Tom had grown quite fond of it even though Cat and Rufus wouldn't call him Sir Tom.

This was greeted by sighs and strange looks from both Cat and Rufus.

'I think what Cat meant was, who should go – you and her or me alone?' said Rufus, who was very close to calling him a stupid boy.

'Oh,' said Tom, only now realising he had actually said it out loud.

Rufus turned to Cat. 'I'm of the mind that you and my nephew should go,' said Rufus, 'My time machine isn't what you would call reliable – damned temperamental at times. Lost my pocket watch between here and home once; wouldn't want Arthur going the same way.'

It was decided.

'But what if he doesn't want to go?' ventured Tom, still smarting from his last suggestion.

'I can't see why not,' said Rufus, stroking his beard as he contemplated the idea, 'but having said that, he can be a bit of a stubborn old cuss at times.' He then shook his head as if shaking something free from it. 'No – I'm sure he'll come on board.' He looked at Cat. 'But it might not be a bad idea to go bearing beads.'

'Beads?' said Tom.

'He means a bribe,' Cat explained.

'Bribe King Arthur?' stammered Tom, horrified, 'He'll be above that won't he?'

'Everyman has his price,' said Rufus, knowingly, lowering his voice as he said it, but then his tone lightened, 'and best not to call him that, positively hates it. It's Art now, his choice – can't see what's wrong with Arthur myself, but there you are.'

Cat listened to Rufus and again found she was having trouble recognising the man sitting before her, especially the part about everyone having his price. She found this positively dark.

Tom hadn't noticed anything and was more interested in Arthur's name change. 'Art?' he said, 'Like as in artisan or something?'

'My boy,' said Rufus, smiling, the old Rufus, Cat felt she knew back, 'sometimes I wonder about you.' Rufus laughed. 'Wouldn't want you counting out my change, Art man, is short for Arthur.' Rufus laughed again.

Tom reddened.

'What beads do you recommend?' said Cat, ignoring Tom's faux pas, thus lessening his embarrassment.

'Last time I saw the old boy, he was going on about how much he missed the old mead – can't stand it myself. A flagon of it should do it and get him a magazine; you know the type,' Rufus winked at Cat. 'That'll bring a smile to the old fella's face.'

Wanting to make amends for his idiocy, an avalanche of magazine genres filled his head. 'What's he into? Cars?

Trains? Woodworking tools?'

'I think you need to be looking at a higher shelf,' said Rufus, tapping at his nose, 'if you know what I mean.'

'Fishing?'

Rufus sighed the sigh of saints. 'Leave it to Cat; she knows where to get her hands on them and sepia versions no less, a much classier type of publication.'

Tom's face was a picture; one that hadn't been developed yet – blank.

Cat told Tom not to worry. 'I'll leave the mead to you then,' she said to Rufus.

'I'm on my way.' Rufus stood up. 'And while I'm gone, you two plan how you're going to handle things when you get home.'

'Careful,' whispered Cat, as he left. She had a feeling there was trouble ahead.

'Won't he have magazines?' said Tom, who had been mulling over the Arthur situation.

'Not sepia ones, very rare. Only a few slipped through the net,' said Cat.

'Net?'

'A few years ago, our time, the enemy thought they were onto a good thing selling sepia versions of a certain type of magazine at the end of the Victorian era. The idea was to get a head start on the magazines of our day, a lot of money in it you see,' explained Cat.

'But why sepia?'

'Too many questions asked if they used colour ones in those days. It would have complicated things – brought it to our notice. They wanted it to stay underground.'

'But you found out anyway?'

'We had a spy on the inside. As soon as we found out what was going on we destroyed the lot, except of course the inevitable one or two that always slips the net in operations like that.'

'Which you, just happen to know the whereabouts of.'

'Yes,' said Cat, not even attempting to look embarrassed.

'So where do we go to get hold of one then?'

Cat told him and in the blink of a time-manipulated eye, they were home, Egypt, ancient Egypt, back to Egypt, home and back again – sepia mag in hand.

'Wow,' said Tom, on their return, 'quite a collection.'

'You never know when something will come in handy,' said Cat, proud of her little hoard of oddities and antiquities.

'And we were really in a pyramid in ancient Egypt?' said Tom, half expecting Cat to confess she had worked a little glamour on him and they had really travelled to some huge lock-up somewhere.

'Of course,' said Cat, 'even the pharaohs' builders had forgotten they'd built that room, nowhere safer.'

'What about the fishing boat?'

'Another story,' said Cat, quickly avoiding any further questions where that was concerned.

Tom would have liked to have delved further about everything he had just seen, but something in Cat's voice told him he would be banging his head against a brick wall – perhaps when this adventure was over? Instead, he sat down and started to unroll the sepia magazine he had in his hands. At least he had something to read while they waited for Rufus to get back. He read the title: Ladies Abroad! Strange, thought Tom, why would Arthur be interested in foreign lady's fashion? But as he started to open it an indignant Cat wailed her displeasure.

'Good grief Tom, there's a lady present.'

Tom gave Cat a look and opened it anyway, at the centre-fold. 'Ooo!' he said, eyes bulging. 'I'll be-'

'Yes you will,' said Cat, 'if you don't put it away this minute.'

It was a very long and embarrassing wait that followed. With Tom trying hard not to look at Cat, while a grumpy Cat, ensconced on her shelf, glared hard at Tom.

Thankfully Rufus arrived back before it got too unbearable. There was a sharp rap at the loo door.

Tom leapt – as far as his dodgy knee would allow – to his feet. 'Who's there?' he said. So numbing had the mini cold war been between him and Cat, Tom would have been hard pressed at that moment to remember his own name.

'Me, Rufus, idiot nephew of mine,' replied an incredulous Rufus.

'Oh, yes,' said Tom. He opened the door and got a smack across the knuckles with a ruler for his trouble. 'Sor-ow! Why did you do that?' said Tom, sucking on them.

'I could have been anyone. You should have asked me for the password,' said Rufus, secreting the ruler somewhere in the recesses of his robe. He moved the spare loo rolls aside and placed the flagon of mead beside them.

'I didn't know we had one?'

'Then let that be a lesson to you.' Rufus saw the discarded magazine. 'You got one then.'

'Mission accomplished,' said Cat.

Rufus went to pick the magazine up.

'Sorry,' said Tom, rubbing swollen knuckles, 'for Art's eyes only.' He quickly picked the mag up and put it in a jacket pocket.

'Ah-ha,' said Rufus, now noticing the frosty atmosphere in the loo. 'Had a peek, eh?'

Tom said nothing and sat down.

'Any problems?' asked Cat.

'What, no. It would appear our man in the mask has skedaddled, taking his troublesome metal pets with him, their tails between their legs, no doubt.'

On the loo, Tom was thinking he couldn't remember any tails.

'Do you think they know who Arthur is? Or where he is?' said Cat.

Rufus mentioned Arthur's new identity again and asked Cat if she would have guessed who he was?

She had to admit she wouldn't have.

'Then I find it very unlikely,' said Rufus, 'but, judging on what occurred earlier they might know more than we think. I also have a suspicion they've been watching Tom. Caution therefore is the byword from nõw on.

'Watching me?' spluttered Tom, 'But I thought our identities were secret.'

'From each other dear boy, each other, when one falls, we don't want the whole bally house of cards falling about our ears, do we?'

'But they know us?' Tom wasn't in a panic exactly – not yet.

'If they look hard enough, yes, as we know them.'

'But we didn't, did we,' said Cat, 'Not on this occasion.'

'We weren't looking hard enough, that's all,' said Rufus.

A sort of contemplative silence now hung in the air.

It was broken by Rufus. 'Anyway, what's done is done; we should be about doing. But before we part I want you to have this.' He put a hand into his robe and took something from it which he handed to Tom.

'It's a photo,' said Tom, showing it to a neck-craning Cat. He puzzled at the subject matter for a moment wondering at its relevance then shrugged. 'Of a wing chair?'

Cat, on the other hand, had an idea it was more than just a wing chair. 'Is that your time machine?'

'With bells, lights and whistles,' beamed Rufus, 'an exact copy of that one in the book.' He leant down and gave Tom a nudge. 'I'll let you have a look at it when all this is over if you like.' He stood up again. 'And now, dear people, sadly we must be on our respective ways. Tootle-pip and all that.' And just like that, without another word, Rufus was away and gone.

The silence that he left behind wasn't exactly a stunned one, but in it Tom and Cat were exchanging stupefied looks.

'I didn't realise he was so eccentric,' said Tom, looking down at the photo he still held in his hand.

'Some would say mad,' said Cat, dryly.

'Well, whatever, I'm just glad he's on our side.'

'I wonder if it wouldn't be better if he wasn't,' whispered Cat.

'You don't mean that?' said a surprised Tom.

'I wish I didn't, but there're sides to him I didn't know existed.'

Tom didn't know what to make of Cat's remark. Perhaps it was best not to know.

'We should go,' said Cat, climbing beside the flagon of mead to secure it during transit.

Tom slipped the photo in his top pocket. 'Let's,' he said.

Chapter 35

Having carefully nudged the door open a crack, Tom peeped through the gap into the room beyond. In the sparse light, provided by the smallest of barred windows, he could make out numerous laden shelves and an assortment of stacked boxes.

'What can you see?' asked Cat.

'A storeroom,' said Tom.

'Is it the one?'

'I don't know.' Tom squinted across the room. 'There's a door across from us with light shining underneath.'

'We had better have a look then,' said Cat, alighting from the shelf with the flagon.

'What if it's not?'

'Not what?'

'The right place.'

'I'll question your competence as a traveller and we'll try again,' said Cat.

Tom wasn't sure if she was joking and was afraid to ask. 'What now?'

Cat squeezed between Tom's feet and out through the door. 'Come on.' With a nervous Tom creeping behind, Cat tiptoed across the floor to the other door. They were almost there when Tom rather expertly managed to crack a shin against a crate.

'Fu-' He managed to stop the full expletive by ramming one of his ruler-rapped knuckles into his mouth.

'Ssssch!' whispered Cat, ear to the ground for any sign of response to Tom's aborted outburst. There didn't appear to be any, but Cat was now on full alert.

'My leg,' groaned Tom, through gritted teeth.

'Suck it up,' said Cat, unsympathetically.

'But it's on fire,' said Tom, scanning the shelves for anything that might help, but the room was in too much gloom for him to make anything out clearly.

'I get the picture,' said Cat, 'but keep the noise down or someone might hear you.' She looked over her shoulder. Tom had rolled up his trouser leg and was briskly rubbing at his shin.

'I think it's bleeding,' said Tom.

Whites of eyes flashed in the gloom as Cat rolled hers. 'Can you walk?'

'I think so,' whined Tom, pathetically.

'Then walk over here and open this door.'

'What if they heard us?'

'Heard you,' corrected Cat, 'I don't think so.'

As his hands weren't wet or sticky Tom took this as a good sign he wasn't bleeding after all. He rolled the trouser leg back to where it belonged and sidled up beside Cat.

'They could be waiting for us on the other side of the door with a cricket bat or something,' said Tom, body in one piece, but his mind causing pain – to Cat at least.

'I'm sure I can deal with the situation should one arise.'

'Or phoning the police.'

'Or waiting with weapons of mass destruction,' said Cat, 'I get the picture, Tom and we'll take our chances. Now, if you're ready?'

With a limp that had suddenly arrived from nowhere, Tom hobbled round Cat and placed a hand on the handle. 'You sure it's all clear?'

Cat sniffed at the gap at the foot of the door. She could smell a single human on the other side, but no sense of anxiety from it. 'All clear, so if you could do the honours?'

'Honours?'

'Open the door,' hissed Cat, trying desperately not to show her growing exasperation.

'What if it's locked?'

Oh good grief! thought Cat. She decided to take matters into her own hands. The door handle suddenly started to turn without Tom's help.

'Wha-' said Tom, stepping back.

'A parlour trick,' said Cat, 'nothing more.' She put her weight against the now open door and gave it a gentle push. 'Careful,' she warned.

Chapter 36

The grannies didn't need an invite. They swept in, taking Katie with them. They knew exactly where the others were and with clockwork military precision – apart from one battered individual who ran on batteries – they went swiftly about their business.

Outside the house, the one who had orchestrated the attack waited with an evil, yet contented smile across her lips; this time there would be no mistakes. This time the sword would be theirs.

Chapter 37

For the umpteenth time Tom tried a door handle and peeped through an open door and for the umpteenth time they weren't where they were supposed to be.

'Well?' said Cat, prepared for expected disappointment.

'Nope,' said Tom, carefully closing the door. 'What now?' It had been suggested that if this try bombed out, just as the others had, it would be time for a rethink.

'We sit and think,' said Cat, a small frown almost matching the one Tom was wearing spread across her brow. 'Something's not right and it's high time we found out what.'

They left the storeroom and regrouped in the portable loo.

'So, what we got?' said Cat, sounding your typical New York television detective.

'Aching feet,' replied Tom, sounding your typical grumpy old man. He was perched on his plastic throne in the process of removing a shoe and sock.

'Do you have to?' moaned Cat, wrinkling her pretty little nose.

'It helps me think,' said Tom.

'Think?'

'No, not really, my feet ache and I want to tend to them. We must have travelled miles in the last few days.'

'One: it's not been days and two: forget your feet and use your brain, we're in trouble here. Something doesn't want us to find Arthur and we've got to find out what.'

Tom took a moment to blow on his toes before putting his sock and shoe back on. 'Could it be the enemy?' he said, wishing Cat wouldn't use that word; it made him feel like a spy or something. Perhaps they could come up with something different to call them when this was all over.

'I don't think so,' said Cat, looking thoughtful, 'It's as if the loo itself is having problems – as if it's reluctant to take us where we want to go.'

'Is that possible?'

'Personally, I don't think so, which leaves us with the loo having some sort of problem.' Cat wondered. 'You know what I think?'

Tom didn't – he really didn't. 'No.'

'I think it's being deflected somehow. We always land in a storeroom, which means we are on the right track. Then at the last second – wham!'

'Wham?'

'We shoot off at right angles or something. I think we should go home and have a rummage in the shed; something in there might be able to help.'

'Only if it comes with a manual,' said Tom, thinking the idea a wild goose chase considering how much stuff was stashed in there. He took the photo Rufus had given him from his pocket. 'Perhaps we should go back and ask Rufus? At least he would know if there was something useful in the shed that would help us.' Tom looked at the photo.

Trying hard not to show her surprise at Tom's suggestion, which was a bloody good one by anyone's standard, Cat readily agreed. 'Back it is then,' she said.

But Tom had already changed his mind. 'I don't think that's such a good idea anymore.'

Cat, ready to lambaste the man for his dithering, stopped all thought of it when she saw how pale he had become. 'Tom?'

Tom showed her the photo.

Cat's mouth dropped open. Line after line of spidery writing had appeared across the picture. Cat knew instantly

217

who it belonged to – Rufus, and the message was a chilling one.

It read:

The masked man has Lucy and the kids. Granny-napped!
Waiting for me when I went back for the mead.
Couldn't say anything, wired.
Wants to swap them for the sword and Arthur.
Think of something!
P.S. Sorry for the confusing ride, polarization strip
on back of photo. Had to make sure you saw this
before you got to Arthur.
Rufus.
P.P.S. Come prepared, grannies galore!!!

'They've got Lucy and the kids,' said Tom, forgetting whether Cat could read or not, 'want the sword and Arthur in exchange. What are we going to do?'

As Cat read the note a cold chill crossed her heart. 'Two choices,' said Cat, adopting extreme seriousness, 'we either charge back into the past and try to rescue them, taking that masked menace out in the process, or we go back to just before they were taken and stop it happening.'

The shock he had received from reading the note, to Tom's surprise, quickly ebbed as something else kicked in – firm resolution. Something had to be done and quickly. Like it or not he was a traveller now and he had responsibilities – how he hated that word – to others and right now that meant his family. It was bullet biting time. It was decision time – time to assume his role – it was Tyme time!

'Do we know when they were taken?' said Tom, steeliness about his eyes.

Of course they didn't, Cat realised. 'No.'

'Then we only have one choice, but before we kick some butt, I say we get Arthur on side. The more the merrier.'

A wide-eyed Cat was impressed by this new Tom. How long it would last was another thing, but until then… 'All for one-'

'Let's not get silly now.'

Chapter 38

'You sure you got rid of the strip?' said Cat, glowering at Tom.

'Of course I did,' said Tom, showing Cat the photo and the place the strip had been. 'Must be something else stopping us.' Tom went to put the photo back in his pocket, but missed and it floated to the floor.

'Then what is that?' said Cat, pointing to one of Tom's feet.

Tom went to retrieve the photo, which had fluttered between his shoes, but stopped as he spied something jutting from beneath his shoe. He picked the photo up and lifted his foot to inspect his sole. It was the polarised strip.

'How did that get there?' said Tom, apparently genuinely mystified.

'Get rid of it.'

'But I…'

'Just do it.'

Tom peeled it from his shoe and threw it into the umpteenth-and-one storeroom they had now visited and closed the door on it.

'Perhaps now?'

Tom again put his mind to the matter at hand. Arthur, here we come. Finally!

The storeroom they stepped into differed little to the storerooms they had been privy to recently, but something about it raised their hopes. This one felt right.

They crossed to the door, but just as Tom went to turn the handle, he paused. Something had been niggling at him since the hunt for Arthur had begun. He needed to know something before they went on. He turned to Cat. 'Why were all the toilets in the storerooms,' he asked.

Cat shrugged. 'Your world, not mine.'

Fair do's, thought Tom. He turned the handle.

Someone was whistling.

'It's him,' whispered Tom, almost ecstatic, 'I'd know that tuneless warble anywhere.'

'You sure?' asked Cat, wishing she could cross her toes.

''Course I am,' Tom assured.

This didn't exactly fill Cat with optimism.

With surging confidence he pushed the door wide and stepped into the shop beyond. A microsecond later he was flat on his face, behind a counter, with the full force of Cat between his shoulder blades.

The astounded shopkeeper, who stood behind the counter with them, was frankly, well, astounded, but had no time to react as the sound of the shop door opening drew his attention.

The shopkeeper tensed then let slip a relieved gasp. 'Oh, it's you!' he said, sounding relieved and managing to keep more than a semblance of level-headedness after what he had just experienced.

'Well that's a nice welcome,' said the customer, shaking her brolly and placing it by the door, 'perhaps I should take my trade elsewhere.'

'Sorry,' said the shopkeeper.

The customer gave the shopkeeper a concerned glance. 'It's okay, I'm only joking. Are you all right?' The man looked positively ashen.

Behind the counter Tom tried to prise his head from the floor. I recognise that voice, he thought, and tried to say so, but

221

the same white light that had held Rufus so effectively back in the past did its job again and sealed his gob shut before he had chance to utter a word.

'Yes,' said the shopkeeper, somewhat distracted, but he managed to compose himself, 'yes, sorry. What can I do for you, *Lucy*? 'The post?' His eyes kept darting to the struggle going on by his feet. Luckily Lucy didn't appear to notice.

'Has it arrived yet?'

He knew what that light was.

'Mister Smokowski?'

Mister Smokowski suddenly decided he couldn't cope with both the strange goings on and a customer at the same time. One had to go and he didn't like the way the cat was staring at him. He made his choice.

'Eh? No... sorry. Er... I have to do something. Is there anything else I can help you with before you leave?' Why had he said that? He was trying to get rid.

Lucy knew a brush off when she heard one. 'I... no,' she said, changing her mind, 'no thank you.' She gave Mister Smokowski a concerned look and went to go on her way, but stopped when she saw him appear to almost jump back from something behind the counter. She tried to see what it was.

'You sure you're okay, Mister Smokowski?' said Lucy, trying to peer behind the counter and taking a step closer.

But Mister Smokowski noticed her interest and gaining a few of his senses quickly moved through the gap left by the open counter flap. 'Yes, yes,' he answered, smoothing his apron, 'just busy, that's all. See you this evening.'

'The post?' Lucy repeated.

'I'll bring it with me,' said Mister Smokowski, shaking his head. 'Tut-tut, the postal service these days, but what can you do?'

Lucy backed away. 'You won't forget them?' she said, as she was ushered to the door.

'What? No. See you later then.'

One last gentle piece of guidance and Lucy was safely outside. Mister Smokowski then quickly turned the open sign round to show he was closed, pulled the blind and locked the door. He stood there for a moment collecting his thoughts, back pressed against the blind, staring at the counter. What the hell was going on?

Chapter 39

'Was that our Lucy just then?' puzzled Tom, who, now free of the light and Cat, was using the counter to pull himself upright.

Ignoring Tom and his question for the moment, Cat leapt onto the counter and stared across at Mister Smokowski who was still leaning against the door. He was staring back at her. She could see the questions bubbling up behind his eyes. She decided to beat him to it and hoped it wouldn't be too much of a shock for him. 'Mister Smokowski?' she asked.

'Cat?' said Mister Smokowski, taking Cat by surprise.

'You know me?' said Cat, warily.

'You know her?' said Tom, his head popping up from behind the counter.

'Heard of you.' Came a cryptic answer.

'You're famous,' said Tom.

The ignoring of Tom continued.

'He said you might come one day.'

'Rufus?' asked Cat.

'Yes.' Mister Smokowski levered himself from the door and took a step forward, he seemed to be looking for something. 'Have you anything for me?'

'Mead-'

'A flagon?'

'Yes.'

'Anything else?'

'A magazine.'

'What sort?'

'Sepia,' said Cat, wondering where this was all leading, so deciding to keep the magazine's content a secret for the moment.

'Ah,' said Mister Smokowski, nodding sagely. It appeared he didn't need to know.

Behind Cat, Tom had managed to haul himself up and was now arranging his clothes and dusting himself down. He thought he might have a private word with Cat later about the excesses of force displayed, but for now his mind was set on more important things, also he just happened to be a tad in awe at meeting Arthur again even though the man standing before him looked a lot leaner, shorter and downright different than the last time he had seen him. Disguise, he supposed. Could do wonders with plastic surgery these days.

'Smokowski... I mean Arthur... sorry, I mean Art, how are you?'

Mister Smokowski frowned at Tom.

Tom edged through the gap in the counter. 'Remember me? Of course you do. I mean you knighted me. Good grief, listen to me, babbling like a star-struck teenager. Should I kneel or bow or something?' Tom started to bow.

'What are you going on about Tom?' said Mister Smokowski, looking the very much puzzled shopkeeper.

Cat sat. 'You were expecting us,' she said.

It was Smokowski's turn to straighten up ruffled attire. He nervously smoothed his apron. 'One day perhaps, but not like this. I imagined a more orthodox approach. A phone call maybe – to prepare me, that sort of thing.

Appearing to have forgotten the urgency of their visit, Tom was struggling onto one knee.

'They've got Lucy and the kids,' said Cat.

'But I...' Smokowski thumbed at the door behind him.

'Which means they are taken sometime later today.'

A sudden click echoed through the shop. Cat tensed, but it

225

was only Tom's dodgy knee as tried to get up. He had recovered from his spell of awe and was back on track when he heard they might have a time for the abduction. 'We've got to get them back,' he said, grimacing as his knee protested.

'And that's where you come in,' said Cat, to Smokowski. 'The sword's waiting for you in the loo. I thought we could take them by surprise, you swinging Excalibur, me swinging magic and Tom... Tom backing us up.'

'Whoa,' said Smokowski, 'hold your horses one minute.'

'Why aren't I swinging anything?' said Tom.

'Times running,' Cat pointed out.

'But you've got it all wrong,' Smokowski protested.

'Rufus said you might be a bit stubborn, but I thought under the circumstances-'

'I am not being stubborn,' argued Smokowski, 'you've got the wrong end of the stick.'

'What stick?' demanded Tom.

'If you're worried, Tom here could act as a decoy,' proposed Cat, surprised that the great warrior Arthur might be.

'Decoy?' said Tom, not liking the sound of that.

Mister Smokowski threw up his hands in despair. 'You're not listening,' he said, 'you've got the wrong man. I'm not Arthur.'

Chapter 40

'And you are sure you said nothing?'

Rufus glared up at the masked man from the chair he had been trussed to earlier. 'How could I? You had me wired.'

The masked man, his mask repaired or replaced, started to pace the floor. At last things were going his – their way. He stopped his pacing and faced Rufus. 'I think your nephew is a lot like you, but doesn't know it yet,' he said, smiling or was that sneering, beneath his mask.

'He is nothing like me,' snapped Rufus, hoping to all that was holy that the masked man was wrong.

'He's reckless, a fool. He's just like you. He's coming and he'll walk straight into my trap, him and that damn cat. And don't think I don't know you tipped them off. And don't try and deny it, because that's you all over Rufus – a meddler. You wouldn't have been able to help yourself.'

Things were beginning to sound personal and Tom had said he thought he recognized the man's voice. 'Do I know you?' said Rufus.

The masked man snapped his fingers and two ninja grannies left their positions by the bedroom door and came to his side. He said something to them and they left the house. He then put a hand to his mask as if preparing to take it off, but stopped short and let his hand fall away. 'No,' said the man, 'no you don't.' This time there was a sneer behind the mask. 'And it doesn't matter anyway. I have you. I have them,' he glanced at the bedroom where, a now solitary granny kept guard, 'and soon I shall have the sword. That is all that matters. And then,' the man let forth a cackle, not perhaps your mad scientist sort, but a crazed one all the same, 'I shall have the Earth.'

The man cackled a little more then stopped abruptly, mid cackle. He looked towards the front door.

'They're coming. I can feel it.' He started for the door. 'Soon all will be mine.' He opened the door and left it slightly ajar. 'Wouldn't want to make it too hard for them,' he cackled, from somewhere outside.

'Nutter!' shouted Rufus, after him.

A couple of seconds later the door swung open again. The masked man entered and took something from his coat. 'Glad you reminded me,' he said, 'you've also got a big mouth.' He produced a roll of duct tape and wrapped what was left around Rufus's mouth. 'Never did know when to keep it shut, did you Rufus?'

Rufus shook his head furiously. It was all he could do.

The masked man walked behind Rufus and patted his head. 'There-there, soon be over.' He then left to wait for Tom and the others to arrive.

Chapter 41

'What you talking about Smokowski?' said Tom, thumbing his lapels.

'Did Rufus tell you I was Arthur?' asked Smokowski, looking, with some disdain, at Tom acting like some forties film gangster.

'Yes,' said Cat, 'he told us to give you the mead and the magazine.

Smokowski knew instantly where their problem lay. 'He lied,' said he, 'they're just a signal to me, so that I know Rufus sent you and you're on the up and up.'

Cat arched an eyebrow, which was another talent she possessed. 'Why would he do that?' She watched Smokowski's reaction to the question very carefully and was surprised to see his eyes wander to Tom. Curious, thought Cat.

'Why are you looking at me like that?' said Tom, catching Smokowski's look.

Smokowski cleared his throat. 'I think what we have here, in the best tradition of cop movies, is a situation.' The expectant expressions suggested he carry on and explain. 'Rufus, in his inimitable fashion, appears to have passed the buck.' Smokowski waited for a response. None came. 'Let me explain.'

It turned out that Arthur had indeed been in a worse state than Rufus had thought and the hospital, the best one this side of the military, could do nothing for him – didn't know how to. There were tests and more tests, but Arthur wasn't dying of his wounds, he was dying of old age. Within a day of arriving at the hospital, Arthur had aged five years.

Something had to be done and fast, and as Rufus blamed himself for Arthur's predicament, thinking something along the time jump must have caused the problem, he pulled out all the stops until there was only one option left open to him. It was a myth, but if it existed then he was the man to find it. The fountain of youth.

'You're joking, right?' said Tom, chuckling. 'You expect us to believe that?'

'What happened next,' said Cat, obviously believing.

'You can't trust him,' Tom protested, 'Rufus said he'd be stubborn, he's just throwing us a line. He doesn't want to help. We'll just have to go it alone.'

'Hear him out,' said Cat.

'But…'

'Please continue, Mister Smokowski.'

Mister Smokowski did.

Rufus, against all the odds, found it and brought back a flask full of the precious liquid. He administered a few drops to Arthur's dying lips and stepped away, hoping he had done enough. As it turned out, he had done more than enough. The response was amazing – instant, but not quite what Rufus had been expecting. What happened next had Rufus reaching for the whiskey. Instead of just healing Arthur, it regenerated his body to a time when he had no ills. When the liquid was finished with him, Arthur was no longer an old man waiting for death, but a young man in his twenties, full of it. It had worked, but too well.

'So you're telling us,' said Tom, 'that Arthur, thanks to this mythical fountain of youth, is now a young man and wandering about outside?'

'Yes,' said Smokowski, 'well, no, not exactly.'

'There you go,' said Tom, 'full of beeswax, what did I say?

230

We should go.'

'What I mean is that he was a young man, but Rufus hid him back in time, about twenty years ago.'

'So, that would make him a man in his forties wandering about outside?' said Cat, 'Where outside?' Cat thought Smokowski was telling the truth, but keeping something back for himself.

'I… er.'

'I… er, what?' said Tom.

'I think I find myself in a difficult situation.'

'Not as difficult as ours,' said Tom, growing a little angry.

Cat stepped in as Smokowski took on the appearance of a man in a right old pickle, one that was about to go off. 'What aren't you telling us?' she asked him, softly.

Smokowski's eyes once again wandered to Tom. 'All right, I'll tell you everything I know, but, sorry Tom, only to Cat.

'What!' stormed Tom, hardly believing what he had heard, 'But we've been friends for nearly twenty years. You have something to say, you say it in front of me.'

'Tom,' said Cat, quietly, 'I think you should calm down and let Mister Smokowski here tell me what the heck it is he wants to tell me. Remember Lucy and the kids.'

Tom wasn't happy, but did as Cat asked. With a couple of glances over his shoulder he sloped off to the magazine rack so Smokowski could get off whatever it was he had on his chest.

'Well?' said Cat, when she felt Tom was out of earshot, 'what is it you can tell me, but not Tom?'

Smokowski told her.

'Holy snowballs in hell!' said Cat.

231

Chapter 42

'You what?!' yelled Tom, all anatomical failings forgotten as he hopped with anger around the shop. 'You what?!' he repeated, the strong likelihood that hysteria was imminent. 'Bollocks! That... that, good for nothing? I don't believe you.'

Tom did some teeth gnashing and some stomping that he would feel later once he had cooled down. 'It can't be him,' he further ranted, 'he just can't be Arthur.' His knee now joined in the protesting, but under its own agenda. Tom quickly pulled rein and hobbled over to the counter which he leaned on. 'I won't believe it.'

But sadly for Tom, it was true and as much as he disliked the idea, he was going to have to lump it. Not that that would be easy. Not after what Cat had just told him. Not after finding out that Arthur, so called King of the Brits, was the ex-husband of his daughter – father of his grandkids. Not easy at all.

Mister Smokowski took the opportunity to try and put his case – tried to explain to Tom that he was just a foot soldier, that some travellers had them, their identities kept secret even from their trusted familiars. He tried to tell Tom how sorry he was that it had been left to him to break the news. He knew how much Tom disliked the man for running out on his daughter like that, but he also tried to explain that not everything was as it seemed.

But Tom chose to ignore him and fell into a sullen trance, turning his back on his friend.

'Will he be all right?' whispered Smokowski to Cat.

'I hope so,' said Cat, whose own sympathetic noises when telling Tom, had also been ignored. 'I've seen flickers of Rufus in him.'

A smile appeared on Smokowski's lips. 'There's hope then, as long as it's only a small flicker.'

Cat couldn't agree more, but now wasn't the time to be weighing up the pros and cons of being like Rufus; there were more pressing matters that needed dealing with. 'Will you come with us?' asked Cat, choosing to make plans without Tom while he was in the state he was.

Smokowski nodded, it was the least he could do. 'Of course I will, from what you've told me you'll need all the help you can muster. And as Rufus saw fit to name me as Arthur, how about I play the part when we get there? We could hold the element of surprise if they're expecting an older man, as I suspect they might be.'

'If you're sure,' said Cat, admiring the man's nerve.

Smokowski laughed. 'Hell no, but like you it's part of my job description. Anyway, about time I had me a little adventure in my life.'

Plans, as far as was it was possible to make without knowing how Arthur would fit into them, were now made. Tom was coaxed. Weapons were gathered, which amounted to Excalibur, Tom's saver, Cat, and a toy plastic sword that Smokowski removed from a display as a substitute for the real thing. It was hoped that seen from a distance no one would notice it wasn't the real Excalibur. Tom was coaxed some more. Smokowski struggled into a ski suit. Finally they were ready. All they needed now was the final member of their team.

As Tom was slumped in a grumpy, unresponsive heap on the toilet, it was left to Smokowski to take the first step into Arthur's domain. He shivered. Not that it was particularly

233

cold; it was the room that he had stepped into that had caused it. Everything in it gave the impression of ice or snow – all sterile whites, blues and silvers. That and the fact he was standing somewhere in the Arctic Circle.

Cat trotted after him. There was no sight of Arthur, but there were two other doors.

'Can't be far,' said Smokowski, sweating in his ski suit.

'You've been here before, haven't you?' said Cat, forever the astute one.

'You noticed,' said Smokowski, smiling, 'Just the once, with Rufus, bloody cold outside. He sent you on a wild goose chase so we could get Arthur here without anyone knowing.'

'I just didn't know him, did I?'

Smokowski allowed himself a small laugh. 'I doubt he truly does either.' He reached out and turned the handle of the nearest door and opened it. Arthur was inside; sound asleep and snoring on a bunk.

It wasn't the warmest of reunions. Smokowski's part in it rankled, even though Arthur had agreed to everything – the having to leave without saying a word. But the non contact with his family, he hadn't counted on that – on being a virtual prisoner for so long. Week's maybe, months even, but years – his only contact with the world, Rufus. It was no wonder he was angry.

'Let me up!' growled Arthur, from his prone position on the floor of the bedroom.

'Not until you promise you won't try and throttle Mister Smokowski again,' said Cat, standing amid the white light keeping Arthur pinned to the floor.

'But he lied,' said Arthur, trying, without any success, to pick himself up off the floor.

'I didn't,' protested Smokowski, 'I only did what I was told to do. I thought I was doing the right thing. I was told you

234

were in danger; your family was in danger. I didn't know he was going to keep you here for so long and what could I do about it anyway? It was Rufus.'

The howl that greeted the mention of Tom's uncle could have come from one of a number of creatures, real or mythical, that you wouldn't want to meet during daylight, let alone down a dark alley somewhere. 'Where is he? Had enough of doing his own dirty work has he?'

'He's being held captive,' said Cat.

This brought a half laugh from Arthur. Receiving some of his own medicine is he? Well serves him right and if that's why you're here, to ask me to help rescue him, you've another think coming. He can rot for all I care.'

'They've got Lucy and the kids as well.'

The sudden interruption surprised Cat and Smokowski. Arthur, straining to see who had spoken, though he thought he knew, was allowed to do so.

Arthur's whole attitude suddenly changed. 'Tom?'

'You okay, Tom?' said Cat.

'I'll survive, but I need answers.'

'You must hate me,' said Arthur, from below.

'I just want to know what really happened, the truth. Was it all Rufus' doing?'

'I played my part,' Arthur confessed.

'Let him up, Cat.'

'I don't know,' said Cat, looking at Smokowski as he took steps to the door.

'He won't hurt anyone, now that he's going home.'

'Home?' said Arthur, 'I'm going home?'

'But first we have to sort things out between us and free your wife and kids, and, as Cat is so fond of saying, time is running. Cat.'

It was a lot tighter in the loo and way more tense as they prepared to go back. Arthur, reunited with Excalibur, glared at

235

Smokowski, even though it wasn't his fault. Tom was glowering at Arthur, even though he'd said it wasn't his fault. And Cat, she was seething inside and out at Rufus, who it appeared *was* at fault, for *everything*.

The journey was brief, the arrival a relief, as cat and humans fairly burst from the portable toilet. With the freshest of air now filling their lungs things started to simmer down enough for Cat to fill the new arrivals in on what they were up against and to concoct some sort of plan of action to deal with them.

'Now,' said Cat, when they had finished, 'has anyone got any questions about what we are about to face or the plan?'

'Ninja grannies?' exclaimed Smokowski.

'Clockwork robots?' puzzled Arthur.

'Plan?' said Tom, a tad sarcastically.

'It's the best I could come up with at short notice,' said Cat.

'You never mentioned ninja grannies back at the shop,' said a worried Smokowski, 'did you?'

'What is this clockwork?' asked Arthur, having only lived before and after the onset of the concept. There were clocks in Hope End, but it wasn't the most urgent of needs for Arthur to know how Rufus kept them going. In the house he had shared with Lucy, everything had been battery operated.

'Old Smokowski here, charges the house, waving his plastic sword and we wait in hiding for whatever crawls from under a stone or drops from a tree. That's your plan?'

'Now I hear it back, I suppose it might need a little revision,' said Cat, who, by her own admission and background – feline, wasn't amongst the top strategists in the world.

'I suggest we charge them head on,' said Arthur, swinging Excalibur above his head, 'Hiding is for sissies.'

Tom looked at him. 'Sissies?'

'I watched a lot of teen movies in the Arctic,' said Arthur.

'Fair do,' said Tom, nodding.

'I suggest I wait in the loo until it's all over,' suggested Smokowski, not liking the sound of those grannies one single bit.

'And I suggest we take it as we see it, spy out the lay of the land and go from there,' said Tom, strangely the most rational one amongst them, for the moment.

Cat was out of suggestions so Tom's motion was adopted.

As they came in sight of Merlin's house, Tom had another idea. 'I've just thought, what if Art here was to put the sword in the stone right now? That would spoil their evil little plan.'

It was a thought, but as Cat pointed out. 'We may need it, Tom,' said Cat, 'If we put it back now who knows what that masked madman might do to Lucy and the children.'

Tom hadn't thought of that. 'Damn it, Cat, you're right,' he said, clenching his fists. 'What now?'

'We do as you said, lay low, wait and grab an opportunity if and when it arises.'

'And if one doesn't?'

'Plan B,' said Cat.

'What's plan B?'

The others closed in a little to listen.

'Art's idea.'

'Good grief,' said Tom and Smokowski.

'Ah-ha,' said Arthur, flexing his muscles, 'but please call me Arthur. Art is what Rufus called me when he visited.'

But B was the backup, for now they would continue with plan A – no one was keen on a suicide mission – and laid low.

For a while there was nothing, nothing to suggest the masked man or his entourage were around, but just as one or two of them were beginning to feel their age, the door to the house swung open. The masked man appeared with someone by his side. It was Lucy.

'I know you're out there,' he shouted, in no particular direction. 'All I want is the sword, give it to me and no one gets hurt.'

'Not until the Earths disappear,' said Tom, under his breath.

'Let me go down,' said Arthur, hand tightening around the hilt of his sword, 'I'll deal with him.'

'Let's not be too hasty,' said Smokowski, placing a tentative hand on Arthur's shoulder. 'Look over there, to the right, by the woodpile.'

All looked. They weren't easy to spot, but two headscarves could just be made out above the fence of a small pen.

'Is there anyway you can disable the grannies?' said Smokowski, turning to Cat.

'I'm not sure. I've only come across the odd one now and again and they were taken care of hand to hand. I could try to generate a power surge, but the trouble is they're clockwork, or at least most of them are and we don't know how many of them are hiding down there.'

'It's worth a shot,' said Tom. 'If it works we've near as damn it won. If not, we're no worse off than we are now.'

'It could also give away our position.'

'Now you're sounding like a movie general,' said Tom, smiling. 'Go on, give it a go. They already know we're out here.'

Cat was convinced. 'Okay, but keep your eyes closed until I give the all clear.'

Eyes shut around her, Cat started to concentrate. Above them, ominous looking clouds began to gather.

'What's happening?' whispered someone.

'Sssch!' hissed someone else.

Hair began to rise on necks. Fur stood on end. The clouds blackened, electricity built and the sky was suddenly rent by an all mighty crash and flash of unbridled power which hit the ground twenty or so feet from the house. The masked man and Lucy were thrown to the ground. A moment later a solitary granny, slightly damaged, slipped from her hiding place in a tree.

'Blast,' said Cat, the only one who had seen what had happened.

'What?' said Tom.

'Can I open my eyes now?' said Smokowski.

'Double blast,' said Cat, as below, a multitude of grannies now emerged from their hiding places.

'By my shield,' said Arthur, when he saw them.

'You can say that again,' said Tom.

'My eyes,' said Smokowski.

'Yes,' said Cat.

Smokowski opened his eyes which immediately opened wider. 'Great galloping grannies!'

'You can say that again,' said Tom.

Quick thinking was now called for and as Cat appeared to be the only one qualified at the moment, she did some.

'Tom.'

'Yes?'

'The saver. Arthur.'

'Yes?'

'Prepare for battle. Smokowski.'

'Yeah?'

'See if you can find a way in while we keep them at bay.'

As they prepared for a fight, the masked man recovered and dragged a struggling Lucy indoors.

The grannies advanced.

Cat, claws sharp and cruel, Arthur, muscles bulging, sword swinging, went to meet them. Tom rummaged frantically in his pocket for the saver.

'Where the hell is it?' he said to himself, as the sound of metal on metal started to reverberate through the air. At last

239

he found it. Fumbled it. Gripped it again, Concentrated on it. It changed. It wasn't what he had been expecting.

Granny after granny fell to the ground, but Cat and Arthur were in danger of being overwhelmed. 'Tom!' shouted Cat, 'Where are you?'

'Coming!' Came a reply amidst what sounded like an engine starting. And come he did and battle was met.

The grannies broke off their attack on Cat and Arthur and converged as one on this new enemy. The one making that rat-a-tat noise.

Cat, fur matted, Arthur, sweat covered, stood and watched in amazement as Tom took the fight to the grannies in what could only be described as a mini-tank/walking frame combo on wheels. Rat-a-tat-tat went its guns as it mowed down wave after wave of charging grannies.

The battle lasted less than a minute, but the result was one for good guys everywhere. What few grannies there were that survived being mowed down took to their heels.

Tom steered his tank over to where Cat and Arthur were standing and switched it off. 'Do you think that's the lot of them?' he said, clambering from it.

'If it isn't, I doubt we'll have any trouble from them after that,' said Cat, in awe of what she had just seen.

'I thought they were mindless fighting machines,' said Tom.

'Not totally mindless, but not stupid either.'

Tom picked up the saver, now a manageable size again and slipped it into his pocket.

'Well done, said Arthur, patting Tom on the back, 'I wouldn't have thought of anything like that given a million years.' He was as impressed as Cat was, if not more so – him being a warrior.

Tom puffed out his chest and then sucked it back in again. He couldn't lie. 'Nor I,' he admitted. 'I asked for a suit of armour for the older gent with weapons as standard. I couldn't think of anything else.'

'All's well,' said a grinning Cat.

'Look,' said Arthur, suddenly. He was gesturing to a waving Smokowski.

'Look's as though he's found a way in.'

Tom and Arthur were both for rushing down to him, but Cat had other ideas. Smokowski was waved back and plan C was put into action.

'Ready?' asked Cat.

'Ready,' said Smokowski.

'Then let's go.'

Plastic sword in hand, Mister Smokowski led the way to the house, confident that it was clear of granny robots. Cat followed one step behind.

Circling the house and coming from the other direction was Arthur. Tom had made tracks and was in the toilet.

Smokowski and Cat were no more than thirty feet from the house when the door opened.

'That's far enough,' shouted the masked man from inside. 'Throw the sword on the ground and back away.'

Cat glanced to the left. Arthur wasn't in position yet, she would have to play for time. 'Give it up,' said Cat, stepping round Smokowski, 'you can't win and you know it. Your robots have been destroyed and we have you surrounded.'

The masked man poked his head round the door jamb to get a better look and laughed when he saw the two of them standing there. 'Shouldn't one of you be round back then?' He was going to laugh again when it clicked there should be another of them. The door opened further so that the masked man could get a better look at his surroundings. 'Where is he then,' he yelled, meaning Tom, 'the apprentice?'

The "apprentice" was at that precise moment closing his eyes and hoping for the best.

'He's run away,' said Cat.

The masked man laughed. 'You know what, Cat?' I half believed you then.' The masked man now stepped through the doorway. He had Lucy by the neck. 'Now throw the sword over here and tell that idiot of yours to show himself or the lady here gets it. I won't tell you again.' He held something nasty against Lucy's throat for emphasise.

'I don't like this,' whispered Smokowski, 'where have the others got to?'

'I don't know,' Cat whispered back, 'but I think we should do as he says. Put the sword on the ground.'

Smokowski laid his plastic sword on the ground and stepped away.

The masked man became animated. 'What… what? I said throw it. It's no good to me over there. Throw it over here.'

Plan C was now running into a problem. If Smokowski threw it over, the masked man would see in the way that it travelled through the air that it wasn't the real sword.

'Now!' screamed the masked man, growing irate, the nasty object at Lucy's neck moving dangerously close to her jugular. 'NOW!'

'Is this what you want?!'

The sudden interruption by a strange voice took the masked man by surprise. He had hidden when the fighting had started so knew nothing of the real Arthur. 'What the-?' He turned towards the stranger. 'Who the hell are you?' He demanded, strengthening his grip on Lucy.

'The one you've been waiting for. I am Arthur Pendragon and this,' said Arthur, hoisting his sword above his head, 'is Excalibur.' Arthur gave the sword a swish. 'Now let Lucy go and upon my oath I shall lay it at your feet.'

But the masked man hadn't been the only one to be surprised on hearing Arthur's voice and having turned when the masked man had, Lucy now had a clear view of him.

242

'Darren?' she said, looking puzzled, 'is that you?'

'Darren?' said Cat.

'Rufus chose it for him,' Smokowski explained, 'thought it a bit trendier than plain old Arthur.'

Confusion was now mounting in the masked man's mind. 'Darren?' he repeated, looking from the real Arthur, to the fake Arthur, to Lucy and back again. But they wouldn't fool him. This new Arthur was much too young. 'Good try,' he said, turning back to face Cat and Smokowski – Lucy going with him. 'But I know who the real Arthur is, don't I Smokowski. Now throw it over here.'

Another puzzle – how did he know Smokowski? Cat wanted to know and she still needed to play for some time.

'How do you know Mister Smokowski?' she asked.

Every fibre of his body told him he was being played, but he couldn't help himself – baddies never could. 'Always had my suspicions he was not who he said he was. Appearing out of nowhere like that all those years ago. But the clincher was when that old duffer Rufus was in the loo with you and told you Arthur's new name. I didn't buy that listening gear in a corner shop you know, no offence Smokowski, it's a real piece of kit like spy's use.'

It wasn't what Cat had asked, but it bought time and put Rufus in a totally different light for the moment. Of course he hadn't been able to tell them Arthur's real identity. But at the same time he had put Smokowski in danger. But... Cat stopped there. There was no point in going on. Rufus did what he did and that was the end of it.

And that is where the masked man came to his senses and listened to what his body had been telling him. He was being duped somewhere, somehow? He knew it. He stepped clear from the door, Lucy with him. 'Throw both swords over here. Now!'

This time there was no playing for time; none was needed. Arthur and Smokowski both looked at Cat. It was about time the masked man got what was coming to him. 'Give him the swords,' she said.

What happened next had the masked man, in order of occurrence, confused, surprised and finally unconscious.

The swords flew through the air straight and true, or at least one of them did – the real one. The other, Smokowski's plastic one, sort of swayed and wobbled and weaved before landing on the ground and breaking in two. This had the masked man confused.

The real sword – Excalibur, flew through the air straight and true and didn't stop until it splintered the door jamb beside the masked man's head. This surprised the hell out of him.

And before he could react to what was going on, before he had a chance to turn his anger onto Lucy, before he could do anything about anything, a good old-fashioned truncheon, made from good old-fashioned seasoned timber, made contact with the back of his head. This sent him crashing to the ground in an unconscious heap.

'He had one inside then?' said Cat, as all clustered round the downed masked man.

'Good call, Cat, next to the bedroom,' said Tom, still wielding the saver truncheon, 'seems you were right about our Rufus thinking an outside loo was too much of an inconvenience.'

'Journey okay?'

'A bit bumpy,' said Tom. 'It didn't like it much, wouldn't fancy trying to travel through time in it on my own.'

'But it worked, that's the main thing.'

'Thank goodness.'

'Shall we take him inside?' asked Smokowski.

'Good idea,' said Cat. 'Arthur?'

But Arthur, who was itching to go inside and have words

with Rufus, found he wasn't in a position to do anything right then. Questions were being put to him by a rather irate ex-wife. Questions like: where the hell did you go? And: why? So Tom and Smokowski took the strain.

Inside, while the masked man was trussed up, while the kids were released, while Rufus was untied – again, Lucy continued her grilling. Moving from Arthur, who shouldn't think for a moment she was finished with him, to Tom, to Rufus, whom she thought was dead – and why wasn't he? – to Smokowski. Hitting each in turn with interrogation and enquiries and demands to know what the hell was going on? They in turn fielded excuses, shied away or passed the buck. Marc and Kate looked on, bewildered. Cat stayed quietly in the background.

That is until Lucy completed a full circle and returned to Arthur. Cat took the opportunity, now that Smokowski was free of the verbal barrage, to sidle over to him.

'I think,' whispered Cat, when she got there, 'that perhaps is now a good idea to find out who that masked man is.' Smokowski agreed and together they rounded on the unconscious villain.

Smokowski slipped the mask from the man's face. 'Good grief!' said Smokowski, when the deed was done.

'Do you know him?' asked Cat, making sure she wouldn't be heard by Lucy and add to the problems. Thankfully she hadn't realised that it was Cat who had been doing the talking outside – who would?

'I sure do,' said Smokowski, 'and I believe I now know who his accomplice is.' He told Cat his thoughts and she immediately went on red alert.

'We've got to go,' she said, urgently, but with an underlying tone of excitement.

'Where?' said Smokowski.

'Back to when we picked you up, with a bit of luck we

might be able sort two problems out at once.' Her intuition was working overtime. She cast a quick glance at Lucy. 'Get Tom and Arthur and meet me in the toilet.'

That, though, was easier said than done.

'But we've got to go,' groaned Smokowski, as he took the full force of the Lucy.

'No one goes anywhere until I get some answers,' snarled Lucy, actually showing her teeth.

'But we have to go to the toilet,' said Tom, which in hindsight wasn't the cleverest thing to say.

'What, all of you! Are you trying to wind me up?'

'On the contrary,' said Cat, who had, quite frankly, had enough. Not that it would matter Lucy knowing there was a talking cat in their midst if they could kill those two birds they were aiming for with that one stone.

It shut Lucy up a treat, just as planned. And while she stood there in stunned silence, grasping for words that wouldn't come, they made fast their getaway.

Chapter 43

The four of them crammed into the loo. 'Where are we going?' enquired Tom, who needed to know so that they could get there.

Cat told him. She then told him why.

'Gadzooks!' said a stunned Tom, for want of a better word. 'Them? But I thought he was dead.'

Cat put him further in the picture.

'But won't that change the future… now… you know what I mean.'

'It will be as if nothing happened to them. They'll not remember a thing,' said Cat, that certain smile back.

Tom looked worried. 'You sure they'll be okay?'

'There'll be no more questions,' said Cat.

Tom brightened a little; he could live with that, but that didn't mean he had stopped worrying. He had little choice though; he would have to trust Cat on this one.

'Shall we go?'

Tom closed his eyes.

They trooped through the storeroom, through the shop and out the back door where they clambered into Smokowski's aging van.

The journey was short, but took longer than it should have done as Smokowski doggedly kept to a thirty mile an hour speed limit even when signs dictated he could do otherwise. Tom sat in the back wondering if there was a flat cap in the shed he could present to the man.

They arrived hoping they wouldn't be too late, even though it had occurred to all of them that if they were they would know better next time, and stopped a distance from Lucy's house, but within sight of it. All appeared quiet, but appearances could be deceptive and sure enough, a couple of minutes later, a little old lady came into view, dodging furtively from bush to bush. She stopped at the foot of the steps that led to the front door and spoke into her handbag. Moments later another two old ladies, one they recognized as being the battery operated one, sprinted from somewhere across the road to join her. They took up positions beside the door and then seemed to hesitate, as if they were waiting for something or someone.

Arthur wanted to go then, strike while the iron was hot, but Cat stopped him; told him to wait; someone was missing.

They didn't have to wait long, walking down the street, as if she didn't have a care in the world, came a fourth old lady, but this one was different, she moved and acted human.

'Bloody heck,' said Tom, seeing who it was, 'you were right, Cat.'

'Arthur,' said Cat.

'Yes.'

'Do you think you can deal with the one on the right?'

'No problem.'

'On my signal. I'll take the two on the left.'

'What about me?' said Tom, fingering the saver in his pocket. 'I can help.'

'Sorry, Tom,' said Cat, thinking about his last saver contribution which, although brilliant, was obviously still in the experimental stage. She couldn't take the chance in a built up area. What if he accidentally nuked everyone? 'We've got the grannies covered. You and Smokowski deal with the old lady.'

Tom wasn't happy, but at least he was playing a part.

'Wait until the old lady reaches the foot of the steps,' said Cat. 'Ready? Go!'

It was over in a flash. Excalibur, wielded by Arthur did its job, separating a granny's head from her shoulders before she had the chance to react. Cat took out the battery granny with a well-directed power surge and turned her back on the other one who instantly crumpled and disappeared into a black hole.

The human granny, the leader, having made it to the second step reached into her handbag, but Smokowski, showing the agility of a much younger man, took her out with a flying tackle before she could remove anything. Tom, a shade slower, arrived just as the light went on in the hall.

It was a close call, but all managed to hide before the door opened, Tom and Smokowski taking the old lady with them.

'Hello?' said Kate, her head appearing, 'Anyone there?' She took a step out and looked this way and that. 'Hello?'

Lucy called to her from inside. 'Anyone there Kate?'

Kate shrugged, 'No, must have been a cat or something.' She had one more look about then closed the door and returned to whatever it was she had been doing in the lounge.

At roughly the same time, somewhere in the past, in a house where Merlin lived, a mother and her two children suddenly ceased to exist.

Arthur and Cat were the first to venture from their hiding places – Arthur amazed at finding the grannies he and Cat had destroyed had vanished.

'Where did they go?'

'Just had time to do a little light cleaning,' said Cat, lifting her tail.

With Arthur none the wiser, they went to find Tom and Smokowski.

They found them hiding behind a large shrubbery, hunched over the old lady. Tom looked up as they approached; he was in a bit of a state.

'What's wrong?' said Cat.

'She's dead, that's what. He's killed her.'

'He's right,' said Smokowski, his face almost the same colour as his hair. 'I can't find a pulse.'

Cat went over to the body and sniffed. No sense of life but... She moved along the body until she drew level with the old lady's head. Is that a... it is. 'You wouldn't have,' said Cat, bringing puzzled looks, 'because she's not human, look here.'

They looked.

'At what?' said Tom.

'Her neck.'

The old lady's neck was twisted at an unnatural angle. He looked, had a reaction retch, but stopped short of actually throwing up when he noticed the wires sticking out from it.

'She's a robot!' sighed a very relieved Smokowski, who had already convicted himself of murder and thrown away the key.

'But she can't be,' said Tom, swallowing something nasty that had lodged in his throat, 'I was only talking to her... when was it?' He moved closer and inspected the damage.

Cat raised *that* eyebrow. 'Not a robot, Tom,' she said, 'but rather a very convincing android.' She turned her back on it. 'Which means either the real one is in hiding or was replaced by this thing some time ago. Time, I think, to pay Clyde a return visit and ask a few searching questions.'

Was it him, thought Tom, or was Cat beginning to sound like a certain famous but fictional detective? Hang about, who did she say? 'Who?' said Tom.

'As in Bonnie and...' said Cat.

'As in who and who?' said Tom.

Smokowski explained.

'And now gentlemen, if you don't mind and for your own safety, I suggest you vacate the area, I want to finish tidying up.'

Chapter 44

They arrived back at Merlin's not long after Lucy and the kids had vanished from it. The masked man, now unmasked, was where they had left him, but now conscious. Rufus though wasn't where they had left him.

As they vacated the loo en masse, they discovered him standing menacingly close to the now unmasked man, waving a knife in his hand that Bowie would have been proud of.

'No!' shouted Cat, when she saw what was happening.

Rufus turned away from the now unmasked man and lowered the knife. 'It's not what you think, Cat.'

'What is it I think?' snapped Cat, tartly.

'I was going to release him.'

Tom, Arthur and Smokowski, all horrified when they saw the knife in Rufus' hand, were now mortified on hearing what he had meant to do with it; even if they were more than relieved to hear he hadn't intended far worse.

'You were going to let him go?' said Tom, 'after all that he's done.' Tom was starting to fume – uncle or no uncle…

Cat stepped forward in an attempt to defuse matters before they got any worse and eyeballed Rufus until he got the message and put the knife on the table. 'Now, I think you should tell us what the heck is going on here.'

Rufus slumped into the rocking chair, which would have provided a little comic relief if he hadn't grabbed hold of the table to stop the thing from tipping backwards and settled down, looking every inch the elderly gent that he was. He took a moment to compose himself and told everyone they had better make themselves comfortable, as it was going to be a long story.

It was.

It all began a long, long time ago and there was a woman involved.

Rufus, playing the role of the experienced older man, had taken a shine to a certain young lady who happened to be spoken for. This didn't stop him. Suffice to say the young lady's husband wasn't at all happy with the goings on when he found out and grew very angry whereupon Rufus and the young lady decided it might be a good idea to high tail it out of there.

But the affair didn't last long. The young lady, realising her mistake fled, ashamed of what had gone on and spent the rest of her days exiled by guilt and grief, afraid to contact her husband. She died alone and unhappy, having pined her life away.

Rufus, on the other hand, continued his life in his own merry way, even when old buddies of his told him of her plight; he thought nothing of what had happened, that is, until now.

'Rufus!' said a dismayed Cat, when he had finished. But what had his story to do with the man tied to the chair?

But Rufus wasn't finished yet. There now followed the twist every good story should have. He stood up and gestured to the masked, now unmasked man. 'I think you all know who this is seated here, but bear with me for a moment and let me introduce you to Arthur Dewhurst, the husband of the young lady in my story.'

Which is where the masked, now unmasked man, took up the story.

The now unmasked man, who knew nothing of the fate that had befallen his beloved, was, unbeknown to Rufus, also a Traveller. He spent the next few years brooding and plotting and brooding some more, but never coming up with that perfect idea that would wreak just revenge on the man that had destroyed his life. Instead he slowly grew old and disillusioned. Until, he heard about the sword. Knowing that Rufus had taken on the part-time mantle of Merlin, an idea blossomed in his mind. But did he have time? Then something happened that felt like a sign from above; Rufus had gone missing. Knowing that Tom couldn't take up the travellers' mantle for five years he realised he did have time. He would have his revenge yet. And then another sign appeared – a ninja granny. He managed to best it, but an idea sprang up. He took the granny to bits and from the ashes rose the phoenix. Trial and error ensued until he had the latest Emily Dewhurst modelled on how he perceived she would look in her dotage. An unseen bonus was the grannies adopting each new Emily as their leader. Revenge on the world would finally be his along with the chance of a new life with his android wife, away from interfering twits like Rufus. And it would be such a cold, cold dish when it was finally served.

The room was in deathly silence when he finished.

Rufus broke it. 'And that is why I was letting him go.'

'And you think he would have just got up and walked away?' said Cat. Of all the things she may have thought of him over the years she had never had him down as naive.

Rufus didn't answer.

'Would you have walked away, Mister Dewhurst?' said Cat.

Arthur Dewhurst also said nothing, but the doleful eyes of a man going nowhere changed to ones of burning hate.

Cat had her answer. She wandered over to Tom and the others. 'I have an idea,' she said, 'but first, Arthur, get some rope.'

Rufus raised no objection when Arthur tied him to the rocking chair or kept back any of the information Cat asked him for, but when Cat asked Arthur to do one more thing for her he strained at his bonds. 'No!' he yelled, 'not that.'

But Cat was not one for u-turns, no matter how helpful he had been. Arthur found the wing chair with all the bells and whistles and chopped it to pieces. When he returned, Rufus was quiet. Tom stood beside him holding tape.

'You wanted to be Merlin, Rufus, now's your chance to be him and only him.' She gave him a stare that told him she was serious and then turned to Smokowski. 'Will you look after them until we get back?' He said he would and Cat trusted him.

It wasn't far to the stone and as Tom and Cat held their breaths, Arthur drove it home. It was over, Tom's first ever mission was over and a success. Now for the loose ends.

Tom sat on the loo deciding which question he wanted to ask. He chose the one aimed at Arthur. 'Why didn't you ask Rufus why he kept you hidden away for so long when you had the chance? I would have been down his throat.'

Arthur gave Tom a tired look. 'What's done is done,' he said. 'I can't turn back the clock, I'll just have to take my chances with Lucy and hope she understands.'

Cat sat on her shelf shaking her head. It was a sad gesture because she knew it couldn't happen, but she had a proposition for Arthur that might cushion the disappointment. She would tell him when the time was right.

'Good luck with that,' said Tom, as much in the dark as Arthur. He asked Cat the other thing on his mind. 'Why didn't Dewhurst do what we just did?' he said, 'I don't understand that.'

'Only he knows the answer to *that*, Tom,' said Cat, 'but it's academic if everything goes right when we get to the other end. Tom?'

'Yes?'

'You know what to do.'

They travelled forward, yet into the past – Rufus' shady past and arrived with time to spare at a well-known lover's lane. A secret tryst was due to go down. Instead, it was Rufus that went down, felled by Tom's trusty truncheon. They dragged him away and waited for Missus Dewhurst to arrive. She did – waited around for ten or so minutes, then, having had time to reflect on her actions thought better of what she was doing and went home to her husband. Back in Merlin's house a chair suddenly emptied and the ropes that had bound Arthur Dewhurst fell silently to the floor.

Time for celebration? Tom patted Arthur on the back and Arthur reciprocated, but Cat was about to play the party pooper. She waited until they got back to the loo before giving Arthur the bad news.

'She can't know,' said Cat, feeling Arthur's pain and disappointment, but rules were rules, 'it would put everyone in danger.'

'Then what do I do?' said Arthur, 'I can't go back to the Arctic.'

'You won't have to if you agree to what I suggest.' She told Arthur what it was she had in mind.

It wasn't perfect, but what was in life? Cat wanted to go back to when Arthur was incarcerated in his Arctic prison and stop it happening. The future would change, but hopefully not too drastically; it wasn't as if it were a historical event.

'Will I remember anything?' said Arthur.

'No,' said Cat.

'What about Lucy and the kids, is it fair of me?'

'Did you want to leave them?' said Tom.

'No,' said Arthur, 'but they've got a life now.'

'Not the one they would have chosen, I think,' said Tom.

Cat, quiet, had a solution she didn't want to share, but felt this was a special case. 'I can change it back,' she said, 'if

256

things don't work out, but then you are on your own Arthur, no further meddling.'

It swayed Arthur's decision as Cat thought it might. 'Then I agree,' he said.

It was messy; Cat didn't think it wouldn't be. A lot of memory juggling had to be done. At least she wouldn't be running into herself, what with Rufus having sent her then self on some wild goose chase. The headache she had after would last a good hour, but it was a success. In the loo, a waiting Tom watched as Arthur simply faded away.

When Cat got back Tom was waiting with a very valid enquiry. 'Won't Rufus and ol' Smokowski be different when we get back?'

Cat smiled and made a confession. 'I placed Smokowski and his shop in a time bubble when we left it and Rufus in one at the house. They'll remember everything and it'll be a sort of punishment for Rufus.'

Tom didn't pretend he understood so let it wash over him; he'd been doing a lot of that lately. 'So what now?' said Tom.

'How do you feel about a piece of cake?' she asked, 'once we get Smokowski and put Rufus in his place.'

Strangely enough, Tom *was* feeling a little peckish.

Chapter 45

'Now,' said Cat, her serious face on as she, Tom and Smokowski prepared to leave the loo, 'prepare yourselves for changes, they should be small and personal, but they will surprise and remember, only you will know how it was before this all began.'

Tom put his universal translator on a shelf, opened the loo door and stepped into his garden. The mission was over and he was home. To say it was a relief to finally be back home would be an understatement; he felt like kneeling and kissing the ground.

Smokowski, an armful of cards and the present Lucy had ordered, picked up on a stopover so he could get changed and pick them up, joined Tom and grabbed his arm. He ushered him to the side gate. 'Better not be late,' he laughed.

'Better hadn't,' smiled Tom. But where was Cat? 'Cat?' he said, looking round.

Cat was stood by the loo's open door. 'You go on,' she said, 'I'll turn up in a while. I've a few things I've got to do.'

Tom frowned and nodded, then let Smokowski lead him round to the front door.

As Tom put his key to the lock he paused and turned to Smokowski with a worried look on his face. 'Suppose there's no party when we go in?'

Smokowski shrugged his shoulders. 'We won't know until we go in,' said he sagely.

Tom put the key in the door, turned it and went in.

'Surprise!' shouted Marc and Kate, firing poppers into the air.

'Happy birthday, Dad,' said Lucy, giving him a hug and a kiss on the cheek.

So far so good. 'Well I'll be,' said Tom, feigning surprise.

Lucy grabbed Tom by the arm. 'Katie, can you take the cards and present from Mister Smokowski, who I thought had forgotten them,' she gave him a scornful, but playful look, 'and take them into the lounge. Granddad can open them later.'

There's one. When has Kate ever been happy being called Katie?

Lucy led Tom into the kitchen where the cake and surprise guests were waiting – some guests more surprising than others.

'Happy birthday, Dad,' said a male voice.

Tom spun on his heels. I've a son?

'Hey, sorry Tom didn't mean to make you jump.'

It was Arthur.

'You okay, Dad?' said Lucy, shaking her fist at Arthur. 'He's always doing that, aren't you Darren, lurking.'

It's Darren.

There was laughter from across the room, the odd relative and pub crony and another surprise or rather, two.

'You've joined us at last,' said Arthur Dewhurst, smiling like the cat that got the cream.

Yah!

'Ha, he means the "over the hill club",' said Emily Dewhurst.

Double yah!

The surprised look on Tom's face was misconstrued as puzzlement.

'They mean pensioner, Dad,' said Lucy, stepping in and making a gaga face at everyone. 'I don't know Dad, sometimes I wonder about you.'

Tom was doing some wondering of his own as it sunk in that the Emily Dewhurst joking with him was the real one and not some android. Truth was, as much as you prepared yourself for the changes it wasn't the same when you actually faced them. He was struggling. He scanned the room for Cat, but she was nowhere to be seen. The party carried on. He would have to carry on. And after a while, as time passed and no further surprises of great consequence turned up to shake him, he found he was actually starting to enjoy the changes to his life; his daughter certainly seemed happier than she had for a long time.

It was card and present time. Tom opened them with the appropriate ooh and ah here and there until he had one left – Lucy's.

'Go on,' she playfully egged, laughing, as Tom held it at arm's length, 'open it.'

Tom did. It was a flat cap. He popped it on his head and everyone laughed except for Lucy.

'That's odd,' said Lucy, looking baffled.

'I still like it though,' said Tom.

Lucy laughed. 'I meant it's not what I ordered. It was supposed to be a box set.'

'A box set?' said Tom.

'Yeah,' said Lucy, 'the whole series of that seventies sci-fi programme you like so much.'

'Still, you seem to like your hat, so no damage done I suppose.' Lucy gave Tom a hug.

The party started to gradually wind down from there 'til the only partygoers left were Tom, Smokowski, Darren, Lucy and the kids. It wasn't long after, that Smokowski decided it was time for him to take his leave.

Tom saw Smokowski to the back door and walked with him through the garden to the side gate.

'See you tomorrow?' said Smokowski.

'That or yesterday,' laughed Tom. He closed the gate after Smokowski, who was laughing as he left, and stood a moment, thinking about the day. Was it really just a day?

'Nice cap, Tom, a present?'

Tom snapped out of his musings and looked down into the eyes of a smiling Cat.

'Where have you been?' said Tom, not sure what he was feeling at that precise moment. He decided, as a man, not to go there. 'You missed the party.'

'Loose ends,' she said, 'took me a little longer than I thought. Any significant changes I should know about?'

Tom laughed. 'Yeah,' he said, 'it would seem I'm now a big sci-fi fan.'

'Can't all be perfect, but I shouldn't worry, one of my loose ends,' grinned Cat. 'How are Lucy and the family?'

'I don't think we need worry about them,' said Tom. 'Question though?'

'Shoot.'

'How come *I* didn't change?'

'You were protected, the moment you first stepped into the loo.'

'Ah-ha,' said Tom, none the wiser. 'Shall we go indoors and introduce you to the family?'

'Why not?' said Cat. 'Oh, and by the way, how'd you feel about a little trip to Atlantis?'

'What?'

'Only joking. Got any chicken?'

Other titles by
Stefan Jakubowski
Published by ZYGMUNT STANLEY

STRANGE RELATIONS
ISBN 978-0-9554244-2-7

Truly original, intriguing, amusing and touching – altogether a compelling read.

Richard Ross, joiner, part-time local football referee, ordinary man, is about to get a shock. It's time to meet the relatives. But guess what? They're all dead. Even worse, they are his past lives and all share the same soul – his!

With help from his Strange Relations, an angel named Joe, and Roberta (Australopithecus Robustus), Richard has to learn the last lesson of life so all will be allowed to journey towards the Light. Richard is the last of a very long line and everyone's last chance.

One small problem though – Richard is in a coma and time is fast running out.

'Impossible!' blurted the Chaplain.

'Why?' said Geoff, 'Thirty-nine years ago I'd have said it was impossible for me to be sitting in a room talking to three ghosts. Let alone be one.'

'That was improbable, not impossible,' argued the Chaplain. 'What I mean is that it's impossible for a ghost to occupy a mortal's dead body, even if they do share the same soul.'

'But Richard isn't dead,' Laura pointed out, as gently as possible.

DEAD PECULIAR

ISBN 978-0-9554244-0-3

You're dead – end of story. At least that's how Richard Ross saw it.

But he knows different now. Now that he's dead that is!

When Richard Ross entered the afterlife he thought his worries were well and truly over. When will he ever learn? Trapped, with all hell breaking loose around him he needs help – the living kind.

Can Marvo, a hapless hypnotist, and Rosemary Bloom, a plant psychic, really come to his rescue? Who knows!

With his dead relatives beside him, Richard sets out on a dangerous journey that will take them deep into their past. For Richard things are about to change from strange to peculiar. Dead Peculiar.

The Chaplain swallowed hard, he knew he had no chance if the beast attacked. 'What do I do?'

'Flutter your eyelids, would be my guess.'

'Be serious, I'm in trouble here.'

'I was, I think he likes you.'

The Chaplain gulped. A moment ago he was worried about being ripped apart, but now the ball was in a totally different and very worrying court.

'What do I do?' repeated the Chaplain.

'Keep still,' advised Sammy.

'I can't, I'm shaking too much.'

'I think he likes it.'

'What?'

'The submissive bit. Look he's sniffing, he wants to sniff you.'

It was all too much for the Chaplain. Blown cover or no blown cover, he was not about to stand there and have his bits sniffed by some great slavering beast.

MISCREATION

ISBN 978-0-9554244-1-0
There's life.
There shouldn't be.

Creator Brown has been at it again. But then what can you expect from someone who occasionally ignores the odd zero – especially as he happens to work in billions and trillions.

But Brown is the least of the problems for the Chief Creator who has just been handed other disturbing news. The Anarchist is about to rise, from certain bits of wreckage.

Serpens the self deluded, self proclaimed tutu wearing Anarchist, banished from the Hall of Creators for certain improprieties and as punishment doomed to travel the universe for all time in a claustrophobic meteorite with his meat-head minions has, as luck would have it, crash-landed on Brown's misaligned calamity. Time for a plan – something he's not very good at – to escape the planet and pursue his doubtful claim to be ruler of the universe. But it is going to take time – a whole evolution of it.

Enter man. To be precise, Musca "the explosion was nothing to do with me" soot-smeared idiot son of the very recently deceased Chieftain. He plans to take the survivors of a certain devastating incident to a mythical land called OHM – there's no place like it. Trouble is they don't want to go. Not with him anyway.

Let the lunacy begin!